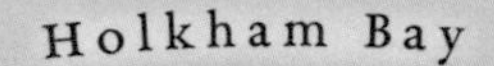
Holkham Bay

Marshes
Lady Anne's Drive
Ancient House
Railway
The Victoria Inn
Holkham Village
Freeman Street
Wells-next-the-Sea
North Gates
Pleasure Gardens
Grotto
Palmer's Lodge
-Holkham Park-

A HAUNTING AT HOLKHAM

Also by Anne Glenconner

Lady in Waiting
Murder On Mustique

Anne Glenconner

A HAUNTING AT HOLKHAM

HODDER &
STOUGHTON

First published in Great Britain in 2021 by Hodder & Stoughton
An Hachette UK company

1

A CIP catalogue record for this title is available from the British Library

Hardback ISBN 978 1 529 33640 5
Trade Paperback ISBN 978 1 529 33642 9
eBook ISBN 978 1 529 33644 3

Typeset in Celeste by
Palimpsest Book Production Ltd, Falkirk, Stirlingshire

Printed in USA with Lakeside Book Company

Hodder & Stoughton Ltd
Carmelite House
50 Victoria Embankment
London EC4Y 0DZ

www.hodder.co.uk

For my parents Tommy and Elizabeth the 5th Earl and Countess of Leicester

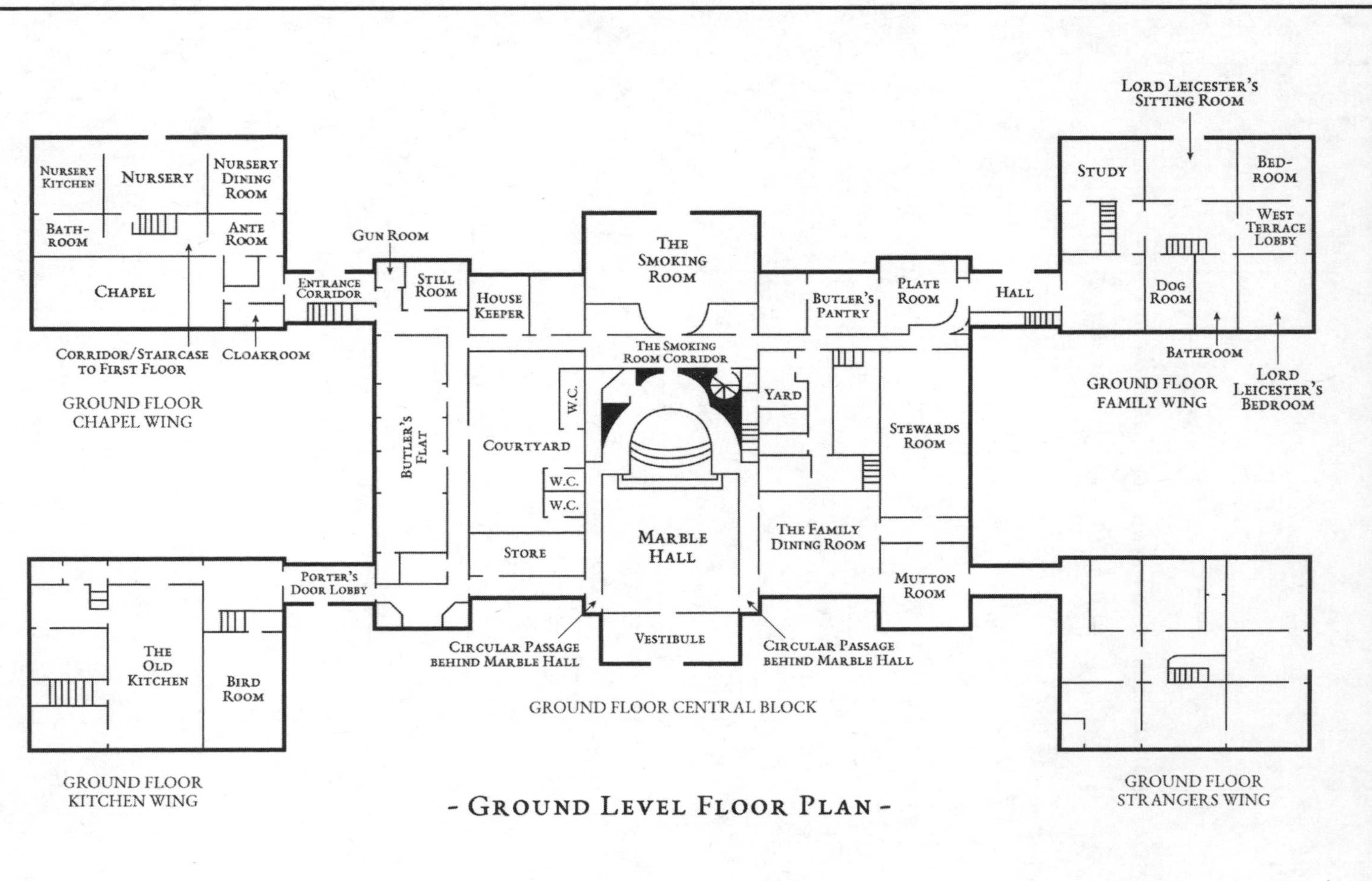

- Ground Level Floor Plan -

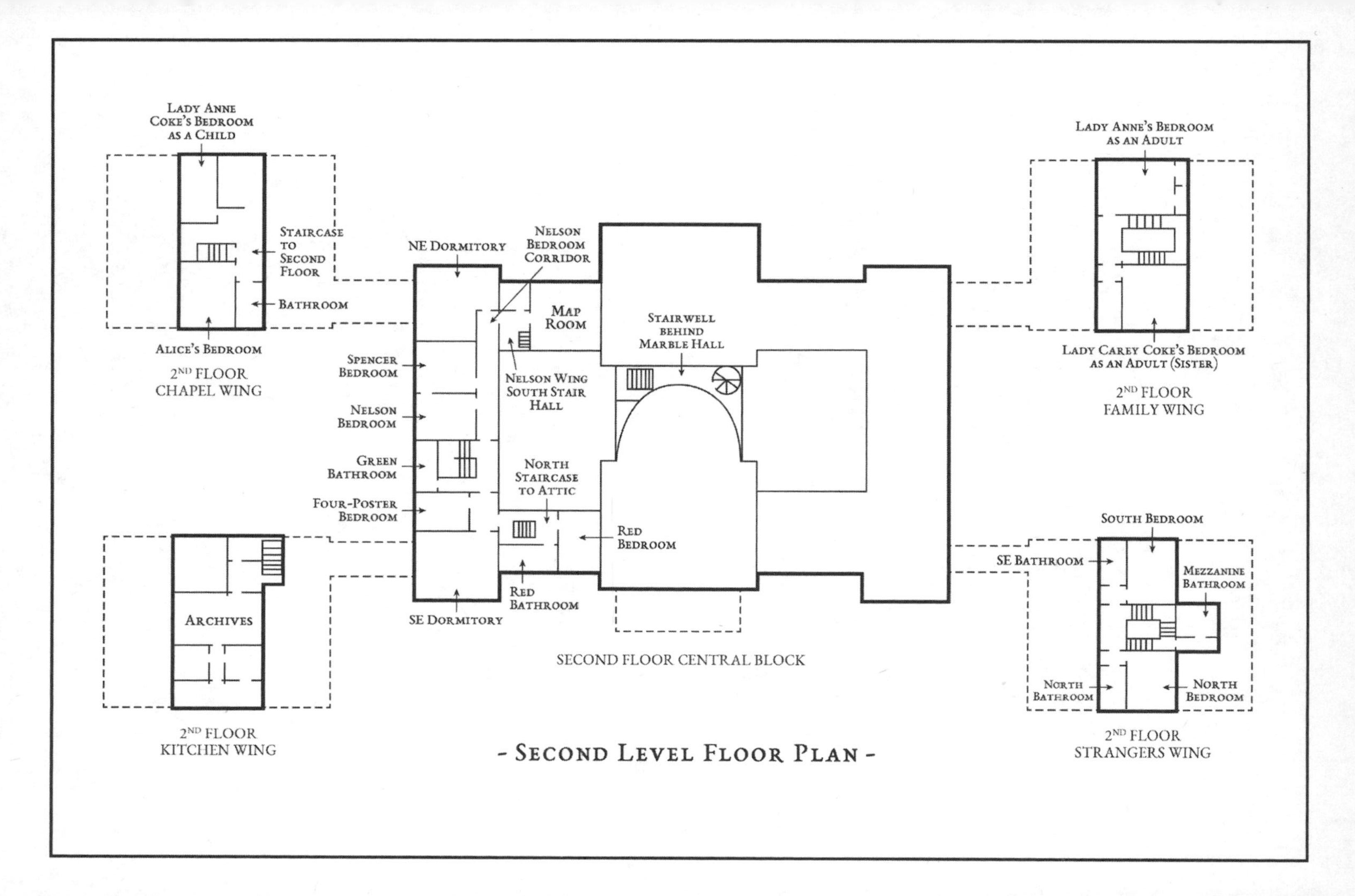
Lady Anne Coke's Bedroom as a Child
Staircase to Second Floor
Bathroom
Alice's Bedroom
2ND FLOOR CHAPEL WING
NE Dormitory
Nelson Bedroom Corridor
Map Room
Spencer Bedroom
Nelson Wing South Stair Hall
Nelson Bedroom
Green Bathroom
North Staircase to Attic
Four-Poster Bedroom
Red Bedroom
Red Bathroom
SE Dormitory
Stairwell behind Marble Hall
SECOND FLOOR CENTRAL BLOCK
Archives
2ND FLOOR KITCHEN WING
Lady Anne's Bedroom as an Adult
Lady Carey Coke's Bedroom as an Adult (Sister)
2ND FLOOR FAMILY WING
South Bedroom
SE Bathroom
Mezzanine Bathroom
North Bathroom
North Bedroom
2ND FLOOR STRANGERS WING
- Second Level Floor Plan -

1.

January 17th 1950

THAT DRATTED TELEPHONE. Always ringing when Mrs Rosen had her hands full. Here it was a quarter past eight already by the hall clock and she had half a dozen little jobs to do before taking the tea trolley into the lounge at nine. Clearing up the dinner plates always took longer than she thought it would. You'd think she'd know, after all these years, that the gentlemen travellers couldn't help splashing their soup around, but it came as a surprise every time.

It took a moment to find a place to set down the clean tablecloth before she could answer the phone's wheezy jangle. The lobby area was padded with winter coats – scarfs and hats jostling for space on the pegs, and more galoshes and overshoes underfoot what with the weather this week being so mucky.

The pale Bakelite phone summoned her with more of a rattle than a ring, which explained why none of the gentlemen in the lounge had heard it. Another thing that needed seeing to. Mrs Rosen managed to balance the table-cloth on a pile of magazines set out on the hall chest by the phone and note pad, and keep them from falling onto the floor with her hip while she picked up the heavy receiver and lifted it to her ear.

'Scunthorpe 478? Yes, good evening . . .' A roar of laughter greeted some successful anecdote in the lounge. 'I'm terribly sorry, I didn't catch that. Do you need a room? It's two shillings a night, and that includes a light breakfast as well as dinner and tea. Oh, I'm sorry – one of our guests? No, I don't think we have a gentleman named Cook with us . . . Oh it is spelled C-O-K-E? I see. Well, my husband didn't mention a young lady, but he served at dinner, you see, while I was in the kitchen . . .' She paused to let the person on the other end of the line speak. Now she straightened up smartly and the tablecloth and magazines slithered onto the linoleum floor. She barely noticed. 'Oh yes, I see. If you would just bear with me one moment, madam.'

Mrs Rosen's youngest was trying to scoot by, but she was too quick for him. She grabbed his collar and pointed at the fallen glossies and tablecloth. As he gathered them up, she set the receiver down with great care next to the phone, then undid the ties on her apron and hung it among the greatcoats of the travelling salesmen. Now she looked there *was* a lady's coat hanging among them. A pale brown duffle coat with big wooden toggles, and a floral scarf tucked round the hood. Very pretty. She touched her hair. Jimmy gave her an odd look and she scowled at him and pointed till he got the message and took the clean cloth into the dining room.

She opened the door to the lounge. All men as far as she could see, crowded around the little tables with constantly filling ashtrays between them. Other than tobacco the air smelt dark and sharp, that hair cream the gentlemen used.

The noise of conversation died down as they saw her open the door.

'Is Miss Coke here?' she asked, pronouncing it properly to rhyme with 'book' and still not quite believing such a person could be in her lounge, but the refined female voice on the telephone had seemed quite certain. 'Miss Anne Coke of Holkham Hall?'

A slim arm appeared, waving above the heads of the room's other occupants, and Mrs Rosen watched as a tall, slender young woman, a girl really, not more than seventeen, with blonde shoulder-length hair held neatly off her face and brushed-out curls, rose out from among the salesmen like a Venus rising from the foam of commerce. She was holding a book and had been sitting on the corner sofa. Her finger was trapped between the covers, marking her place.

'Telephone call, Miss Coke. From your mother, at Holkham Hall,' she couldn't help adding.

'Thank you so much, Mrs Rosen,' the young lady said. The salesmen shuffled their chairs out of the way to let her by and stared. The ones who had spoken to her at dinner looked, slyly smug, the ones who had ignored her, profoundly disconcerted.

'This way,' Mrs Rosen said, and led her out of the room as if there could be any confusion as to where the telephone was. Mrs Rosen closed the door on the lounge and the men left behind stared at the closed door.

'Holkham Hall? Isn't that some enormous pile in Norfolk? Earl of Leicester's place?' a ginger-haired man who travelled in toothpaste asked the room in general.

'On the coast and a stone's throw from Sandringham,' an

older gentleman with an iron moustache replied. 'Miss Coke is the granddaughter of the Earl of Leicester.'

'No!' Ginger said. 'She told me her family run a pottery and she's hoping to sell vases and Toby jugs to the fancy goods shops in Grimsby and Skegness!'

'That's right.' The gentleman with the iron moustache had thought the ginger-haired fellow was a little full of himself and enjoyed seeing him temporarily flustered. 'I do the King's Lynn run at least twice a year. They converted the old laundry at the Hall. Nice things they are making there too, got some artistry to them. Pretty little set with snow-drops on them.'

The door opened again and the young lady returned. She looked, if possible, a little paler than she had before. Several of the men stood up.

'I'm terribly sorry, I left my bag by the sofa. Might someone pass it to me?'

The handbag, more of a briefcase really, was retrieved and Iron Moustache had the privilege of passing it into her hands.

'Not bad news, I hope, Miss Coke,' he said. He had a kind, avuncular face. Anne had met him once or twice on these selling trips, and he had absorbed the news of her aristocratic lineage with calm courtesy and the minimum of fuss. He had been happy to share his knowledge of sales too – the best days to visit certain shops and who liked to chat, but never bought. Samuels, that was his name. Marcus Samuels. She swallowed.

'I'm afraid so, Mr Samuels. My grandfather has died. I must go home at once.'

The men murmured their sympathy and concern, and those smoking put out their cigarettes as a sign of respect.

'I am sorry to hear that,' Mr Samuels said. 'A very fine gentleman. And you are determined to drive back tonight, Lady Anne?'

Her blue eyes widened slightly to hear herself addressed as 'Lady Anne'. A small thing, but it carried a great deal of change with it.

'I feel I must.'

He nodded. 'We shall let you pack, but I think perhaps the gentlemen here and I can come up with a list of useful numbers and a few names. A few garages and guest houses along your route in case you run into any trouble with that little car of yours. Yours *is* the Mini Morris, isn't it?' She nodded. 'You'll be going through Sleaford and Holbeach, I imagine. We can do that, can't we, chaps?'

The chaps were quite sure they could.

'That's very kind.'

'A pleasure, my lady,'

'Thank you so much,' she said, hardly knowing what she was saying, then she withdrew to speak to Mrs Rosen and gather her belongings.

'I see it now, of course,' Ginger said. 'Breeding.'

Mr Samuels sniffed meaningfully and took his notebook out of his pocket.

'Right, gentlemen. Let's make sure Lady Anne gets home safe.'

Anne went to her room and began to pack her few odds and ends into her suitcase. The case with her samples from the pottery, carefully wrapped in sheets of newspaper, was still in the car. Then she sat down rather suddenly on the narrow bed, her wash bag on her knee.

'Oh, Grandpa!'

A fall, her mother had said on the telephone, he had missed his footing on the cellar stairs between the chapel and the gun room. How could he have done? He knew every stone and step in Holkham, every brick and polished flag. Had her mother said something about a stroke? Wasn't Grandpa too young for a stroke? He was not even seventy yet. He had only become Earl in 1941 when his own father died at ninety-three. Anne had thought of him as in his prime and he had seemed quite well when she left Holkham three days ago. He was enjoying the tail-enders, getting the best out of the last weeks of the shooting season and filling the game room with pheasants, while Anne, her sister and her mother worked in the pottery opposite. They charted the progress of their own days by the sound of the guns, the distant thunder from the coveys around the kitchen garden.

She saw her tears had fallen on her leather wash bag and wiped them off before they stained. And Dad was the Earl now! Already! He would be in an awful state. He had become so nervous since the war, everything had to be just so, as if not arriving for dinner on the stroke of eight meant the entire house would collapse around their ears. Now there would be another round of death duties and that would drive him potty. But worse than all that, what would the house be like without Grandpa in it?

Anne lifted her head. Whatever had happened, whatever

did happen, sitting here wouldn't help matters. She stowed her bag and hair brushes, pyjamas and stockings and clicked the case shut, picked up her briefcase and carried them both downstairs to collect her coat, scarf and the condolences of her fellow travelling salesmen.

2.

It was a long, cold drive. The car was her mother's runabout – a rattly beast with a clutch that could get sticky and subject to terrible draughts. It was not as if she could go on her sales trips in her father's Bentley. Anne concentrated on the road.

The pottery had been her mother's idea. When she and Dad had finally got back from Egypt at Christmas in 1943, Elizabeth, Viscountess Coke, had seen one of the Italian Prisoners of War throwing a pot on a homemade wheel in the Holkham brickworks. Once her war work with the land girls was done, and the country had lurched from the delirium of VE Day into the cold dawn of post-war austerity, she remembered him and his pot. Lady Coke saw the opportunity to earn a little money, and Lord only knows they needed it. The old laundry became what her father referred to as 'the potting shed'. There Lady Coke and Anne's sister Carey and half a dozen craftsmen fashioned mugs and bowls, vases and pots, all proudly stamped with the Holkham name. At first Anne helped in the works, but she got so bored with the fettling and sponging, she begged for another job. What about sales? They could go to trade fairs together, but someone still needed to go door-to-door, visiting the fancy goods shops in the coastal towns.

Her father thought Anne was too young. Her mother thought the experience would toughen her up and that was no bad thing before she was launched as a debutante. Lady Coke won the argument, and Anne discovered to her delight she was rather good at selling. The training aristocratic young ladies like herself enjoyed had taught her how to appear easy and pleasant with all types of people, even when she felt rather shy on the inside. It had also taught her to be clear about her wants and needs and show a little backbone when necessary. Buyers at several shops had thought that getting an advantageous bargain would be easy when dealing with this delicate-looking child. They had inevitably found themselves ordering rather more than they had expected, at rather higher prices than they had intended, and thanking Miss Coke afterwards for the opportunity.

Thinking about the road, if her petrol would last and listening to every rattle and click of the car kept grief at bay. The fact of her grandfather's death was, somehow, outside the car in the dark. Dawn was breaking as she drove along Holbeach High Street and as she recognised her surroundings, the eight-hundred-year-old wool church ahead of her, the store frontages, all shut up and silent, she realised she was only fifty miles from home and the reason for her long night's drive seemed to fall in on her again with the light. She turned off the road and stopped the car outside the church, indicating her intention carefully to the deserted streets, parked and pulled on the handbrake, then covered her face with her hands and had the proper cry her heart had been longing for since she had put down the receiver in Mrs Rosen's guest house.

Just ten minutes, she told herself, have a good weep and then be ready to face everybody at the Hall. Her father would be torn between grief and work for the estate; her mother and sister would be dealing with the servants, all of whom were devoted to the old Earl. Had anyone told the King? Of course, her father would have sent word at once. When would the visits of condolence begin? A fall. Her grandfather had had a fall and Maria had found him. Anne tried to remember the last thing she had said to him. She had gone to say goodbye to him before leaving for this trip, of course. He had been in the manuscript library in the Family Wing with Mr Mullins, the Holkham archivist and librarian, their heads bent low over some ancient volume, thick as thieves as ever. It had been such an ordinary, quick goodbye. He had wished her good fortune and told her to drive carefully, which she always, always did, but he had been intent on examining the book in front of him.

She got out her handkerchief and dried her eyes, checked her flowered headscarf was still in place in the rear-view mirror, then climbed out of the car. She needed to feel the air on her face, cooled and salt-sharpened by the North Sea. She watched the great all-encompassing sky of Norfolk, unbroken by hills or mountains, and the sun rising to the east, a cool pale-gold disc showing above the horizon now and burning off the mist from the long marshes. Bronze Age fishermen had trapped eels there just as their descendants did today, and King John had lost his jewels into the receiving waters. She should be glad to remember her grandfather like that, absorbed in his treasures, sharing a moment in time with some anonymous fourteenth-century illustrator, his hand resting where the master's had, linked by paper and ink across all those oceans of time.

Anne got back into the little car. As she turned back onto the road through King's Lynn and on to Holkham, the little rattling cough in the engine deepened.

The cough became bronchiolar after she passed through King's Lynn, catching site of the boats setting off to catch the still hours of the morning. She willed it not to get any worse, and the idea it might, began to turn into panic in her chest. No. Not now. She would not have one of her panicky turns now. She just needed to get home. She clutched the steering wheel tighter, as if that would help. Then the engine died just west of Docking. Ten miles! That was all! She twisted the key and pushed down on the clutch, until the push became a stamp and her frustration and panic overwhelmed her.

'I'm not sure that is a good idea.'

The male voice at the passenger window made her jump and she put her hand to her chest as she turned around to see who had addressed her. Still, the voice startled her out of her dark place, and she was herself again, like she had jumped back into her own skin.

A youngish man, in his late twenties perhaps, in a heavy

sweater, his longish blond hair uncovered in the morning chill, was bending down and looking at her through the window.

'I know,' she said. 'Oh blast! I've flooded the engine and I am *so* near home!'

He looked up and down the narrow road; as he straightened up to do so Anne noticed the door to one of the Cross Lane flint cottages was open. He must have heard the last gasp of her engine as he was at his breakfast.

'You may have done. We can't have you blocking the road though, or Old George will have a fit when he comes through with his cart. If you put it in neutral, I'll give you a push and we can steer you onto the side of the road for now.'

Anne pulled herself together. 'Yes, thank you.'

She put the car into neutral and wondered if she should get out to help push and steer through the open driver's door, but the car was already in motion. She turned the wheel, and the car rolled uncomplainingly onto the grass just beyond the row of cottages.

Now what? If this man had a telephone in the house, perhaps she could ring the Hall and ask Smith to collect her. He probably didn't have a telephone though. Most of the people near Holkham regarded them with suspicion. Mrs Pullen, one of the daily ladies, had told Anne that she wouldn't have one in the house as people only ever used it to rush bad news to you, and who wants that? She had a point.

She climbed out of the car again and looked at her watch. Just past eight o'clock in the morning.

'Where do you live?' the young man said, dusting off his

hands. 'I can drive you home if you are in a rush. The garage on Pound Lane opens in an hour though, and Mike will probably be able to patch her up if you'd rather wait.'

'I live at Holkham Hall,' Anne said. 'And I would like to get home as soon as possible.'

His eyes sparked with understanding. 'Oh! Are you one of the granddaughters? I heard about the old Earl's death in the pub last night. My condolences.'

'Thank you.' She put out her hand. 'I am Anne Coke.'

He looked at her gloves, then at his own hands, grimy from pushing the back of the car. 'I'm Charles Elwood, a temporary tenant of your family. Give me a moment to wash up and I'll drive you to the Hall. When I get back, I'll set Mike on this old beast.'

He turned back towards the cottage at once.

'Thank you, Mr Elwood!' she called after him.

He raised his hand as he turned in to the cottage but didn't look back.

Elwood? Not a local man. His cottage had stood empty since the war and like the two next to it was rather dilapidated. Her grandfather was planning to get on to these ones as soon as the new cottages in Burnham Thorpe were complete.

She craned her neck slightly to see in through the living room window and caught a glimpse of a rather bare interior. Was that an easel?

He re-emerged and twirled his car key through his long fingers.

'Do you need to get anything from your car? A bag, perhaps?'

She blushed. 'Yes. Of course.'

'I'll just pull the car around.'

His car was a little Ford Anglia and pottered along the final miles to Holkham with throaty enthusiasm.

Now that she wasn't driving, Anne realised how tired she was. She pulled off her flowered headscarf and ran her fingers through her hair, trying to tidy up a little.

'Were you close to your grandfather?' Charles asked.

'Yes, I was. Particularly when I was little. I thought he was marvellous. When the war started my sister Carey and I were sent up to stay with my cousins in Scotland. Then in 'forty-three she got measles and as Mum and Dad were about to come back to Norfolk, I was sent down to stay at Holkham in advance to be out of the way while Carey recovered.

'How come you are a tenant of Holkham?' she asked.

'I was in the Scots Guards during the war, came back and went to art college after I was demobbed and have been looking for somewhere to paint. An old army friend said your family might have a few places going cheap, so here I am.'

Anne frowned. 'You've been here through the winter? It must have been jolly spartan.'

'I had enough heat in Italy to last me a lifetime. And my needs are simple, luckily enough.'

Something in his dry tone made the wheels in Anne's brain turn slowly and the parts locked together.

'Oh, you are the communist! I've heard about you. Dad said you had quite a good war, then picked up some strange ideas.'

'Yes, but luckily he hadn't heard about the strange ideas before he agreed to rent the cottage to me for a year. And if by a good war you mean I didn't die or run away, yes, I suppose I did. You call your father "Dad"? I assumed you called him *pater* or *Daddy*.'

Anne bristled. 'I live in Holkham, not a Jeeves and Wooster novel.'

'Would a lowly son of the soil like me be able to tell the difference?'

'You don't *sound* like a lowly son of the soil.'

'My mother made me practise to the radio so I could get a nice job.' His voice was bitter. 'I think she rather wanted me to be a butler. And I'm not a communist, I'm a democratic socialist. Every intelligent man in the country is these days. After the last fifty years who could possibly be anything else? Families like yours have kept families like mine down for centuries. You should never have allowed us an education.'

'Then you'll be delighted to hear my family will probably be crippled by the second run of death duties in a decade. Because, as I think we mentioned earlier, my grandfather died yesterday.'

He flushed and went quiet while Anne stared, furious and upset, out at the passing hedgerows.

Charles cleared his throat. 'I'm sorry, Miss Coke. That little tantrum was unforgivable. I've been on my own too much. Arguing with the class system in my head and I took it out on you.'

'That's quite all right,' she said tightly.

'It really isn't but thank you for saying so.'

She certainly didn't feel like forgiving him yet. She stared out at the bare fields, feeling the heat in her cheeks and blinking quickly, then the flint and brick wall of the estate was on their left, running alongside her as if in welcome. The keeper in the south lodge had heard the car; he had already opened the iron gates across the avenue for them, and waved them in. Charles drove slowly through, raising his hand in thanks.

'I came home to paint, not preach. I'm rather betwixt and between at the moment. Everyone in London thinks I'm a crazed war monger. Everyone here thinks I'm a bohemian or a communist. It's been a rather lonely winter. Though last night everyone in the pub was talking very fondly of your grandfather. Seems it was worth even talking to me to praise him.'

'Did you tell them your opinions about the English class system?' she asked.

'No, I thought I'd save it all up to rant at one of his grieving relations!' he replied, shaking his head. That made her smile.

He drove slowly up the avenue, climbing the gentle undulations of the land in a dead straight line towards the obelisk, a straight arrow up towards the grey and empty sky.

Then they reached it, and below and beyond them was home. Charles whistled.

Holkham Hall, in all its Palladian splendour, caught the morning light – a high escarpment of butter-coloured stone joining land and sky, the great south portico with its massive Corinthian columns, flanked by the Chapel and Family Wings, each one divided into three regular parts. The whole frontage had a stately, symmetrical rhythm, embellished by the lake to the west, and the conservatory to the east.

The avenue curled down the slope towards the Hall, and now a visitor would see the terraces in front of the house and the fountain. St George, his sword raised to slay a dragon spewing water from its jaws, and swans, seashells and dolphins sending jets in great arcs around him.

Elwood noticed a line of people, a queue snaking out from the side of the house. Men in jackets and women in hats and gloves.

'Who are they?' Charles asked.

Anne looked out of the window. 'They are some of our tenants. They have come to pay their respects to Grandpa.'

'I see.'

The avenue led round the edge of the south frontage, past the top of the lake and round to the north side of the house.

'Where shall I let you out?' he asked quietly.

'Here is fine, Mr Elwood.'

The car's tyres scrunched on the gravel and he drove up the final curve of the road to the entrance, glancing up at the stone lions as he did, and let the car come to a gentle stop.

Anne let herself out, then reached over to pluck her suitcase out of the back seat. Shreeve, the butler, was waiting at the top of the shallow flight of stairs, his hands clasped behind his back.

'I shall see to your car,' Charles said. 'Please don't think about it today.'

She took the key from the pocket of her duffle coat and handed it to him.

'That's very good of you, thank you. And thank you for bringing me home.' She picked up her suitcase and briefcase and walked away. Charles watched her slim figure disappear into the Hall.

3.

'DID YOU HAVE engine trouble, Lady Anne?' Shreeve asked as he took her suitcase from her and opened the door from the vestibule into the Marble Hall.

'Yes, but close by and Mr Elwood said he'd deal with it. Where is Mum?'

'Lady Leicester has just finished her breakfast and is in her sitting room. Lady Carey has gone to the pottery and your father,' he paused, 'your father is with the Captain and Reverend Howard. Would you like to see your grandfather, Lady Anne?'

'People are lining up along the terrace to see him.'

'Your mother has arranged the Book of Condolence at the chapel entrance, but we haven't opened the doors for the tenants as yet.'

'Thank you. Yes, I shall. And how is everyone? How are you, Shreeve?'

He blinked. 'Bearing up, my lady. Bearing up.' He looked for a moment as if he was about to say something more, then changed his mind.

Anne took off her gloves and coat and handed them to

him. 'I shall go and see Mum after I've visited Grandpa,' she told him. 'If you can let her know I'll just be a few minutes.'

He nodded and Anne turned left out of the Marble Hall, then right in the direction of the chapel, along the passage between the internal courtyard and Shreeve's offices. Her ancestors peered down at her from the walls of the anteroom. She put her hand on the door, breathed deeply, then went inside.

It was a high, narrow chapel, full of light. The walls were lined with red and white alabaster to the height of the gallery, then rose a further storey to the roof in white plaster and large windows. Above the altar was a soft-edged masterpiece by Guido Reni, the Virgin Mary, her flowing hair lit with the light of heaven, her hands stretched wide in welcome and wonder. She was flanked by St Cecilia and St Anne. A triumvirate of women to watch over a very masculine household as they prayed so hard for sons. Perhaps they should have chosen different saints. Anne had two sisters, Carey, only two years younger than herself, and Sarah, born at the end of the war, the doll and delight of the whole family and their greatest disappointment.

Anne's father was now the fifth Earl of Leicester. When he died the title and the estate would go to his third cousin, a man none of them knew living in South Africa. The knowledge of that had caused Grandpa great pain, though he had loved little Sarah as much as any of them. Poor Grandpa.

The fourth Earl of Leicester of Holkham, Thomas William Coke, Knight of the Order of St John, Lord Lieutenant of Norfolk, lay in the centre of the chapel, his head towards the altar, as if on a bed, his hands crossed over his chest. The benches had all been cleared out, which made the chapel feel very still and empty. Two of the gardeners, John Hope and Peter Franklin, in starched shirts and Sunday coats, stood on either side of the altar facing him, their heads bowed.

They glanced up surreptitiously when Anne came in and she nodded at them, but no one spoke as she walked up the aisle and looked down at her grandfather's face. He was gone, she saw that at once. The figure in front of her was a memory of him, like looking at a portrait or a photograph rather than the man himself. A narrow face, like his son's, with the same high forehead, a carefully trimmed moustache. She touched his long, musician's fingers, bent down and kissed his forehead, then, with one hand still resting on his hands, lowered her head for a moment and offered up her prayers for him. They weren't words though, her prayers in that moment, but a tumble of images of him in life: setting records to play on the huge oak gramophone in the statue gallery; in heated conversation with the gardeners, his voice bouncing off the brick walls; fretting over the account books; the warmth and pleasure with which he talked about the house, the art and treasures that lined the walls and filled each niche, bookshelf, table top.

She raised her head, brushed his cheek with her fingertips one last time, then left him there with the candles and the fresh flowers and his silent guardians and went to find her mother.

Shreeve had been waiting for her to leave. Behind her she heard the doors to the entrance corridor open, heard the murmur of the mourners waiting outside, the coughs and clearing of throats as the people of the village, the estate, the tenants of Holkham's fifty thousand acres, prepared to offer their own farewells to Lord Leicester.

Lady Leicester was in her working clothes when Anne found her in her sitting room. She was sitting at her writing desk, staring out across the gardens, fountain pen in hand, but the sheet in front of her blank.

'Mum?'

She jumped up and crossed the room with quick strides, then hugged her daughter hard.

'Anne, you look shattered! You must have driven all night! You shouldn't have done that, though I'm terribly glad you did. It's all so unutterably sad. Shreeve sent up tea, bless him, and bread and butter. Come and sit down. We've had so many messages of condolence already, and your father is worrying about what to put in *The Times*. What a disaster – Tommy's only been gone a few hours and I miss him like the blazes already.'

She led her daughter to the armchairs by the fireplace and pushed food and tea on her. Lady Leicester had only been nineteen when Anne was born, and she felt more of an older sister than a mother at times. Especially when Anne was still at school just after the war and Lady Leicester had challenged her two older daughters to climb every tree on the avenue.

'What happened, Mum?' Anne said. The tea was strong and very welcome.

'We don't know, darling. Which makes it all even worse. Maria found him at the bottom of the stairs yesterday morning and we have no idea how long he'd been lying there.'

She watched her daughter's face attentively.

'I'm sorry it took so long to get the news to you, Anne, but I couldn't find your call book for hours and the Hall was full of doctors and policemen.'

'Policemen?' Anne asked.

'Yes, as it was a sudden death, you see, but it was clear he must just have slipped on the stairs and taken an unlucky fall. They were very decent and your father sent them packing pretty sharpish. The coroner's hearing will just be a formality.'

Anne put down her bread and butter, her appetite gone. 'I hate the idea I was wandering around Scunthorpe being all bright and cheery with the sales staff when Grandpa was dead.'

'I know, darling. I'm sorry but it couldn't be helped. Look, I had better tell you now. Maria is blaming Lady Mary. She swears she saw a white cat in the cellars last week and now claims it was an omen.'

'They think the ghost killed Grandpa?'

'You know Lady Mary can play horrible tricks sometimes. You were terrified of her when we came back from Egypt. I was quite worried about you. I thought living here with only Grandpa and her for company had turned you quite odd.'

Anne didn't know what to say to that, so she sipped her tea.

'And he encouraged you!' Lady Leicester said fiercely.

'I enjoyed finding out about her, Mum.'

'Carey says she still gives her little shoves along the passages around the kitchen. Thank God she hasn't made her way into the pottery. Probably far too snobbish to haunt the old laundry.' Lady Leicester studied the air around her with narrowed eyes. 'Remember if you ever break any of my pots, I'll send for the vicar and have you exorcised!' Anne smiled.

'Oh, by the way, what did you do to my car? Shreeve said you'd had trouble.'

'It got me as far as Docking, then conked out. I got a lift the rest of the way from an artist who is renting one of the cottages.'

'Oh yes! Charles Elwood! Your father thinks he is trying to turn everyone in the village communist.'

'He's a democratic socialist, apparently. And hasn't had much success converting anyone.'

Her mother wrinkled her nose. 'Delighted to hear it! One of your father's army friends recommended him, so we thought he might be all right. I don't suppose Tommy will allow one of his paintings in the house even if he is Constable reborn.'

'He offered to get Mike to see to the car.'

'Well, good for him. But he must be a bit strange. Who else would take on John's old place? Though even the peppercorn rent we are charging him makes a difference.' She waved her hand, dismissing Elwood, communism and the dilapidated cottage, then leant forward, her elbows on her knees and her expression suddenly serious.

'Anne, there's something else. It's a little strange but . . .' She got up and picked up a large black velvet pouch from her writing table, which she handed to Anne. 'This was in your grandfather's pocket when he fell. Open it up. Tell me what you think.'

Anne pulled open the ribbon drawstring and tipped the contents of the pouch into her lap. The winter sun was shining low through the plate-glass windows and it seemed as if she had tipped a cascade of rainbows into her lap.

'The Coke necklace?' she said at once.

But something was wrong. The weight of the necklace in her hand as she lifted it felt unnatural; even the rainbows weren't right. The facets of the stones seemed dampened, the play of light within them clumsy and lifeless.

'But this isn't the necklace, Mum. It's a copy.'

'Yes!' Elizabeth replied, throwing herself into the other armchair again and staring unhappily at the interloper as it dangled from Anne's fingers. 'I knew you'd see it! I did too, though it took me a lot longer.'

Anne felt her head spinning. 'Mum, what on earth is going on? A fall like this, and a fake necklace in his pocket? What exactly did the police say?'

'Nothing! I told you – Dad saw them off the premises pretty quickly and we haven't told them about the necklace.'

'But, Mum . . .'

'No, Anne! Your father insisted and I think he is quite right. Whatever that' – she waved with disgust at the necklace – 'means, it can't bring Tom back, but the police would see it as an excuse to kick up a fuss. Your father will *not* have a lot of policemen crawling around the house asking questions. It would simply be too shaming. And what if it got into the press? And you know it would! The King was here shooting hare only a day or two ago with your father. What if the police decide to go and ask him about your grandfather or a diamond necklace? No. It's absolutely out of the question.'

Anne started to protest again, but her mother cut her off, two spots of colour in her cheeks. 'And not a word to Carey about this either.'

'You haven't told her?'

'No. Your father and I decided to tell you, but why worry Carey with it? We have no idea what it means.'

'But Grandpa!'

'He fell and he was killed, and that's tragedy enough for us to deal with. Come along, Anne. You are nearly eighteen. A little discretion and a little responsibility is absolutely necessary for anyone in our position – you must see this is the thing to do.'

Anne felt her cheeks flush, but Mum only ever spoke to her like this when she was really upset. She was still trying to gather her thoughts when the door opened and Anne's father entered – the new Earl of Leicester, Anne realised with a slight shock. He was tall and rangy, with the high forehead, narrow nose and fine blue eyes common in the family, but his face looked tight with exhaustion. He carried his father's heavy diary, always kept in his room in the estate office, under his arm.

'Elizabeth, the solicitor is coming in an hour. Have you spoken to Mrs Warnes about the funeral arrangements? We'll need to have a marquee for the tenants after the service, of course. I hope the guy ropes haven't rotted. The game lockers are full, but if we offer them nothing but venison puffs, I'll have complaints about not doing Father justice for a decade.' He noticed his eldest daughter. 'Anne! I am glad you are home.'

'Hello, Dad.' Anne put the necklace down next to the bread and butter and crossed the room to offer him her cheek. She was almost as tall as him now. He had always seemed a spindly giant when she was a child, a distant, sharp-edged presence, a disapproving shadow cast by the fierce sunlight of her grandfather's approval. That had been especially true when he and Elizabeth had first come back from Egypt, virtual strangers to their daughters, to find their eldest child devoted to her grandfather, but nervous and prone to nightmares and sudden attacks of terror.

In the years since then she'd grown more used to him again and her nightmares had lessened, but she was still wary of him, his sudden flashes of temper, his insistence on things being done in a certain way. Her mother assured her he had been a very different man when they married, but Anne could not remember *that* father.

It still wasn't spoken of, what he'd been through and seen in North Africa, but as Anne grew up she began to suspect he had been through and seen a great deal. She knew her uncle, her father's brother, David, had been shot down and died in the desert, not of his injuries, but of thirst. He had been a sweet man, happy to play with his nieces, but every time Anne saw his photograph in the library in its heavy silver frame, his lively, intelligent face looking sideways at the camera, and his arms crossed, she tasted sand in her mouth and the war seemed very close and dark again.

'Darling, Anne spotted the necklace was fake at once. I told you she would.'

'Very clever, but has it done us any good?' He slammed the diary down on Elizabeth's writing desk, making the correspondence jump and shudder. 'And what *was* Father doing with it in his pocket? I've been looking through his appointments and can't find a thing to explain it. He and Abner Mullins had an appointment with a man from the British Museum to talk about some of the manuscripts the day before, and Horton and he were visiting tenants in the afternoon. But Horton said that was just usual estate business, and Mullins said their meeting was about checking the condition of the manuscripts. British Museum man was content we aren't keeping the Leonardo Codex in a damp cupboard and Father agreed to some repairs to the north lodge. He had nothing down for the morning, so might have been up to anything, I suppose. He had supper on a tray in the library. Nothing about the diamonds.'

He opened the diary and Anne, looking over his shoulder, saw her grandfather's familiar loose, looping handwriting. Times of appointments were marked down with names, and on the right of the page were brief notations, initials and occasional words to serve as an aide-mémoire. She studied the page, a great fondness for her grandfather, his worries and enthusiasms blossoming inside her as she read his jottings. She had a sudden memory of his face, lit by the red developing light in his photographic studio in the cellars, his enthusiasm and curiosity to see what the chemical bath would reveal, the anticipation, wondering which of his photographs of his friends, family and home had been successful.

'I've been back over the accounts from 1938 and I can't

find any sign of the real necklace being sold!' Anne's father went on, dragging her back to the present. 'No sign of an unexplained deposit in any of the bank accounts either, and if Father had a few thousand in notes stashed in the house he hid it bloody well.' He twisted round to look at his wife. ''Thirty eight was the last time you wore the necklace, wasn't it?'

'Yes, that's right. I did ask Tom if I might wear it when Princess Elizabeth married, but he said he wasn't happy with such a display so soon after the war.' She huffed. 'Though honestly so many woman there were absolutely cloaked in every family jewel they could manage without collapsing under the weight. I swear I saw the Duchess of Devonshire totter under the weight of her tiara.'

'He said you couldn't wear it in 'forty-seven then? Perhaps he sold them when my grandfather died in 'forty-one. Certainly things were a little tight at that time and we were away in Egypt by then, so we might not have heard.'

Anne shook her head. 'No, Dad. The real ones were still here in the winter of 1943. Grandpa showed them to me.'

Her father ran his long fingers over the top of his head. 'You are quite sure, Anne? It is important.'

'Quite sure.'

He gave her a careful assessing look, then nodded shortly.

'Tom would hardly have shown off a fake, darling! Not to his granddaughter,' Elizabeth added.

'No, that's true,' Leicester conceded.

'Dad, are you sure you shouldn't tell the police about the necklace?'

He stared at her as if she blasphemed.

'Absolutely not! I will not have my father's death turned into a penny dreadful mystery.'

'But, Dad—'

'No, Anne! And I expect you to respect my wishes. Good God, you are about to be presented at court! We'll have press photographers crawling around the place anyway. You'll never find a decent husband with some scandal like this hanging over Holkham.'

He turned a page in the book. 'If we can't retrieve the diamonds, we'll have to hush it up in some way. Not the sort of thing that will escape notice in the end though. The only thing that seems strange in Dad's diary in the last few days is this.' He pointed at a name, heavily underlined. 'Every other name I recognise, but who is Lavender Crane?'

'How strange,' Elizabeth said. Her face suddenly brightened. 'Oh, wasn't she the governess we hired for Anne? You and I never met her, darling. She left just before we came home.'

Anne stared at the name on the page. It seemed to shimmer and shake, grow until it filled the whole of the page, that heavy underlining, the careful deliberate outline of each letter.

'Anne? That was her name, wasn't it? Miss Lavender Crane. She came highly recommended. I remember crowing over our luck in Cairo. She probably wrote to Tom asking for a reference.'

'Excuse me, I'm so sorry.'

Anne stepped backwards from the table and, suddenly blinded by tears, made her way through her mother's overstuffed sitting room, across the narrow hall and into the bathroom. Before she knew what was happening, she was kneeling on the cold floor, her body shuddering, and throwing up violently into the lavatory. Lavender Crane. Even her name was enough to break Anne into a thousand tiny pieces.

4.

ANNE WOKE EARLY the next morning. Maria brought her breakfast tray and opened the curtains. She was normally such a brisk and lively presence in the house, usually you could feel her suppressing the urge to chatter even as she observed the usual protocols. She had been devoted to the Earl though, having joined the household with her brother, one of the Italian prisoners, just after the war, and her cousin, Gina.

'Is my father up yet, Maria?' Anne asked, taking her tray and pouring her tea. A simple breakfast, toast and butter. Her pot of jam, marked with her name, was getting rather low and there would not be a new one until the beginning of the next month, not with sugar rationing still so tight.

'Yes, my lady,' Maria said. 'He's in the office already. We're all very glad to have you home. Reverend Howard is to visit at three to discuss the music for the funeral, and Lady Leicester would like you and Lady Carey there too.'

Anne went through her usual morning routine quickly and dressed, shivering, in one of her outfits. Long skirt and thick stockings, one of the Fair Isle jumpers her aunt in Scotland so loved to knit, bless her and bless the sheep on the estate for the yarn too. She and Carey would have to scrape every coupon they had together to buy material for mourning clothes. Anne thought of the jam pot. Perhaps it was no bad thing she'd have to do without it for a week or two. The great greasy breakfasts she ate while out on the road selling the Holkham pottery wares were beginning to thicken her waist a little and her first season as a debutante was just around the corner.

She fetched her order book from her briefcase and took it downstairs and out to the old laundry that was now the domain of her mother and Holkham Pottery. However dismissive her father might be, her mother's little business now employed five people as well as herself and her two daughters and seemed to be thriving.

Carey, had at fifteen an artistic talent Anne had never possessed and a liveliness Anne felt she had lost at some point during the war, as if it had been looted from her like an artwork and she had, since then, been searching for it among the ruins of her memories. They had stayed up late in Carey's room last night talking about their grandfather and worrying about their father and the estate. Anne had not mentioned seeing her old governess's name in the day book, or her reaction to it.

When they had been reunited at Christmas in 1943, Anne's parents returning from Egypt and Carey and her nanny Billy Williams arriving from their cousin's Scottish estates, Carey had sensed something had happened, but she didn't enquire too closely, waiting perhaps for her sister to confide in her.

Anne never had, not about that anyway, and perhaps Carey took Anne's new nervousness, looking over her shoulder and freezing suddenly whenever they heard footsteps approaching, as a sign she was worrying about Lady Mary as everyone else did.

Carey was already at work at her design table, drawing abstract swirls. She saw Anne and put down her pencil.

'For the new piggy banks! They are going to be very odd-looking pigs, great long eyelashes and these paisley shapes over their backs. Do you think they will sell?'

Anne studied them over her sister's shoulder and thought of the shops she had visited up and down the coast, the sea wind pulling at her headscarf as she came in, her smile bright, and asked to see the owner. Some of them were sweethearts, gave her tea and biscuits in the backroom as she unpacked her suitcase of samples. Others looked at her with faces like thunder, arms folded, as she knelt on the cold floor unwrapping jugs and vases. She thought of their range of souvenirs, tea things and fancy goods, the butter dishes and vases people bought as a treat while in a holiday mood. After six years of war and another five of sugar rations and clothing coupons, they needed all the colour they could get.

'Yes, I rather think they will. And they'll stand out in the shops. *And* they are made to encourage young people to save!' She made her voice a bit more severe. 'A moral lesson, Carey. People will spend a few shillings for some colour, especially if they don't need to feel guilty about it.'

Carey looked at her sideways. 'Are you sure you want to do the orders today, Anne? There's no rush.'

Anne nodded. Funny how grief for Grandpa was never out of her mind yet could still spring up from the corners of her heart with renewed force.

'Yes. It will stop me moping.'

Or thinking about the fake necklace and her father's refusal to inform the police. The whole thing was making her rattled and nervous. Not to mention that strange mix of panic and nausea she had felt seeing Lavender Crane written in her grandfather's diary.

Enough of that. Concentrate, Anne. They went through the orders together, discussed delivery times and worked out the bills Mrs Fisher would need to type up and the supplies that should be ordered. For a while Anne felt calmer; work had a pleasing forward motion to it. Carey though, after half an hour, was itching to get back to her drawing board, and Anne said she would finish up the paperwork for Mrs Fisher herself.

'We'll have to get new cards printed for Mum,' Carey said over her shoulder from the doorway. 'Do you think your buyers will pay extra to have their delivery notes signed by a countess rather than a mere viscountess?'

'Most of them are far too hard-headed for that. They'll just leave the note somewhere visible on the table so the other salesmen can see it,' Anne replied.

Carey heard something and looked out of the window behind Anne. 'Oh! Your knight in painted armour approaches! Or it might be Mike, I suppose. Either way, someone is coaxing Mum's car into the stable yard.'

Anne put the cap on her fountain pen and stood up.

'Have you seen any of his work, Carey?'

'Elwood's? Yes, he had a show in King's Lynn over the summer when you were learning how to be a maid at Powderham Castle.'

'I wasn't learning how to be a maid, I was learning how to run a house!'

But Carey carried on, ignoring her protests.

'He's good. Bit of a Camden School type, so rather old-fashioned. But yes, he's very good, I think. I'd tell Dad to buy some of his work if we had two farthings to rub together.'

They walked into the main space of the pottery side by side, but Carey returned to her drawing table and Anne walked out alone into the forecourt to see who had brought her car back.

It was Elwood. He had managed to get his bike and painting gear into the rear of the little car and was now extracting them rather clumsily and cursing as he stumbled backwards over his folding easel.

'Mr Elwood, here, let me help you,' Anne said, hurrying across the gravel and picking up the easel to give him room to manoeuvre.

'Thank you!' Then when he had got the bike out and had put it down on its kick-stand so it wasn't leaning up against the rather battered paintwork of the Mini Morris, he brushed the dirt off his hands and smiled at her. It was a good smile, crinkling the skin around his eyes.

'Good morning! Mike says the fan belt just needed a tweak and there's no charge. I hope you don't mind me using it to bring my bike up.'

'It's very kind of you to bring the car back,' Anne said as he handed her the ignition key. She saw the keyring, a plaited doll that Carey had made for her years before she had any keys to attach to it, and felt a little embarrassed. 'Can I offer you tea?'

'No thanks.' He glanced down at her shoes. She was wearing her everyday, everywhere lace-ups. 'But I wouldn't mind a walk before I find my spot and get painting. I'll just be sitting on my arse all day once I start work.'

She blinked.

'Sorry! Too long in London, I've forgotten to watch my tongue.'

He seemed actually sorry.

'That's perfectly all right. Would you like to see the view from the monument?' She pointed up the slope to the monument to Coke of Norfolk, a Corinthian pillar more than a hundred feet high with a wheat sheaf on top, placed in an exact line with the centre of the Hall.

'Lovely!'

He had an air of vigour about him today, a joyousness and freedom. Anne wished she could borrow some of it and spray it on herself when she needed a lift, like scent.

They walked along one of the paths and across the great northern lawn, cropped by the deer on the estate. The air was still chill with the notes of autumn but the sun was warm.

'How are you all doing?' he asked after a while.

'Fine, thank you,' she said swiftly, realising at once this was a terrible lie. All the feelings she had squashed down while working with Carey roared back into life. He didn't attempt to say anything more until they had reached the monument and turned around to look at the sweep of the lawn, the house and obelisk on the horizon. Anne had always loved this view. It was the one place she didn't feel the vague sense someone was observing her from the shadows, ready to pounce. But then, she couldn't see the Ice House from here.

'It's a hell of a place,' he said, and for some reason that made her laugh.

'Yes, it is.'

He pursed his lips and bounced his leg, trying to keep something in. He failed. 'But you have to admit it's ridiculous one family gets to enjoy all this wealth and privilege while people starve in the village.'

'Nobody is starving in the village,' Anne replied smartly, 'and they never have while my family has been at Holkham. And as for wealth and privilege – well, it's not like Holkham or anything in it is ever really *ours*. We are just custodians and worry about it our entire lives, then pass it on for someone else in the family to worry about when we die. Though my cousin may inherit the title and not much else.'

He looked confused. Everything bubbled up to her lips. She was suddenly very angry with him.

'Death duties, remember? My great-grandfather, the third Earl, died in 1941. And right up until he died he insisted on living in a "fitting manner". My poor grandfather spent the war and the years since just trying to hang on and pay the taxes due on the inheritance. The army made a mess of half the Hall, there are no servants to look after it and hardly anyone left to work the land and the place is falling apart around our ears! Now Father has to cope with another set of taxes just as we thought it might be possible to get back on an even keel, and the whole shebang, if there is anything left, will go to a cousin we have never met because I'm a girl and only have sisters.'

Charles cleared his throat. 'I am talking in general principles, you know. I promise when the revolution comes you won't be condemned out of hand.'

'That's a comfort. Do you think that's what they told the Russian aristocracy?'

'Cousins of yours, were they?'

'No.'

There was a long pause. The wood pigeons cooed behind them and Anne caught the scent of woodsmoke on the air. It made her think of the cellars where the logs were stacked for the hungry fires that still left the Hall freezing, of her grandfather falling with that damned necklace in his pocket. She twisted sideways and wiped a tear from her eye, hoping he didn't see.

'I'm sorry to hear things are tough,' he said. 'I suppose it must take an awful lot of energy keeping up appearances and all that. Being what people expect you to be. When you are an artist people just expect you to be undisciplined and bad-tempered, so that suits me down to the ground. As you've probably already noticed.'

She looked sideways at him and he did look sorry. And kind. That little spurt of anger disappeared and now the misery and upset returned, like the tide charging up the creek.

'I don't mind all that, really. The keeping up appearances stuff. Or at least, we're all used to it, it's just . . .'

She stopped herself and sat down on the steps below the plinth.

He watched her, his forehead puckered with concern.

'Is there something else, Lady Anne? Honestly, I'm not some sort of crazed zealot, even if I have behaved like a bit of a brute towards you. If I can make it up to you in any way.'

She couldn't keep it in any more. 'There is a diamond necklace, rather valuable and it has gone missing. My grandfather was carrying a fake, a copy of it, in his pocket when he died. He fell down the stairs and the maids and the cook are saying our resident ghost, Lady Mary, did it. Anyway, we can't work out what happened to the original necklace and have no idea why on earth Grandpa had the fake in his pocket! It would all be grim enough already, but my father is terribly worried about the necklace causing a scandal.'

'Good Lord!' He took out his cigarette case and offered her one. She shook her head, then stared at the ground, listening to the flare of his cigarette lighter, his first inhale and exhale. Why had she said all that? She didn't want his sympathy, and she didn't think complaining about her hard luck was going to convert him from being a socialist or a communist or whatever he was.

He glanced sideways, seeming to sense she needed a moment to recover. 'You know, whoever commissioned this monument found a sculptor who really knew how to do sheep. That's something for your family to be proud of.'

She looked round and found herself staring up at a small group of the animals supported on one corner of the plinth.

The sheep were very lifelike, and rather smug. That made her smile briefly.

'It is a strange business about the necklace though!' he went on, still examining the sheep. It made it easier to talk to him, somehow. 'Do you have any idea when the original disappeared?'

'I saw it just after I started living here in 1943. I was rather lonely, and Grandpa showed it to me to cheer me up.'

'When you were here by yourself?'

'Yes, with my governess.' She shuddered, but he didn't seem to notice that.

'And no one has seen it since?'

'I think it was gone by 'forty-seven. My mother asked to wear it that year and Grandpa said no. But why on earth was the fake in his pocket when he fell?'

'What do the police say?' he asked, straightening up and flicking the ash of his cigarette into the grass.

She shook her head.

'They haven't been told? I see.'

Anne felt a bubble of misery and shame in her throat. 'How can you? I'm so sorry to blurt all of that out. I absolutely shouldn't have told you and Dad would be livid if he knew I had. I think it must be something to do with you being an outsider. Everyone else within fifty miles has known me since I was a child, and that makes it very hard to speak to anyone sometimes. But do you mind awfully not repeating any of what I said?'

'I'll keep it to myself. I promise. Part of my new resolve not to be a brute.' He smiled at her as he said it, but she must have believed him; she felt relieved now, not scared.

'By the way, how long do you have to live round here before you stop being an outsider?'

'My family have been here about five hundred years, so we're just about all right.'

He laughed softly.

'No, that's unfair. Some of the Italians who were here as prisoners during the war stayed on, and they are part of the community now.'

He grew serious again. 'Lady Anne, I'm sorry to ask, but are you afraid there was something . . . strange about your grandfather's death?'

It felt very uncomfortable to have someone say it out loud. Could she trust him? Some instinct was telling her she could and should. 'I am rather. Why did he have that fake in his pocket? But Father won't have it spoken of. The scandal is a worry, with me about to start my first season. I won't inherit, so I'll have to find a husband who will inherit something grand enough for Dad to be happy. And he'll do anything to avoid embarrassing the Royal Family.'

'Even ignore the circumstances of his father's own death?'

'Oh yes. It's his – our – duty. And whatever happened, Grandpa is dead and we must try and cope.'

She didn't realise she had started crying again until she found herself accepting his handkerchief. Dad would give her such a rocket if he knew, spilling the family secrets and then weeping all over a communist.

'But it bothers you?'

'It does,' Anne said, and closed her eyes. Suddenly the air felt cold and she felt that deep horrible fear again, as if she was about to lose her mind. A sense of enclosure, a damp chill.

'Lady Anne?'

She opened her eyes again. She had twisted his handkerchief into a tight band around her fingers, cutting off the circulation so the tips were dead white.

'Please call me Anne. I'm sorry. I don't know what's wrong. I used to have funny fits of panic quite often after Mum and Dad came home, but I haven't had a proper one in ages.'

'Stress can do funny things to a person. I've seen enough of it among the men I served with.'

It was all too ridiculous. 'But I wasn't at war! I was here with my grandfather living my privileged life, for goodness' sake!'

He finished his cigarette. 'It's none of my business, but when I saw you yesterday, you were obviously just very sad about your grandfather. It seems to me today you are rather agitated. Better to see it through, don't you think? Find out what has got you so upset? Rather than suppress it?'

'That's not really our way. But in any case, how can I find anything out if my father won't tell the police about the necklace?'

He was quiet for a while, then asked: 'Is it a *good* fake?'

'What? The necklace? Yes. It's an exact copy. It was only when I held it I realised it wasn't the real thing. Why do you ask?'

He shrugged slightly. 'It might not answer the question as to why your grandfather was carrying it when he died, but if you could find who made it – and it has to be someone in London really, doesn't it? – perhaps you could find *when* it was made, and that could help you towards an answer.'

'That's a rather good idea.' Her shoulders slumped. 'But I can't just ring round the likely shops!'

'Perhaps you know someone who could call on your behalf?' he suggested lightly.

Anne frowned, then her brow cleared. 'You know, I think I might.'

They went back to the stable yard to pick up his bike and painting gear, then walked together through the north gate, past the alms-houses and cottages of Holkham to the public telephone box on the corner outside the Victoria Hotel. Anne had to borrow some change for the call from Elwood, then she burrowed into the pocket of her duffle coat for two sharply folded pieces of paper. The last number on the second page was what she was looking for.

She dialled the number and waited for what seemed like forever until a very pleasant-sounding female voice answered. Yes, her husband was at home, and would be pleased to speak to Lady Anne.

A pause, then that kind avuncular voice from Mrs Rosen's hotel.

'Lady Anne? You got home safely, I hope?'

'Yes, thank you so much, Mr Samuels.' She swallowed, now or never. 'Mr Samuels, do I remember correctly, you trade in all sorts of costume jewellery?'

'I do.'

'I have the most enormous favour to ask you.'

She could almost hear his smile. 'Let me fetch a pen, and then you can ask away.'

When she hung up the receiver ten minutes later she felt both nervous and relieved. It was better to be doing something, and she was sure that Mr Samuels could be trusted.

Charles was waiting on a bench outside the pub and stood up when he saw her emerge.

'Success?' he asked.

'I hope so,' Anne said, and thrust her hands into her pockets. The air was cold and the salt marshes in the distance looked rather bleak. 'He will write to me.'

'I was talking to the landlord while you were on the telephone,' Charles said slowly. 'Did you know a boy called Johnnie Fuller during the war?'

'Yes! We were friends. Why?'

'According to the landlord, he went missing three days ago.'

5.

1943

'WHY CAN'T YOU just go to school in the village like me?'

Anne shrugged and continued weaving together the fronds of bracken. On a summer's day it would be absolute torture to be so near the beach, but not be allowed to go into the sea, but the autumn air rather killed the desire to sea-bathe. It was good to be in the Donkey Wood though, it was their particular kingdom and they knew where all the blackberries could be found and had a network of forts and hideouts stretching from one edge to the other. Sometimes she and Johnnie saw soldiers being trained from here, crawling under coils of barbed wire with their rifles in front of them, or jumping over walls and into ponds in their heavy boots while the sergeant major shouted at them. They must be doing target practice or PT runs today however, as the training ground was quiet.

'I'd hate to be you,' Johnnie said. He was sitting astride his bike. It was new, to him anyway; his brother had bought it in a junk shop in King's Lynn and fixed it up for him last time he was home on leave. It was painted a lovely dark green and the spokes shone with careful polishing. 'Imagine having a teacher to yourself all the time. Just sitting and staring at you while you are trying to do sums.'

'I quite like sums,' Anne said. The plait wasn't coming out right and her fingertips had gone green. She dropped the bracken back onto the ground and dusted off her hands. 'It's all the English I'm worried about. I never know what to write in my compositions.'

She had to sound casual talking to Johnnie about it, but the idea of a new governess worried her. Up in Scotland she had shared in her cousins' lessons, and their governess had mostly concentrated her attentions on James. Anne had sat behind them, staring out of the window and looking forward to the moment she could go and join her sister in the park. She occasionally got easy pages of maths problems to do, and comprehension exercises, which were rather fun. When James struggled through their basic Latin, Anne was allowed to draw portraits of Kings and Queens, as long as she wrote their dates and major incidents of the reigns underneath the pictures.

She would be going to school in a year, so she wasn't sure why she needed a governess at all, but Grandpa said it had been decided in a series of very expensive telegrams with her parents in Cairo, so the matter was obviously not up for discussion. She had much rather just be with Grandpa. Only this morning he had been playing her Beethoven on the huge gramophone player in the statue gallery. She had danced around to the music, under the kindly gaze of Diana the huntress. Grandpa clapped when she finished and told her all about Beethoven and how even though he was deaf he had changed music forever. It was much more fun than the lessons in Scotland.

'Shall we go and look at the prisoners?' Johnnie asked. He glanced at his watch, another present from his brother. 'You have an hour before tea.'

'The Italians?' Anne got to her feet and picked up her own bike. It looked a bit shabby next to Johnnie's, but she could still ride faster than him when they raced down the avenue, even though he was a boy and two years older than her.

Johnnie made a face. He knew Anne preferred the Italians because they smiled and waved; some of them were even allowed out to help on the farm and round the estate – the Hall carpenter had taken one on as an apprentice as his lad had been called up and the joints in his hands had started giving him problems – but Johnnie liked watching the few Germans held in their own separate hut, sure they were going to escape the second he took his eye off them, and felt thrilled and terrified as a result. They did look particularly evil. He obviously sympathised about the governess though.

'Italian then.'

They got a good welcome. The prisoners who hadn't been assigned farm work were obviously bored, and the two children racing up and down in front of their camp was at least something to look at. The guards pretended not to see them. The camp was a series of Nissen huts with wire fences around them. When the trees were bare, they might just get a glimpse of the church on the hill, but mostly their view was just the trees.

To the north they could look through their wire fencing,

over the flint and brick wall that ran around the whole estate, and look at the salt marshes and pines beyond.

It wasn't surprising, then, that they waved at the children and cheered when Johnnie managed a wheelie. He was pleased, even if they were the enemy. Or sort of. It was a bit confusing now most of Italy had been liberated and joined the fight against Hitler.

When they raised their hands over their heads to clap, the targets on their uniforms caught the light, like roundels on the wings of a Spitfire, showing their guards where to shoot if they escaped.

When they got tired, they waved one final time and started pushing their bikes towards the lake and the house.

'Mr Fletcher was showing Grandpa the game book last night,' Anne said, 'and he said the keepers are dying to catch some of the Germans escaping so they can write "two brace of pheasant, five ducks, one German" in it.'

Johnnie laughed. The sky was beginning to darken already. 'If the Germans escape, they will probably do it all at once and the gamekeepers won't stand a chance. They are only bringing the most evil and dangerous ones back to England. Mum has started locking the doors and windows in case they get as far as our house. You should have a plan of how to escape the Hall if Hitler invades. He'll probably want to live there.'

'Hitler won't invade now, will he? I thought we didn't need to worry about that any more. That's why I was allowed to come back to stay with Grandpa.'

'George said he might, just to stop us invading France and if he does, I bet he'll still want to come here.'

Anne scowled down at her handlebars. 'If he does come to Holkham, I shan't run away. I shall fight him.'

'You're a girl.'

'Well maybe I'll pretend to welcome him in, then I'll put poison in his tea!'

'He'll probably live in Buckingham Palace. But maybe he'll want to visit Holkham,' he added quickly when Anne looked offended. 'You can poison him then!'

Carey would be so jealous if Anne got to poison Hitler by herself. They had come up with the plan together, and even made up some possible poisons from pencil shavings and the scrapings of old medicine bottles till Billy, Carey's nanny, had made them throw them all away because of the smell.

She would quite like to poison the German prisoners, they looked so awful and scowling. She had said as much to Grandpa and got a lecture on the Geneva Convention. Anne wasn't convinced. The Italians were nice, but Anne blamed the Germans for making her parents move to Egypt and for the sweet rations, and for the dusty, sad, shut-up feel of the Hall. If it wasn't for the Germans Shreeve, the butler, would have time to help her polish her bike so it looked as nice as Johnnie's, or at least there would be plenty of gardeners to help, like there used to be.

They reached the kitchen garden, the great lake stretching out in front of them, the church of St Withburga on the rise to the east, the village where Johnnie lived to the west and the great sweep of the Hall laid out in front of them. He looked at his watch again.

'What's your governess called?'

'Miss Lavender Crane,' Anne said. 'Some of her luggage came yesterday and it was written on the label.'

'Lavender? Sounds like someone in a story book,' Johnnie said. 'You better hop it or you'll meet her with grass stains all over your trousers.'

6.

MRS WARNES, THE housekeeper, gave Anne a significant look when she had propped up her bike in the stables between the Bentley and the governess cart and rushed in to wash up for tea, but she needn't have worried. Miss Lavender Crane did not arrive. Anne was waiting in the nursery in the Chapel Wing with her hair brushed, shoes polished and in her knee socks and short green wool skirt at four thirty precisely, but after twenty minutes of waiting, Ruby came in to tell her Miss Crane's train was delayed and Anne was to have her tea and go to bed.

'I'll be up at half past eight to see you are ready for bed, Miss Anne,' Ruby said. 'And if Miss Crane hasn't arrived, I'll sleep in the maid's room next to yours as usual.'

Ruby had been looking after Anne since she arrived back from Scotland, and although she was very nice, she always seemed to have three other places to be. Anne ate her tea quickly, bread and butter and milk and a sausage and an apple, but no cake of course, so Ruby could 'get on'. Said she would be perfectly all right by herself, then went scurrying through the house so she could watch for Miss Lavender

Crane's arrival from a window in the south tribune at the end of the statue gallery.

It was long after dark when Miss Crane did arrive, but Anne was still watching from the window as long as she could stand the cold, then dashing back to the vents between the statues to get a little warm air from the heating pipes for a minute before returning to her post. It was colder inside the Hall than outside. Finally, just when she was afraid she'd have to go to bed before anything happened, she saw the lights of the Bentley coming down the avenue in the pitch darkness. She ran through the statue gallery and was in time to see Smith, the chauffeur, open the car door and a slim figure step out. Then she tiptoed through the dining room onto the narrow-pillared walkway that ran around the Marble Hall.

Grandpa had promised they would bring in a Christmas tree as usual this year, war or no war. Even if there was no sugar for cakes, some traditions were sacrosanct. The tree would be installed here in the Marble Hall, the grand entrance to Holkham, lit with hundreds of wax candles that had to be lit with special long tapers, and Anne and her grandpa would hand out presents to the village children. For now the hall was as Thomas Coke, the first Earl, had intended it. A huge open area like an amphitheatre, with columns of pink alabaster reaching up to the domed ceiling and a grand staircase leading towards the state rooms and galleries. Around the edge, at the level of the state rooms and hidden behind the pillars, some of the collection of Coke statues cast their pale glances down at new arrivals below them. The Marble Hall was the only bit of the house that really, truly looked like itself. The state rooms – the salon, the formal dining and drawing rooms – were all covered in dust sheets; the Strangers Wing was all shut up as nobody stayed the night even when there were shoots and the Kitchen Wing had been taken over by the Royal Engineers along with half the stables. Anne felt a bit sorry for Miss Crane. Holkham was not its usual self.

Anne hid behind one of the pink alabaster pillars and peered cautiously round the edge. The door to the vestibule opened and a woman walked into the hall, then paused, looking up at the shadows of the domed ceiling, while Smith brought in her bag and handed it to Shreeve, who was waiting quietly in the shadows. Smith huffed a little as he did. It must have been rather heavy.

Miss Lavender Crane was carrying only a tiny leather handbag, held over the crook of her arm. It shone. Her coat was long, and of grey wool, and she wore a hat in a matching colour, perched on her elegantly rolled black hair. Her shoes had high heels and her skirt, rather tight, came down to just below her knees so Anne could glimpse the gleam of her stockings. Her grandfather must have been watching for Miss Crane's arrival too. He came in through the salon, smoothed the hair back from his head and walked down the grand staircase to greet her while Miss Crane was still looking up at the ceiling. She was very beautiful, Anne thought, large eyes and a wide mouth, her skin pale and powdered and her lips a dark pink, like the sun on the red bricks of the Ice House.

'Miss Crane? Welcome to Holkham! Your train was delayed?'

He offered her his hand and shook the fingertips of her grey glove.

'Lord Leicester! Thank you, yes, a terrible journey but of course the troops must take priority. I am so sorry to have missed tea.'

'Can't be helped,' Leicester replied. 'You'll meet Anne in the morning, but once Shreeve has shown you to your room in the Chapel Wing, come and join me for a drink in the long library and we'll talk a little about your duties here. It's in the Family Wing, where I live.'

'I hope I will not get lost, Lord Leicester,' she said. Her voice was low and had a smile in it. Anne liked it.

'No doubt you will from time to time, but you'll get the hang of it. The Kitchen Wing and Strangers Wing on the north side of the house are out of bounds. The Family Wing and Chapel Wing, where the nursery and schoolroom and your and Anne's rooms are, are both to the south with the state rooms between them. Shreeve will give you directions. I'm afraid we no longer have a footman in the nursery, so we must all do a bit more for ourselves.'

'Of course, Lord Leicester,' she said. 'I am delighted to be here.'

Her grandfather nodded to her and went back the way he had come while Shreeve led Miss Crane through one of the doors on the ground floor. Anne slipped round to the other side of the pillar to watch them go, and as Shreeve opened the door off the hall for Miss Crane to pass through, she glanced back over her shoulder as if she had felt Anne looking at her. She smiled slightly, as if she had learnt something interesting, then followed Shreeve. Anne looked at her watch. She might have time to find out a bit more about Miss Lavender Crane's duties too before Ruby came to check she was in bed.

Grandpa said the long library was one of his favourite rooms in the house, after the statue gallery, and now the state rooms were draped in dust sheets it was where he entertained the guests he still had and often passed his evenings there. As soon as the door from the Marble Hall shut softly behind Miss Crane, Anne burst from her hiding place and ran round the side of the hall, through the salon, and the south drawing room and south tribune and across the landing into the Family Wing, then pulled open one of the hidden doors in the corner of the classical library and disappeared into a warren of secret corridors, with rough plaster walls and flagged floors, which the servants used to move around the house.

Anne had only been living in the Hall officially for two weeks, but she had spent a lot of time here before they got sent to Scotland to get away from Hitler. She and Carey had spent weeks staying at the Hall over the summer and at Christmas, and spent hours with their cousins exploring each secret corner of the house from the long attics, filled with furniture and huge pictures in heavy frames, to the cellars where their voices echoed and became rounded and unearthly.

Finding her way in these corridors then was like picking up a story book she had once learnt by heart and the pattern of all the secret corridors and doorways unfolded in her mind, crisp and clear as they had ever been. The Hall was like a forest, the main rooms were clearings, obvious to anyone who looked, but if you really knew the house, you knew all the secret places, the linen closets made into bathrooms or WCs, the dressing rooms, storage rooms, back corridors and dead ends, the cellars, a labyrinth of arched and echoing corridors and rooms leading one into the other, stacked with logs for the boiler and wine for the table so they smelt always of fresh-cut wood and the must of old bottles; the back corridors were so narrow in places some of the daily ladies who came to clean had to turn sideways and walk along them crabways with their mops and buckets, and in places they were wide enough for two footmen carrying breakfast trays to the ladies in their bedrooms to walk side by side.

Anne ducked into the snakelike corridor that ran round the edge of the library, turning right and left till she reached the narrow in-between space between the door back out onto the central staircase, and the secret one that opened next to the fireplace in the library itself. She leant up close to the library door and pushed it very gently so it opened the merest crack, not enough to notice if you were in the room. The corridor was in darkness, the type of velvety and complete dark that made the idea of sunshine seem ridiculous somehow. Enough light spilled from behind the fire screen in the library to set the shadows leaping round the room. They looked like they were cast by fighting animals, perhaps the lion and tiger locked in mortal combat in the mosaic above the mantlepiece. Perhaps they *did* fight whenever there weren't people to look at them and had been fighting for more than two thousand years since one of Emperor Hadrian's craftsmen had laid out the tiny squares of marble in Italy for the first time.

She shivered, waiting in the chill of the corridor, the air so still and cold it seemed to be frozen around her, and wrapped her cardigan more tightly across her chest. A cobweb, stretched by her opening the door even this little bit, brushed across her face. She pushed it away, not frightened, but tense in her bones, alert as a hunting dog.

A sudden flood of light from the door into the manuscript library. Shreeve, moving in that strange, smooth way of his, came in and checked the blackout curtains, then turned on the table lamps. A soft, yellow light, but they cast enough of a glow for Anne to see into the room properly. The shadows stopped dancing so much, the animals stilled again. This really was the perfect spot. Shreeve went out for a moment, then returned with a silver tray. Sherry, and cheese biscuits. Anne's mouth watered. She really was terribly hungry, even if Ruby had remembered her tea. It had been a bit of a worry since she'd arrived in Holkham; before the war when they stayed here, the Chapel Wing had two footmen for the nursery as well as the nannies and governesses who travelled with the children. Now Anne was all by herself there, and as each mealtime approached, she worried Ruby might forget she was sitting in the nursery waiting for her tray. They hadn't forgotten her yet, but now Miss Crane was here, she'd be able to stop worrying completely.

She was still enjoying this thought when Grandpa came in. He warmed his hands at the fire, then looked at the fighting animals. Anne studied his profile from her hiding place. His face was thin and looked drawn. He was so busy at the moment, the Home Guard in the temple, and the Royal Engineers in the old kitchen and stable yard, and the prisoners in their huts on the north edge of the park. All these new people around the place, but the house had never felt so empty.

Miss Crane did not keep him waiting long. The door from the manuscript room opened again, and she approached the Earl in his pool of firelight with an easy confident step. She had taken off her hat and gloves and her wool suit seemed rather tight around her chest as well as her hips. Anne thought, with a thrill of pride, that she looked like an illustration in a film magazine, not like her cousins' governess at all whose hair pins were always falling out. The Earl invited Miss Crane to sit and poured her some sherry and Anne was delighted to see when she sat down it was on the far side of the fireplace, so Anne could see her properly.

At first, they spoke about the weather and her journey; she had come from London. That got them on to talking about the war, which was a bit more interesting. Grandpa told her about the POW camps on the estate, and the aerodromes full of American pilots, and the training grounds and the beaches the airmen used for bombing practice, and then they talked about Stalingrad for a while, which had been such a great victory for Joseph Stalin and a sock in the eye for Hitler, and Grandpa muttered darkly about how Hitler was clearly a madman, and one could never know what someone like him might do when backed into a corner. That reminded Anne of what Johnnie had said, and in spite of herself she looked over her shoulder to see if Hitler was creeping up the corridor behind her with a knife between his teeth. He wasn't, but she felt something move in the darkness, a whisper or a breeze in the distance, and for a moment creeping along here in the dark with the night drawing in, and not being able to burst out into the light and warmth of the library, seemed to have been a terrible idea. Then she heard her own name and, forgetting the feeling presence at her back, her attention returned to the room.

'I think Lady Coke, my daughter-in-law, wrote to you with suggestions as to the curriculum Anne is to follow?'

'Yes, she did, Lord Leicester,' Miss Crane said and sipped some sherry. 'A very sensible outline for a young lady in Miss Anne's position, I thought. History and geography, with an emphasis on England and the Empire. She would like Anne to have a solid understanding of mathematics, not the theoretical elements, but enough to be able to make up and read household accounts correctly. She would also like Anne to have a grounding in the classics of English literature, and the history of art.'

Her grandfather nodded. 'Vital. I do not want my granddaughter to make a fool of herself in public. She seems, I am glad to say, naturally curious about the world and about art too. I hope you will encourage that. Without overstimulating her, of course. Well-informed, but not bookish, interested and engaged. That is the sort of lady I wish Anne to become.'

'Lady Coke tells me Anne is not a particularly artistic child? Though I understand her sister is.'

'No, Anne has not inherited her mother's artistic talents as Carey has. And her sister has more natural grace than Anne does too. Anne is a bit of a tomboy but dancing lessons can wait until after the war is over. Encourage her to be more graceful and keep her back straight – that will do for now.'

'What about music, Lord Leicester? I play the piano and can teach singing.'

'Anne has no voice!' He laughed again. 'You'll hear her at church, a lot of volume and usually in tune, but it's like hearing a baby elephant sing. Her tone makes it sound as if she is singing into the belly of a whale. If you can improve that, I would be grateful.' He paused. 'She does have a natural appreciation of music, however. I was playing her the Pastoral Symphony only today, telling her about its composition, and I am pleased to say she listened and thought about what she had heard. As far as the great composers are concerned, I shall teach her myself.'

Miss Crane didn't reply, but nodded, a neat precise movement to show she understood.

'She had better learn French too,' the Earl said. Anne could tell he was getting bored now. Thinking of music probably meant he wanted to play his violin or listen to music as he did most evenings.

'Can you tell me, Lord Leicester, a little more of what Anne is like?'

Anne suddenly rather wished she hadn't come to listen. A little curl of dread twisted her stomach. Her grandfather didn't say anything for a while.

'She is an ordinary little girl. Loving, perhaps a little soft about animals and trees and so on. But not too dreamy. The servants are fond of her. I always say if you want to know a man, watch to see if his people like working for him. So, an unremarkable child but one of whom I am very fond.'

The curl of dread twisted into a lonely hurt, like a bruise. She had heard enough. Anne let the door close, let herself out into the central landing and began the long walk back to the nursery wing, through the state rooms and the ghostly outlines of the furniture, into the chapel gallery then upstairs to her room at the very top of the wing. She checked the blackout curtain was down and switched on the electric lamp. The switch was stiff and hurt her fingers, then she caught sight of herself in the mirror and brushed the last remnants of the cobweb out of her hair.

She would sing quietly now, and she wished she could draw as well as Carey did, but her lines always went wonky for some reason. She did look very ordinary. She sat down heavily on the high bed and the springs creaked. What was wrong with being ordinary anyway? Ordinary was good.

She wished suddenly that Hitler had been creeping up the corridors, that he would turn up so Anne could show she *could* do remarkable things. She imagined Grandpa saying, 'you know, Anne, you might look ordinary but you did a remarkable thing.' Then he could write a letter to her parents and they'd realise Anne had remarkableness in her. Then they wouldn't mind about her not being able to draw or sing, or not being a boy.

She lifted her chin. If Hitler came here, she would show them. She imagined getting a medal from Churchill and being very, very gracious about it. But Hitler might not come here. Perhaps the evil Germans in their little camp would break out and take Miss Crane captive and Anne could rescue her. The gamekeepers would probably get them first though. So what was left for Anne to do? She brushed her hair fifty times and got into bed as Ruby came in, without complaining.

7.

Miss Crane looked just as glamorous in the morning light as she had done the night before. She was waiting for Anne in the nursery when Anne arrived, hair brushed and socks pulled up straight, for her breakfast.

Her skin was lightly powdered again today, and she wore a pale-coloured lipstick. The travelling suit was gone however. Instead she wore a pale green sweater with a matching cardigan over her shoulders and a long dark felt skirt. Around her neck was a small gold cross on a chain and when she smiled her teeth were very white.

'Good morning, Anne. I am Miss Crane.'

'Good morning, Miss Crane.'

'You may sit down.'

Ruby came in with the tray. Porridge this morning and toast. The surface had cooled, of course, it took so long to carry the porridge from the kitchen, but Mrs Rowse always warmed the bowl and cover and made sure it came absolutely scorching off the new range, so even after its long journey to this wing, there was still a warm bit in the middle.

Ruby winked at her as she set down her toast and Anne tried not to be nervous.

Miss Crane looked pleased with her breakfast; she touched the bowl with the family crest on it. Ruby had placed it in front of her so the ostrich with the horseshoe in its mouth was exactly at twelve o'clock, and there was something about the way Miss Crane picked up the heavy spoon, as if she were weighing it.

Lessons began at nine. Miss Crane had rearranged the furniture in the schoolroom, but then no one had really arranged it in the first place, it had just settled into position. Anne was the first person to have lessons here since her father and uncle a thousand years ago.

Now there was one desk in the middle of the room with an ink pot and a dipping pen on it and some sheets of paper. Miss Crane had set up a blackboard at the front of the room where the morning light would fall across it.

'I am told you like to read, Anne. What are you reading at the moment?'

Anne was on safe ground, and Miss Crane was smiling. Her fingernails were perfectly polished and her hair as neat and shiny as when she arrived. No ink stains or worn patches or loose pins or pencils sticking out from her pockets. Her smile was still very friendly though and she held a long ruler in her hand for some reason.

'I have just finished reading *Tarzan*, which was terribly exciting. And I was reading *Riders of the Purple Sage* by Zane Grey, but it was my cousin's book and I had to leave Scotland when they all got sick with measles, so I don't know what happens in the end. I have some fairy tales in my room and I like Lambs' *Tales from Shakespeare* too, and would love to see an actual play. I did see some before the war, but I was very small and they were children's plays. We put on some of our own for the Polish airmen in Scotland, but we weren't very good even if some of the costumes we found were splendid.'

Miss Crane tilted her head to one side. 'If I ask you a question, Anne, answer that question, but do not rattle on.'

Anne blushed and looked down at the blank piece of paper in front of her.

'A sensitive little thing, aren't you?'

Anne did not know what to say, so she kept quiet.

'I shall write a list of the books you should be reading. Is there any modern literature in this house, or any books suitable for children?'

Miss Crane sounded tired, as if the thousands of manuscripts and bound leather volumes in the libraries weren't real books at all.

'My father and mother's books are in trunks in the Red House in the village, waiting for them to come back from the war. My grandfather keeps modern literature in the smoking room, but I don't think he has any children's books. The bookshelf in the cupboard over there has all our books from before the war, and some history books and atlases that my father had before he went to school. And my grandfather said Mrs Warnes can fetch me anything I like from the library in King's Lynn when she goes to the market there. She chose *Tarzan* for me, because market day was the day before I arrived you see and . . .' She was afraid she was chattering so closed her mouth.

Mrs Warnes, the housekeeper at Holkham, was kind to Anne, even though she was just as busy as Ruby and having to do so much herself what with most of the men away and half the maids being land girls now or working in factories in Norwich. Anne's sudden arrival at Holkham without her parents or her sister or her sister's nanny had made life more complicated for her, Anne knew that. Another member of the family to look after meant more rooms to open and keep clean, but Mrs Warnes had made her welcome in her brusque sort of a way. When she was led into her room at Holkham she found her trunks from the Red House had been unpacked, her dolls and toys put on the shelves and her books and her odds and ends – a jewellery box with a Chinese ship on it, a few little china animals and clowns – set out on her mantlepiece. Even some of her old clothes and shoes that couldn't possibly fit her any more had been put in the drawers and wardrobe to make it feel more like home.

'Yes,' Miss Crane said, looking at her carefully. 'I do see. Do you know your Bible?'

'A little,' Anne replied. Everything Miss Crane said felt like a trap all of a sudden.

'Proverbs 22:15.'

'I'm very sorry, but I don't know that one.'

'I am beginning to see why Lady Coke was so keen for me to come to Holkham.' She sighed heavily and turned to the blackboard. Anne watched the words appear in looping lines of white chalk as she wrote. *Foolishness is bound up in the heart of a child.*

Miss Crane looked back at her. 'Read it to me.'

Anne did, quietly.

'Again. What does it say?'

'It says "Foolishness is bound up in the heart of a child", Miss Crane.'

'And will you remember that?'

Anne nodded.

'Good. Now let's see if you are lying or not.'

She picked up the rubber and wiped the words away. 'Write it out.' Anne hesitated. 'You have a pen and paper, Anne. Now do as you have been asked.'

Anne picked up the pen and dipped it in the ink, wondering where the words should go – at the top, as if it was the beginning of a composition? Or across the middle as if she was going to pin it up on the wall? Miss Crane looked over her shoulder and Anne's heart started bouncing about in her chest. Anne's handwriting had been praised in Scotland. Miss Peters had pointed out the evenness of her 'o's and 'e's to her cousin James as an example, but now suddenly the pen felt awkward and heavy in her hand, like she was trying to write with a dinner knife, and the page became blurry. *F-o-o-l—* then the ink spluttered. Miss Crane sighed and pulled the paper away.

'Do it again. Oh dear! Of course, I shall do what I can for Lady Coke, but I shall have my work cut out for me, won't I? Won't I, Anne?'

'Yes, Miss Crane.'

Her hand was trembling now.

'You can hardly hold a pen! Strange, you seemed able to hold a spoon when you were guzzling down your breakfast this morning. Like a little pig. Disgusting. A lady shouldn't shovel her food. Eat little, and with restraint, or we'll have to let out your clothes. No wonder you clump around so much.'

Anne bit the inside of her cheek hard. She would not cry.

A sudden snap. Miss Crane hit the top of the desk with the flat of the ruler and Anne's pen fell out of her hand.

'Don't make silly faces, little pig. Now pick that up and let's start again.'

8.

THE SERVANTS TOOK their lunch before the family, but then they had been up before the family too. Before the war, the upper servants would dine in the steward's room, while the maids and footmen ate separately. Now, with the kitchen taken over by the Royal Engineers and the indoor servants down to seven, they all ate together. It was remarkable what you could get used to. The daily women ate in the maids' dining room, but other than that there was hardly a distinction to be made. Mr Bartholomew, the estate manager, walked down the long avenue to have lunch in his cottage in New Holkham, but they hardly saw him in the actual Hall from one week to the next. The gardeners and their boys ate in the walled gardens.

'Any word from Lord Coke?' Mrs Warnes asked as she served Shreeve. The pie she was slicing was thinner than she would have liked, and the gravy rather watery, but war is war and Cook did what she could. At least they had plenty of vegetables from the kitchen garden still, but no peaches, not with the boys who used to tend the fires that warmed the greenhouses away fighting.

'Lord Leicester hopes Lord and Lady Coke will be able to

get home by Christmas,' Shreeve replied, picking up his knife and fork and examining them for blemishes. The boy who was in charge of polishing them might make a decent footman after the war, and Shreeve was instilling in him the necessary disciplines. If he proved he could keep the servants' cutlery gleaming, he might someday be allowed to polish the silver the family used.

'Such a shame they couldn't be here sooner,' Mrs Warnes said. 'I had no idea there would still be so much to do in Cairo after we beat Rommel. Half of the Italians and all of the Germans in the camps were captured at El Alamein. Seems cruel *they* should get to Holkham before Lord and Lady Coke. It must be lonely for Miss Anne, in the Chapel Wing all by herself.'

'She has a friend in the village, I think,' Abner Mullins said. 'I saw them riding their bicycles together.'

'That's Johnnie Fuller,' Ruby said. 'He's nice enough, mind you his mum is a little high just because she works in a tea shop in Wells, and his dad liked a pint or fifteen. Gower at the Nelson said he didn't know how he was going to afford his rent when Fred Fuller died. Johnnie's older brother is a nice boy though, off fighting.'

Mrs Warnes was willing to eat with the housemaids but did not wish to encourage chatter. She noticed that Ruby blushed slightly when she mentioned the oldest Fuller boy, and absorbed the information but addressed her remarks exclusively to Shreeve.

'Still, now Anne has Miss Crane to keep her company. I hope Miss Crane is settling in? I thought I'd invite her to join me in my sitting room after Miss Anne has her tea so we might discuss any requests she has.'

Shreeve patted his lips and sipped from his water glass. 'Miss Crane is certainly a very elegant young lady. A cut above many governesses. She has hung her certificate in education in her room and set up a photograph of herself in her gown and mortar, holding her diploma. Yes, I think Lady Coke did very well to employ her. And I do apologise, Mrs Warnes, she asked me particularly to thank you for the flowers in her room.'

'She hardly looks old enough to have a diploma!' Mrs Warnes replied, looking pleased and impressed. She paused. 'Perhaps now Miss Anne will leave off patrolling all the service corridors and using the cellar passages to get around. I've told her she should be careful, what with the Strangers Wing shut up.'

Abner Mullins, the house archivist, looked up sharply. His hair had thinned terribly in the last six months and his clothes were loose around his thin frame.

'Miss Anne has been in the cellars of the Strangers Wing?' he asked, his voice taut as a bow string.

'She has the run of the place,' Shreeve said kindly.

'Lord, I wouldn't go down there for all the tea in China,' Ruby said, unimpressed and unaware of the significant looks passing between the senior staff. 'The ghost is always mumbling down there, leaving doors open and lights on. I was taking His Lordship his tea in the long library the other day and she gave me such a shove between the shoulder blades I almost dropped the tray.'

'Perhaps you might warn Miss Crane to avoid the cellars, Mrs Warnes,' Shreeve said, but he was looking at Mullins.

'I shall,' she replied, and though Abner Mullins did not say anything, he nodded his head in what might have been a gesture of thanks.

Anne hardly ate anything for lunch. It was hard to appreciate the pie and potatoes with Miss Crane staring at her. She was afraid she was chewing too much or too little, but she carefully used her knife and fork just as she had been taught, cutting off little pieces and setting down her knife when she took a bite. She could hardly taste the food because of the hot sensation in her throat and backs of her eyes.

After lunch Miss Crane quizzed her on geography. For a moment Anne was hopeful; she was good at geography and had spent hours putting together the county maps of Great Britain during wet afternoons in Scotland. She and her cousins had lots of maps of Europe and Africa too as they were always looking for the countries where their friends and families were fighting, or where the allies were based now the war covered the whole world. Rather than being impressed, however, Miss Crane just looked bored. Finally, she glanced at her watch and declared lessons were over for the day. Anne was dismissed.

She got her bicycle from the stables and pedalled so fast down the avenue she could feel her hair streaming behind her. The corporal manning the north gate for the Royal Engineers returned her salute with a grin, and she skidded through the cottages and up into Donkey Wood. The morning with Miss Crane seemed like a bad dream.

They worked on their redoubt for a while, and when Johnnie asked her about her new governess, she just shrugged.

'You're very quiet, Anne,' he said at last. 'Are you sick or something?'

'No. I was just thinking it's very hard being young during a war, because everyone is off doing remarkable things, and unless Hitler comes here, I will only have ordinary boring things to do. And I would like to do something remarkable.'

'Maybe Hitler will come,' Johnnie said in an encouraging manner. 'He probably has spies all over the place. Right now. Maybe your new governess is one.'

'Maybe,' Anne said. But Miss Crane had just been horrible, not Hitler-ish. And it was Anne's own mother who had sent her, not the Nazis. She threw the stick she had been whittling hard into the autumn undergrowth. She hoped Miss Crane was a spy. Maybe she had tricked her mother into sending her to Holkham. 'But other than keep watch on her, what can I do?'

'I'll keep watch too,' Johnnie said. 'And maybe we can find something else remarkable to do in the meantime.' He paused, then a new idea hit him. 'Do you want to read a comic?'

Anne perked up. Comics weren't allowed in the Hall, and she liked the ones Johnnie had shown her. His mother bought them for him in Wells. He handed her last week's copy of *Hotspur* and began reading the new one himself. A man on the front cover was riding a motorbike and being chased by Red Indians. They had motorbikes too. For a while they lay on the dry earth and turned the pages.

'Wow!'

'What?' Anne said, returning from an adventure to destroy a secret Nazi base in the jungle.

'You have a ghost at the Hall, don't you?'

'Yes. Lady Mary. She keeps shoving Ruby.'

'Have you seen her since you came back?'

Anne remembered that feeling of movement behind her in the corridor last night. 'Maybe.'

'Well then!' He jabbed his finger at the page he was reading. It was the story of a ghost in a castle in Wales and had a big picture of a bearded man floating above the ground while a girl in a maid's uniform cowered in front of him. The maid even looked a bit like Ruby.

'It says here the maid found the ghost's bones behind a wall and he was laid to rest and the bishop said she had been very brave.'

That *did* sound like a remarkable thing. Anne pulled the comic towards her and read, hardly seeing the words as she imagined the Bishop of Norwich giving her an award. Her grandfather wouldn't describe her as an ordinary girl then. And maybe her mother would forgive her for being a bit clumsy and Miss Crane would be so impressed she'd be kind.

'Johnnie – that's a brilliant idea.'

He grinned and wiped his lips with the back of his hand. 'I mean you have to know where she is, don't you? Does she have a special time and place when she appears?'

Anne put a blackberry in her mouth. It was sour and sharp and made her miss jam more than ever, but the burst of juice on the roof of her mouth made her eyes widen with pleasure every time. She considered the question.

'I don't know. I don't think so. Ruby said she creeps up behind her in the service corridor in the Family Wing and whispers in her ear, but she can't understand what she's saying. And Cook, Mrs Rowse, says that she pushes her when she's in the cellar. Mrs Warnes said she can be a shover. Can be any time of day, mind you.'

Johnnie had spotted another clump of blackberries from his prone position on the ground and rolled over to fall on them with a small howl of delight. He didn't offer to share.

'I bet she's around much more at night. I mean, that's always true of ghosts.'

He crunched the berries in a single handful. Anne left one of each clump she found for the birds. She wondered if she should tell him this but decided not to, in case he ate their share.

'You have to take her photograph, Anne!'

'What? Why?'

'Because they would definitely print the story in *Hotspur* if you had a picture! You wouldn't have to find her bones or anything. Why does she haunt Holkham?'

'I don't know.'

'You have to find out. But you have to have the photograph too.'

Her grandfather loved taking photographs. He had a darkroom in the cellar and had let her help develop them twice already. He took pictures of the statues in the gallery, and the horses, and most of the family pictures in the salon and the library were ones he'd taken.

'You need light for photographs, and it's dark at night,' she said.

'There must be electric lights in the corridors, aren't there?'

She nodded. There weren't very many of them though so a lot of the time the passages were very gloomy and full of shadows. She'd have to stay very still so the camera got enough light. She wondered if she'd be brave enough to do that with Lady Mary drifting about. She shuddered.

'You're not scared, are you?' Johnnie asked when she didn't reply.

Remarkable people should not be scared. Not of Hitler, and not of ghosts either.

'Of course not. I shall ask Grandpa if I can borrow a camera. I just have to find the right moment.'

Taking a picture of a ghost would be an exceptional thing to do. No doubt about that.

9.

THE RIGHT MOMENT didn't come for a long time. The more Anne tried to do what Miss Crane wanted the more she got it wrong. What Anne couldn't understand was that glimmer of a smile on Miss Crane's face when she made a mistake. On her second day her penmanship was not much improved from her first and Miss Crane hit her palm with a ruler for the first time. It stung and it was humiliating and it didn't help. By the time the lesson was over both her palms were burning. Miss Crane's pretty face was flushed as if she'd just run up a flight of stairs by the time she was done. At lunch Anne could hardly hold her knife and fork, her skin felt so sore.

Worse than the pain however was what Miss Crane said. Anne's parents were going to be so sad when they came home and found their eldest daughter was such a stupid little girl. Miss Crane would do what she could for dear Lady Coke, of course, but she was no miracle worker. Anne felt herself growing more stupid by the second. She began to forget the names of the English counties. The tap of Miss Crane's pointer on the map reminded her of the slap of the ruler and made her jump, then she couldn't think straight for a moment and Miss Crane gave her no time to answer. She just said the name with a short angry gasp almost at once and struck her pointer on a new place on the map and the same thing happened again.

Johnnie kept asking about the camera and the ghost, so on Friday Anne didn't go to the village to look for him. Miss Crane spent the afternoons, it seemed to Anne, patrolling the Chapel Wing, so she didn't want to stay there either. In the end she went for a walk in the park, confused and fretful. Miss Crane was being cruel and was making Anne more stupid not less, but her mother had specially chosen Miss Crane to teach her. She had discussed her pedagogic methods with Lady Coke, that's what she had said. So, her mother must approve of this? Had Great-Aunt Bridget written to Mum and complained of her? She had been very nice to her and Carey when they were staying there, always thinking of treats for them and making sure she and Carey got the same share of the fun as her own children. Maybe she was just being polite. Anne had grown a lot in the three years since her parents had been away and she *felt* awkward and stupid sometimes, while her cousins seemed so easy and Carey was still quite little. Maybe all that awkwardness had been noticed – Great-Aunt Bridget had seen her hugging her favourite tree in the park once too and given her an odd look, but it was such a nice tree. Anne imagined concerned letters flying back and forth between Downie Park and Cairo discussing the problem of Anne and what was to be done. Perhaps Mum was afraid Dad would be angry with Anne for growing up to be a terrible embarrassment to the family. After all, he was friends with the King, so unless Miss Crane could make Anne more acceptable in society, she would disgrace the whole family!

It started to rain, spitting at first, but as Anne looked up into the broad Norfolk sky, she could see the sweep of the coming squall, grey in the eastern sky and barrelling towards her. She ran up the slope and along the track to the west of the obelisk, the blood pumping through her legs, and reached the little temple in the clearing just as the raindrops turned fat and splashy on the pale stone. She didn't go inside, but the portico gave her shelter enough. The Home Guard had use of the place. It was a little house really and sometimes the old men and boys marched up and down in front of it. No one out front today though. She peered in carefully through the window. Trestle tables with typewriters on them and a couple of men smoking cigarettes. The rest of them were probably patrolling the beach or digging more holes to fire tank mortars from. They all looked smarter now than they had at the beginning of the war, with their American rifles over their shoulders. Lots of them had field glasses too now and spent hours staring into the wide slate skies on the lookout for enemy planes, or the parachutes of spies. She ducked sideways before the men inside could spot her. Johnnie told her they didn't just train with guns, but with grenades and explosives too so they could attack Hitler from behind enemy lines if he invaded. She ran her fingertips over the pitted stonework on the portico pillars – poor temple, it was looking rather bruised – and she wondered what the classical statues inside and the men of the Home Guard made of each other. Then she turned around to watch the magnificent sweep of the squall crossing the park between her and the Hall. The sky was terribly large. Surely if spies did come in by parachute, not all of them could be spotted and run to ground in the woods and fields like a fox.

Someone coughed.

'I am so sorry to startle you,' a man's voice said as she spun around. 'I took shelter here myself. You are Miss Anne Coke, I think? The Earl's granddaughter?'

Anne nodded. The man speaking to her was much younger than her grandfather, and younger than Shreeve too. He wore an RAF uniform, with a flash of wings on his shoulder.

'My name is Captain Horton.' He put out his hand and she shook it. 'I was interrogating some of your German prisoners and was just clearing my head with a walk around the park. Then that squall caught me.'

Anne remembered something she had glimpsed running up to the temple.

'Very glad to meet you,' she said. 'I *am* Anne Coke. Is that your motorbike on the avenue?'

It looked like the one the Red Indian Chief was riding on the cover of *Hotspur*.

He smiled as if she had said something very clever. 'Yes, it is! A Triumph 2000. I'd rather be in a plane, of course, but it gets me around very well and I've been enjoying getting to know the area while I've been stationed here. So, you are a descendant of Coke of Norfolk? It is an honour to meet you.'

'I'm the descendant of lots of Cokes who lived in Norfolk,' she replied, not sure which one he meant.

He had a very thick, very black moustache and his face was tanned. Anne went red whenever she went in the sun, just like her father, but Captain Horton was obviously more like her mother, who looked like an English rose in the winter and an American film star in the summer.

He took a cigarette case from his pocket, snapped it open and offered it to her.

She shook her head. 'No thank you, I don't smoke.'

He knew that of course; one of her knee socks had fallen down as she ran up the hill and she bent down to pull it up, but it was nice of him to treat her like she wasn't a child.

'You don't mind if I do?'

She shook her head. He took one and lit it with a silver lighter. It had wings engraved on it.

'The man I mean was the gentleman who lived here in the last quarter of the eighteenth century. I read all about his land management when I was at college before the war, so it is rather marvellous to be able to visit his home.'

'Oh, I see,' Anne replied, her confusion cleared. 'The one Gainsborough painted! He's in the south dining room. My grandfather has told me about him. He said he was a great innovator.'

'That he was,' Captain Horton replied. Anne did not feel qualified to say much more about him, so she searched for a different topic.

'Did the German prisoners tell you anything useful, Captain?'

'One or two of them did! However I'm afraid I can't tell you what they said.'

'Well *of course* not!'

He chuckled under his breath. 'That's the spirit, Miss Coke.' They could see all the way to the sea from here; the house was hidden by the trees, but they looked down the lawn to the lake, with the rowing boat on it, then the salt marsh beyond the park wall and the line of pine trees on the dunes that hid the beach. Beyond that, sea and sky merged into one. A Spitfire flew low over the water, like the pencil of an artist finding the right place to sketch the horizon before he commits to making a mark on the grey wash of the page.

'Your uncle was a pilot, wasn't he?' Horton asked.

'Yes. Were you in North Africa, Captain? My mother and father are still there.'

'I was, and we lost a great deal of excellent men.' His face went dark and sad for a while, just as Grandfather's did when he thought of Uncle David. Anne had learnt to recognise that look in the faces of the men and women round her. 'Your parents will be home soon, I am sure of it,' he continued more briskly. 'We shall meet again, I hope, Miss Coke. I shall be based in the area for a while, and I'm one of the few pilots who knows some German, so I imagine I'll be back to speak to any new prisoners as they arrive.'

They shook hands.

'It's very nice to meet you, Captain. And please, I know Mr Bartholomew, the agent, would be very happy to talk to you about the estate. His offices are in the stable yard, just next door to where the Royal Engineers have set up. Please do call in and say I suggested it when you come again.'

He touched the edge of his cap.

'That is a very kind invitation, Miss Coke. I shall. The

rain has eased off, I had better get back to base. It is a great pleasure to make your acquaintance.'

Anne watched him jog away through the trees back to the avenue, then heard a burst of laughter from inside the temple. The worst of the squall had passed, so she stepped out onto the wet grass and wondered where in the house her grandfather might be. She would ask him about borrowing a camera today.

10.

Abner Mullins received the message to join Anne and Lord Leicester after tea while he was working his way through the catalogue of paintings at Holkham for the British Museum. His expertise was in manuscripts rather than art, but his position at Holkham had meant he had developed small, discreet areas of expertise in the works and lineage of painters collected by the first Earl during his extended Grand Tour. Several of the most important paintings, historically speaking, were wrapped in dust cloths in the attic. Procaccini's *Lucretia* and Chiari's *Andromeda* displayed rather too much delicately painted flesh for the tastes of some of the previous countesses. When he had taken a careful survey of these particular paintings, during that long autumn before Dunkirk and his son's disappearance, he had found that some of the canvases and sheets had been arranged in what he could only describe as a fort. He suspected Miss Anne, entertaining the Princesses Elizabeth and Margaret at Holkham while their fathers shot together on the estate, might have been behind that. Perhaps not Princess Elizabeth, she was too careful and conscious of other people's property, but the seven-year-old Anne had been a bold and lively child and she and Margaret encouraged each other.

Luckily the paintings had not been damaged while they did duties as playthings and he did not need to visit them again for the task at hand. His work over the previous weeks, and today, was to take careful notes from Coke's diaries and letters, bills of sale and packing lists to provide each painting with its history and provenance so scholars other than he could slot them into their place in the canon of Western Art. The large central table of the manuscript library was arranged with neat piles of these documents in ledgers and document boxes, all bound in black ribbon and labelled in the elegant copperplate of the archivists who had worked at Holkham before him. He was loath to leave when the summons arrived; this manner of work absorbed him so completely his worries and fears were forgotten for a few precious hours. But of course he went; he revelled in the fact that the current Lord Leicester was far more deeply interested in the treasures the house contained than his father had been, or his son showed any sign of becoming.

He assured himself nothing on the table was vulnerable to being displaced by the strange and mercurial draughts the Hall with all its secret corridors was subject to, pushed the fine Kent dining chair on which he worked in this room under the table, and went downstairs to find His Lordship.

Anne stood up promptly as he came in, and offered to pour him tea. She was growing up quickly, Abner thought, still a little girl in her skirt and knee socks, the quick moods on her face, but here, performing as a hostess, she was showing some of the poise of her mother and grandmother and her features were beginning to slim down. The young woman's face just beginning to show behind the girl's.

She handed him the cup, and he thanked her.

'Mr Mullins,' Lord Leicester began, 'Anne has been asking about Lady Mary. I hope you might find a little time to tell her what you know. Do we have any letters? Any odds and ends which might interest her?'

'We do, Lord Leicester. Some of her correspondence, and a great deal of correspondence about her.' He addressed himself to Anne. 'She married the son of the first Earl of Leicester, who built the Hall,' he said, 'but it was, I'm afraid, a very unhappy marriage. It seems she did not want to marry at all and they never got on. She kept to her rooms, and she had no friends here, so she must have been very sad and lonely. Her mother, the Duchess of Argyle, came and rescued her in the end.' He suddenly felt himself struck by the fact Anne herself was in a rather similar position. 'But then she went to London,' he hurried on, 'and had a great many friends and a lot of rather strange adventures.'

'She is not buried here? I thought ghosts only haunted places if they were shut up in the walls or some such thing,' Anne said.

'She is buried in her family vault in Westminster Abbey.'

'Oh. I see. Why does she haunt Holkham then, do you think, Mr Mullins?'

Mr Mullins did not believe in ghosts. He believed in those devilish draughts, old pipes and strange acoustic quirks which carried voices around the walls and wings the same way a whisper could travel across the dome of St Paul's

Cathedral. But he did not want to say that in front of Lord Leicester, who liked to tell stories about the ghost to nervous visitors, or in front of Anne.

'That is probably a question for the vicar rather than myself,' he said, 'but perhaps it is her sadness and distress which haunts Holkham, rather than the lady herself.' His Lordship looked sceptical. 'Or, as Holkham Hall is such a happy place, perhaps it is better to say her sadness appears in odd places and patches from time to time, simply bubbles up very occasionally, like damp under wallpaper.'

The analogy amused Lord Leicester and he gave a short bark of laughter. 'Ha! Yes, like that infernal patch of damp in the yellow tapestry bedroom. The house carpenters have crawled around the attics and under the floorboards a dozen times, and none of them can work out where it is coming from!'

Abner felt a spark of an idea. 'Perhaps, Anne, I might speak to Miss Crane, and we might together do a small study of Lady Mary? If I might steal a little of your lesson time some mornings. We can look through the mentions of her in Debrett's, and in the diaries and letters of various writers of the period. I believe Horace Walpole mentioned her frequently.' Not always in the most complimentary terms, now he thought of it. Wasn't it Walpole who had started referring to her as the white cat?

'That's very kind of you, Mr Mullins. I should like that very much!' She seemed very keen. 'Thank you.'

It would keep her out of the back corridors too, if her interest in Lady Mary could be confined to the libraries, and that would be a blessing for all of them.

'Anne, go to my study, there is a box on the table I would like you to bring me,' Leicester said. 'That's a good girl.'

'Of course, Grandpa,' she said. She sprang up lightly, the urge to be always in movement as strong in her as any healthy young person. And there was the problem, Abner thought, though he kept the sigh of worry internal. When she had left the room, Abner set down his tea cup.

'Lord Leicester, I hope that Anne does not see some parallel between Lady Mary's confinement in Holkham Hall and her own situation.' Leicester raised an eyebrow and Abner hurried on. 'Only she has until so recently been with her sister and cousins, and I know she has a friend in the village, but still she is very much alone here.'

The eyebrow lowered and the Earl's expression became thoughtful.

'It is true, and she has some weeks of isolation still to come.'

'How are Miss Carey and her cousins?' Abner asked. 'Measles can be such a nasty illness. I remember my boy suffered terribly.'

The Earl looked sympathetic and sad at the mention of Abner's son. 'It's knocked them all for six, I believe. Anne was lucky not to catch it, but Carey is recovering well, I'm glad to say. We will not see her at Holkham however until my son and Lady Coke are back in England. Do you have a suggestion, Mr Mullins, as to how we might occupy Anne?'

'Only that perhaps we might give a few more jobs around the house, to occupy and entertain her when she is not at her lessons and the weather makes bicycling to the village less appealing.'

Lord Leicester nodded. 'Yes. That is a good thought. She might, I think, air the Codex and the Bible Picture Book and some of the other manuscripts, don't you think?'

Abner agreed.

'Grandpa, is this what you meant?'

Anne had reappeared with a parcel wrapped in brown paper.

'It is. Now, open it up.'

Anne sat back down on the sofa and unwrapped the parcel on her knee. The Earl looked happier than Abner had seen him since the war began, a kind of Christmas eagerness on his face.

'Oh, Grandpa!'

The brown paper was pulled back to reveal the yellow and black packaging of the Kodak company. Anne opened the carton with great care, and Abner caught sight of the leatherette cover and distinctive square shape – the latest Box Brownie.

'I ordered it after we spent our first afternoon in the darkroom,' the Earl said. 'I was very pleased you came and asked for a camera on the very day it arrived!'

'And this is mine?' Anne said, her voice squeaking slightly. 'I can keep it?'

'It is yours, and yours alone, Anne. Now we must decide what you should photograph.'

Anne jumped up from her seat and flung her arms around her grandfather's neck. He looked pleased, and patted her shoulder.

Abner sighed with relief. This was excellent news. Photographs needed light and there was little of that in the cellars or in the back corridors; if Anne's activities naturally extended no further than the Earl's darkroom, all might yet be well.

'Might I recruit Miss Anne occasionally?' Abner said. 'To have photographs of all the statuary of Holkham would be a wonderful addition to the archives.'

'What do you say, Anne?'

'Of course, Mr Mullins.' Not enthusiasm this time, but genuine politeness.

'Only when the weather is too bad for you to take pictures outside,' Abner added and the child looked relieved, as if she had been expecting to be locked in every day.

The Earl was delighted with the idea. 'Excellent, excellent.'

Abner managed a couple more hours in the manuscript library, making steady progress on the archival work, and only noticed the passage of time when he got up stiffly from his chair again to turn on the electric light. His eye snagged on the thin line across the bookshelf next to the brass light switch, the only sign of the invisible door leading into the service corridors. How had he described it? Lady Mary's ghost like a bubble of sadness and anger in an otherwise happy house. He thought of his son, a blister of pain and worry in an otherwise smooth existence, threatening all the time to grow and ruin him entirely.

He missed his wife every day, but he was glad now that she had died before having to bear her portion of this pain and sadness. War had only been a small cloud on the horizon when she passed. If she knew now, in God's arms, about the horrors of the retreat from Dunkirk, what Paul might have seen and suffered there, she now understood them as a part of God's plan in a way Abner himself was not yet privy to. He wondered what other sorrows were growing in the house, and into what pain or shame they might blossom. David, the Earl's younger son. There was one. The lack of a male heir – there was another. The terrible state of the Holkham finances after the refusal of the last Earl to economise, and all this in the middle of a war with reduced staff in the house and on the estate.

He shook himself. There was too much in this world Abner Mullins could not control, could not fit onto index cards and paper clip into his archives, but some things he could manage. If he could not fight, he could do this work at least to preserve some corner of England and its history, the history of Europe in fact, while the fascists ground so much of her culture under its heel, defiling and distorting what they did not destroy. He returned to the library table, refilled his pen and set to work chronicling the viewing, purchasing and shipping of an idyllic landscape showing Marsyas and Apollo in musical battle. A beautiful picture of Claude Lorrain's. Marsyas would lose his battle and be skinned for it, but this image came from before that dreadful fall. Its colours, Abner knew, were as fresh and full of light as the day the French master had touched his brush to the canvas, and so they would remain long after Abner and his worries were lost among the sands of time.

11.

Anne was shown the treasures from the safe next to Shreeve's rooms on the first Sunday afternoon after the arrival of Miss Crane. As soon as they came back to the house Anne was sent upstairs to take off her church clothes and told to hurry back to meet her grandfather in the plate room.

She had prayed conscientiously in church today and concentrated so hard during the sermon her head was a bit woozy when they walked out of St Withburga's into the late autumn sunshine. She stood next to her grandfather with her hands clasped in front of her while he greeted his tenants and smiled at everyone. Captain Horton was there, she noticed. He had found a seat at the back of the church and was now chatting to Lieutenant Ketteringham of the Home Guard. She saw with satisfaction that Lieutenant Ketteringham was introducing Captain Horton to Mr Bartholomew, the estate manager, and at one point they both glanced in her direction and smiled in a friendly way. Mr Bartholomew was leaning heavily on his stick. He had meant to retire too by now, and hand over the job to his son, but his son had died during the Battle of Britain. Anne wondered which was worse, knowing someone was dead, or not knowing like poor Mr Mullins. Thank goodness Mum and Dad weren't fighting any more. They just had to get home safely now.

Miss Crane was dressed for church, hat and gloves, but, Anne had to admit, looked rather dashing at the same time. Seeing her welcomed into the little group round Captain Horton made Anne blush. Miss Crane would tell Captain Horton how stupid and embarrassing Anne was, and he might be less friendly next time they met. The idea gave her a cold, sick feeling in her stomach. She lifted her chin and resolved to ignore it. There were no lessons today after all. Still, even glancing at Miss Crane, her straight back and glossy hair, made Anne's palms burn. And her wrists.

Anne presented herself at the table in the plate room where the silver was polished, slightly flushed from her hurry to get there as soon as she had changed out of her church clothes. Her grandfather and Shreeve were already there, and when she appeared Lord Leicester smiled and told her to sit down next to him. His Sunday tweed smelt of tobacco smoke.

Shreeve withdrew briefly, and returned with a small stack of oilcloth-wrapped packages and set them down in front of her grandfather, then, having asked if his Lordship required anything else, he withdrew.

'Anne, from now on this will be your job every Sunday between church and lunch,' he said. 'We have at Holkham some very rare and beautiful objects, not just the statues in the galleries or the paintings on the walls, but also these books.'

So that what was in the packages.

As he spoke, he withdrew a thin volume from the first package. It was covered with brown leather, but as he opened it, Anne could see the pages within were a great deal older.

'You know what this is?'

'The Holkham Bible Picture Book!' Anne replied smartly. He had shown it to her once before, before the war even, but the images, in blues and reds, of the garden of Eden and the flood had stayed in her memory and dreams for weeks afterwards.

'Indeed. Made by anonymous monks in the mid-fourteenth century. Now, it is a strange thing with books, even ancient books like these. They want to be read. Leave them shut up, even in the safety of Shreeve's safe, and they might get mouldy and fade. They punish the inattention of their owners. So, every Sunday you must come here and turn the pages so the air can get in and they don't grow resentful.'

He moved the volume to one side and unwrapped the second oilcloth package.

'And do you know this one?'

'The Leonardo da Vinci Codex.'

'And who was Leonardo da Vinci?'

Anne was so entranced she forgot to stay still and swung her legs under the table as she answered, sitting on her hands to resist the urge to touch anything before she was supposed to.

'He was a painter and inventor. He painted the Mona Lisa and the Last Supper.'

The quiet approval of her grandfather was a tangible source of warmth in the chill of the room.

'Well done, my dear. This too needs to be read. Every week now, and turn every page, slowly and carefully, no flicking through it like you might a magazine. Now do you understand, Anne? This is a great responsibility. You are a very lucky little girl, but your position now and in the future will bring duties as well as pleasures. Do you understand?'

Anne nodded. She was not entirely sure that she did understand. Doing your duty at the moment seemed to mean leaving your family and going off to war for years and fighting and being killed, not turning the pages of a book, however seriously Grandpa was speaking.

He began to turn the pages, slowly and carefully and one by one just as he'd described, and as he spoke Anne's eyes swam with the tiny backwards writing and the careful sketches – circles shaded like moons with long lines coming off them, bowls and cups and a little see-saw with children playing on it and all those words.

'Do you see, Anne?' her grandfather said quietly. 'He is writing about water, how it moves and erodes the rocks around it.' He touched another page. 'Here he is studying waterfalls.'

She leant forward, hardly breathing, studying the delicate lines of his drawings and the mysterious writing that bubbled up around them. So the hand that had painted the Mona Lisa had rested on this page. She shivered suddenly as if his ghost had passed through them and was sitting with them now, dipping his pen in his ink and writing, the ideas still pouring out of him so fast that he didn't know he'd been dead for more than four hundred years.

'Now, when you have aired these, you must put them back

in the safe and close the door. Shreeve will leave it open while you are working. Then, until the lunch gong goes you must care for some of the less famous of our friends.' He nodded to the other end of the table. A small stack of leather volumes Anne hadn't noticed before was standing on the green baize alongside a small tray with a brown bottle, a bowl and a cloth.

'The covers must be oiled to prevent them cracking. Those pages you can flick through a little more quickly. They are not so vulnerable or valuable as the Bible and the Codex, but they are still great treasures. I shall show you how to use the oil. It is a recipe perfected by one of Abner's predecessors in the middle of the last century. The archivists at the British Library were so impressed with its qualities, they petitioned my great-grandfather for the recipe.'

'Did he give it to them?'

'Naturally! Now. You'll oil as many as you can until lunch and Mr Mullins will take them away when he comes in on Monday and leave some more for you when he leaves on Saturday evening.'

'What's that?' Anne said, pointing at another oilcloth case her grandfather hadn't opened yet.

He chuckled. 'Ah, now this you need not concern yourself with. It is far better able to look after itself than our poor books, but I thought you'd like to see it. Not to come out of the safe again, however! No playing with it when you put the Codex and Bible away! If I have your promise on that, I shall show it to you now.'

Anne nodded.

'Very well.' This time instead of a book, the oilcloth cover held a narrow jewel box, perhaps two inches high and covered in cracked red leather. The clasp that held it shut was gold. 'You may open it.'

She did. The Coke diamond necklace lay on a bed of white cloth, a diamond sun. A circle of brilliants, with pendant rays all set in silver. It gave off light. Each stone, especially the large ones at the end of the rays, was a dense forest of rainbows, a cluster of refracted light. Anne reached out to touch it, then stopped and looked up at her grandfather.

'You may pick it up, Anne.'

She held it at the top and lifted it up very gently. The links that held the silvered settings clinked in tiny metallic fractured notes as they shifted, as if they were greeting her, and the great stones at the swoop of its arc swung slightly. The rainbows scattered round the room. It was beautiful. Not in the fine human way of the Bible pictures or Leonardo's quick sketches however; the necklace had an awesome, untouchable beauty.

'It's heavy!' she said and laughed and the laugh and the rainbows seemed to shiver together around the room and scatter light all across the green baize.

'It is.' Lord Leicester sat back in his chair for a minute and let his granddaughter enjoy the splendour of the thing. War had made so much of life rather drab, the diamonds gave a light both joyful and unearthly, a promise of better times both past and to come.

'Now, put it back. Remember it is not to be played with.'

Anne set the necklace back in its box. If she could not look at it, it would still be nice to know it was there, shimmering away in the dark.

'Anne? What is that?'

She was just closing the box and the left sleeve of her cardigan had ridden up against the table. Her grandfather was staring at a purple bruise that outlined her wrist under the base of her thumb and across the tender underside of her wrist, just where her skin was so pale her veins were visible between the soft tendons and bones.

'Nothing!' She pulled her cardigan down to hide it again. 'I was climbing over the wall near the beach and slipped and hit it on one of the round flints. It doesn't hurt.'

'You are too old to be climbing over walls, Anne. We have gates.'

Anne blushed. She didn't know why she had lied and was surprised that the lie had come so quickly and easily. That made her ashamed, but telling the truth would have been much, much worse.

Her grandfather didn't mention the bruise again. The necklace was shut away in its box, and they sat together in companionable silence, rubbing the oil mix gently into the leather bindings and rustling through the pages of dense black print.

Anne liked the way the words seemed to sink into the paper, and as they worked her grandfather explained to her about how they were printed. The air was tinged with a scent of lavender, wax and something sharper, an astringent, lemony note, and Anne's mind filled with images of men in London printing shops, arranging the metal letters in rows, the colours of the inks and the weight of the iron presses. All that work to make these lovely pages in front of her now. She thought how those printers and writers would be pleased to see her taking such good care of their books, and the pleasure of it seeped into her bones. Time passed swiftly. As it was Sunday, she and her grandfather had lunch together in the family dining room. It was not as grand as the dining rooms upstairs, but the walls were lined with collections of china and water-colour landscapes, which gave it a friendly feeling. Her grandfather carved the chicken so she got breast meat with a huge slice of brown, crispy sweet skin. Afterwards she was given her sweet ration. Three boiled sweets like jewels. She hid two in her room, then, sucking the third, fetched her bike and headed off to the village to find Johnnie in Donkey Wood, her new camera slung securely over her shoulder.

They spent the time until tea planning the operation with great care. Obviously Anne should practise first. They read the instruction booklet together, and Anne took three pictures of Johnnie, looking carefully through the view finder to make sure he was in the centre of the frame and setting the aperture and shutter speed. The click of the shutter, and the slight resistance as she wound on the film, was very exciting and satisfying. After taking one of him with his hand shading his eyes a little, on the lookout for spies, and another of him in one of the redoubts, he asked if Anne would take one of him with his bike. They decided to take that photograph in the village, and it looked rather good through the view finder. Something about how the light and shadows fell, and his delighted grin towards the lens. His pride shone out with the glow of the autumn sunshine reflected on the red brick walls of the reading room. Anne hoped she'd still see it when the photograph was developed in black and white, and somehow she knew she would.

12.
1950

ANNE STARED AT Charles Elwood in astonishment.

'Johnnie Fuller has gone missing? When was this?'

Elwood pushed his hair out of his eyes. 'The landlord's not sure. A couple of days. But he didn't sound concerned, might just have been telling me the time of day. Your old friend sounds like an unreliable character.'

Anne sat down on the bench by the telephone box. Charles took a seat next to her and lit a cigarette.

'Yes, he is a bit. I haven't had a conversation with him for years,' Anne said. 'Not since my parents came home, really. We'd rather fallen out, and once my sister Carey and I were together again we tended to play with each other. I think Johnnie got a bit prickly about hanging around with two girls. Two *little* girls,' she added. 'His mother died just after the war ended, and he went off the rails a bit after that. My grandfather tried to help, gave him an absolute rocket about his drinking once or twice, but it didn't seem to help.'

'What did you fall out about?' he asked, flicking his match to kill the flame. 'When you were children, I mean.'

'Oh!' Anne half laughed, slightly embarrassed. 'Ghosts! And spies.'

'Important stuff! I got the impression Johnnie going missing for a day or so isn't unusual?' Charles asked. 'How old is he?'

Anne hesitated. 'He is two years older than me – a little more. So he must be twenty now. He did rather lord it over me when we played together, what with him being a boy and older, and his mother bought him comics I wasn't allowed.'

Charles chuckled softly. 'No wonder he thought well of himself. What does he do now?'

'He works at the brickworks on the estate. But I think he's not a very *good* worker. I'm afraid he got one of the maids into trouble and there was a rather rushed wedding last summer. I understand he doesn't enjoy fatherhood a great deal, and tends to disappear off to Wells with his wages as soon as he's paid. Mrs Warnes sends a box of odds and ends to his wife every week. She shouldn't really, as those parcels are supposed to go to widows, but my mother pretends not to notice.'

'Your class spends a lot of time pretending not to notice things.'

Anne felt her anger prickle. 'And people with your politics tend to think simply shouting about every injustice you discover actually changes things.'

He winked at her.

'Oh, you're teasing me.'

'Just a little, Anne. You do seem to know a lot about him, given you haven't had a proper conversation with him since the war.'

She smiled ruefully. 'Such is Holkham! Johnnie's wife, Gina, is the cousin of Maria who still works in the Hall, and Maria keeps us all informed. Honestly, the news seems to sweep around the place. You can't even remember who told you what half the time, but we all seem to know each other's business.'

He leant against the back of the bench, his long legs stretched out in front of him. How easily men moved around the world, Anne thought. They never seemed to worry they might be taking up too much space. 'When is your grandfather's funeral?'

'Saturday. And I must get back to the house, there is so much to be done. By the way, I asked Mr Samuels to write to you with any information about who might have made the necklace. I do hope you don't mind. It's not that anyone would dream of reading my letters at home, of course, but Mum or Dad might ask who a letter they didn't recognise was from, and I'm absolutely terrible at lying.'

Elwood blew out a plume of smoke. It seemed to hang forever in the frosty air.

'I'm happy to act as your postman, but how am I to get a letter to you without raising the same questions?' He frowned, and then answered himself. 'As it happens, I'd like very much to paint from the beach at the end of Lady Anne's Drive. Might you grant me permission to do so? If you do, I shall be there during what daylight hours we have at this time of year, then you can come and see me whenever it suits you.'

'You'll freeze to death!'

He chuckled. 'I have a thermos, and my art to keep me warm. By the way, is the drive named after you?'

'No, of course not. I only became Lady Anne five minutes ago. The drive was built in the early 1820s.'

'You're a walking encyclopaedia!'

She shook her head. 'That's a dreadful thing to say to a girl before her first season, Charles. It's just my grandfather liked me to know about such things. Listen, if you are sure . . . I'll get my father's blessing for you to paint from the end of the drive and I will send you a note saying you have it. You can brandish that at any of the estate workers who might challenge you. The poor beach, it was so lovely before the war. We used to go down from the Hall in the charabanc, the one my father still drives the whole village to church in, all the children and our nannies, and spend the whole day on the dunes in the children's beach hut.'

'And now?'

'You'll see. There's an awful lot of barbed wire still lying around, and bits of the old taxis and buses the RAF and Americans used for target practice. Grandpa spefnt years negotiating with the army and government about the clean-up. That will fall on Dad now, along with everything else. Captain Horton keeps trying to get the arrangements in place, but it's a very delicate job. He keeps telling them, the dunes need to be tended, not just dug up. There are all sorts of weapons pits along the drive too. You'll see.'

'Horton? That's the name I see on the bottom of my quarterly bills, isn't it? He's the estate manager?'

'Yes. He was stationed near here during the war, then took over the estate management from Old Mr Bartholomew three years ago.'

One of the messenger boys from the station turned off

the road towards the gates on his bicycle, towing a little cart of packages from the London train. He saw Anne and waved, and she waved back.

'Anne,' Charles said, frowning over the end of his cigarette, 'has your father spoken to anyone else in the house about the necklace? Aren't there other members of staff who were here between 'thirty-eight when your mother last wore the necklace and now?'

'Oh, yes, lots! Abner Mullins, our archivist, has always been here. And Shreeve, the butler. And our cook and housekeeper too.' She smiled. 'Not to mention Paterson. He's the head gardener and a very keen bagpipe player. He particularly likes playing whenever we have visitors, walking up and down on the terrace and blowing like crazy. But neither my father nor mother would ever ask them about the necklace.'

'They may have noticed something!' he protested, pulling his coat around him.

'Even if they had, they wouldn't say anything,' she said firmly. 'Certainly not the senior staff. It's not just my class who are good at not noticing things, you know. The servants are experts at not seeing things. They have to be, or we'd never be able to all live together as we do.'

He shook his head, but didn't press the point. When he had finished his cigarette, he set off on his bicycle with a wave while Anne turned back towards the house and the jobs that awaited her there.

When Anne went into the estate office on an errand from her mother, Lord Leicester was using the telephone.

'Anne!' Her father covered the mouthpiece with his hand for a moment. 'Wait there.'

'If your photographers trespass on my land,' Leicester barked at whoever was on the other end of the line, 'I will have them shot as poachers! That is what they are.'

Anne adjusted the papers and boxes she was holding and waited for her father to finish.

'It is a *private* funeral!'

Whoever was on the other end of the line was obviously a determined character. When Dad got as angry as this, not even her mother Elizabeth could calm him down. She had learnt, and taught her daughters, simply to wait until the worst was over and her husband was fit to be spoken to again. Stay still, don't roll your eyes and don't interrupt. It usually worked and he became quite reasonable after venting his irritation for a few minutes. The person on the telephone however had obviously some magic power to get a word in without waiting so long.

'Fine,' Leicester said, the bark subsiding into a growl. 'One photographer and one reporter at the church, and send people who know how to behave decently, will you? I will not have some oaf leaning against the gravestones smoking cheap cigarettes while I bury my father. And I will hold you personally responsible for their behaviour. Until then get your leeches off my land. And I expect you to make sure none of the other papers send their people . . . I don't care how you arrange that. Just do it.'

He slammed the receiver back into its place, then took the bundle of papers from her.

'What's this?'

'Letters of condolence from the tenants. Mum says she'll do all the family and friends, but you should handle these. The stationery has arrived from London.'

She put the box on the table and her father opened it. Thick paper, the weight of visiting cards, with the family crest printed at the top, the ostrich trying to swallow a horseshoe, and a black border round the edge. Missives from a house in mourning.

'I suppose we shall be using this stuff until it is time to send out the invitations for your coming out dance,' he said, tracing the edge of the paper with his fingertip. 'When did we say that should be?'

'June, we thought. A Saturday in the second half of the month.'

'Another nightmare. God knows how we will scrape together the money to launch you in a respectable manner. But we shall have to manage somehow. Presumably you'll need clothes.'

Anne blushed. She wanted to remind her father that she had earned almost two hundred pounds in sales just on her last trip. Also, her mother had managed to get hold of a great length of parachute silk and had plans to dye it a pale green that, she confidently asserted, would bring out Anne's pale skin and blonde hair beautifully. He didn't mean to be cruel, she knew that, but he did sometimes make her feel that, just by existing, she was nothing but an expense and a disappointment.

'What else?' he said.

'It's nothing really, but Charles Elwood, the artist who sorted the car out for me, was wondering if he might paint from our beach. I said I'd ask.'

Her father was staring glumly at the thick stack of letters. 'The communist?'

'I don't think he'll have much of a chance to start a revolution on the beach, Dad.'

He gave a grunting half-laugh. 'Good point. Very well, he may paint where he likes.'

Anne hesitated. 'Dad, would you like a hand with these notes to the tenants? You've taken me to visit most of them, so I'm sure it would be all right if I wrote a few.'

He brightened slightly. 'Yes, that would help, Anne. If you can spare an hour. I'll have to do most of them, but you could certainly do some of the labourers and their families.'

Anne fetched her fountain pen from the pottery, then positioned herself at one of the desks in her father's office with a stack of the mourning stationery on her right, and the letters of condolence on her left. The first note she wrote was to Charles, short and formal, telling him he was at liberty to paint from Holkham Beach at the bottom of the drive. She then began to work through her thankyous. She knew all of these families to some degree. Her father had got into the habit of taking her on some of the tours he made round the estate since she finished school. She wasn't sure exactly why. Her grandfather had taken Dad round because they both knew these houses, farms and families would be his responsibility some day, though that day had come sooner than any of them had expected. Anne would never assume that responsibility. Perhaps her father thought it would make her a better helpmate to her future husband, who would probably inherit similar duties.

She worked steadily, trying to add some personal touch to each one and sending her best wishes to the children and relatives of her correspondents. When she was about halfway through, Captain Horton knocked on the open door and came in, a sheaf of papers in his hands.

'Yes, Horton?' her father said, looking up. Anne noticed he had been making slower progress through his pile of letters. 'What is it now?'

Captain Horton was still as handsome as the day Anne had met him at the temple. He had become a regular visitor during the war, and when Mr Bartholomew had suggested him as his replacement as estate manager, he had been welcomed with relief.

'A number of letters that need your signature, Lord Leicester,' he said. 'I believe we should have a London man in to look at the damage in the Strangers Wing. For all the repairs we've made since the war, some of the plaster is still refusing to dry out. I got a name from Mr James Lees-Milne.'

'The National Trust fellow?'

'Yes. He has amassed a great deal of experience in recent years.'

'I bet he has. He knows all our homes inside out now.'

Horton realised for the first time that Anne was in the room. He turned and smiled at her.

'Good morning, Lady Anne.'

'Good morning.'

She wondered why he had never married. She knew all the maids were half in love with him. Ruby had been for a while during the war, but she ended up marrying Johnnie Fuller's elder brother when he was demobbed, and had two children now.

Captain Horton looked down at the page his employer was signing and coughed discreetly.

'What? Oh, Christ. I've signed as Coke, not Leicester. Get another typed up, will you?'

'Of course.'

'Damn it. Thank you, Horton, for taking the Hall repairs off my plate for the moment. It should, I suppose, be Shreeve's job as it is the house itself, but he and Mrs Warnes can barely keep us fed and clean at the moment.'

'I consult Shreeve regularly,' Horton said, carefully. 'I imagine that the house carpenter and his boy will be busy with the tents for the rest of the week, so I've asked him simply to make it safe in the Strangers Wing for now until we can get it looked at properly. We can turn our attention to the old kitchen when the weather begins to warm up.'

'Yes, very good.'

Anne turned back to her letters, trying to make sure she didn't repeat herself or her phrases of thanks too often. The notes would be compared in the villages, and it would not do for people to feel they had received only a rote copy. Anne sometimes felt she spent a lot of her time having to worry about the exact nuances of other people's feelings and thought for a minute with envy of Charles, who could be bad-tempered and no one cared. Still, she lived here, and he lived in that run-down cottage – though the temperature in both probably wasn't much different. Dad had bought half a dozen gas heaters last winter when the whole county seemed to freeze solid in order to get at least some of the rooms to a decent temperature. Ugly things, but they didn't need as much looking after as the open fires and could be trundled off into the service cupboards and corridors when visitors were expected.

She frowned at the next letter on the pile – a very round, feminine hand – written with the pen pressing deep into the paper as if it had been carved by someone used to holding a chisel. She turned it over to read the signature. Ginella Fuller (Mrs). Johnnie's wife.

Anne felt a sudden stab of guilt. She hadn't thought of Johnnie's disappearance since she had said goodbye to Charles. She read the letter more carefully. It was a simple note of condolence. Gina said how glad she was she had come to England, and that the late Earl had always been very kind and patient with her, even making a joke of it when she splashed the soup the first time she had served the King, and how she missed polishing the silver sandwich boxes the guns filled from the buffet in the morning and took out with them for their lunch during shoots. Shreeve must have thought she was a good worker; he normally only let the senior footmen polish silver that would pass under the family's eyes.

Anne turned the page. Gina added her husband was 'away', but knew Johnnie would want to send his sincere condolences too.

Anne wrote her reply, sending her thanks and best wishes to Gina and Johnnie and her hopes that the baby was thriving. Should she say something more? How she remembered playing with Johnnie during the war? No. Better not. She decided to add only that she hoped Johnnie would be home in time to attend the funeral and signed her name. Then she got out her own small notebook from her pocket and made a note to ask Mrs Warnes to put together packages after the funeral for all the families with children on the estate. There was bound to be food left over, and perhaps there were other women, like Gina, who had husbands who were not as reliable as they might be and who would appreciate the help.

The days became very busy with preparations for the funeral. Mrs Warnes and Lady Leicester were their generals, and every woman on the estate from Anne and Carey to the dailies and the wives of the estate workers helped. The tents for the workers and tenants were set up on the north lawns. Beer casks arrived on traps pulled by shire horses and Mrs Rowse prepared a phalanx of game pies and issued strict orders to the gardeners. Not the season for greens of course, but Mrs Rowse tore apart her recipe books looking for ways to dress cabbages and potatoes and eggs in such a way as to make them a fit dish for the family and guests in the salon and the tenants and workers on the lawn.

For two days Anne was too busy organising to think about the necklace, consulting with the gardeners about the flowers and helping her mother with the order of service. Two days before the funeral, however, Anne decided she could slip away for an hour or so and walked through Holkham village and down the drive to the beach.

13.

CHARLES WAS AS good as his word. There he was, sheltered to a degree by the pines on the edge of the dunes and wrapped up in layers of slightly moth-eaten wool, looking out over the beach at the vast sandy expanse of the bay.

She approached quietly along the path and then across the pine needle floor towards him. That smell of seaweed and a sharp, mineral flavour in the air, all mixed with the fragrance of the pine, brought back clear, tactile memories of sea-bathing, the fine sand under her feet and the rough towels rubbing the salt off her skin. He must have heard her coming but he did not acknowledge her, so she waited, watching his gaze flick from the landscape in front of him to his canvas, his palette hooked over his thumb and his whole body taut with attention. She noticed the loose threads around his cuffs and longed for her darning needle; the elbows of his jacket needed a patch too.

How lovely it must be to be so utterly absorbed in something! Her mind was always racing through a dozen different things so she barely knew what was in front of her. One minute she was lost in memories of her grandfather, another she was exerting all her will *not* to remember. She spent the time she should have been concentrating on the funeral arrangements worrying about her forthcoming season, and time she should have been working on the books for the pottery fretting about whatever she'd forgotten to do for the funeral.

Finally, he put down his brush and turned towards her.

'Thank you for waiting, Anne! It's terrible to stop just when you think you might be getting somewhere.' Then he added with unconvincing casualness, 'Do you want to look?'

She did, and came closer. The sky, that looked to her rather blank and uniform today, he had rendered in every shade of silver and pale yellow. The sand was studded in purples and greens.

'It's lovely,' she said, then smiled. 'Sorry, I never know what to say about art.'

'As far as I'm concerned, that'll do nicely.'

He reached into the pocket of his coat and drew out a letter. 'From your Mr Samuels. Jolly decent of him to be so quick about it.'

'Marvellous!' She took it quickly and tore open the seal. Mr Samuels wished her well and said he had a mixture of good and bad news for her. First, the positive. He had identified the craftsman who had made the copy, an elderly gentleman with a workshop and small shop front in Hatton Garden named Lubov. Lubov worked in precious stones as a rule, but enjoyed the challenges of reproducing them too. And Lubov had found the date of the commission. November 1943. Now for the bad news. Lubov had not seen the customer, who had paid in cash and left no name. He had worked from photographs, Lubov added, rather good ones that showed the details of the piece and which had been returned to the customer with the completed copy. He also remembered that the shop assistant who had spoken to the customer referred to their client as a gentleman, and had told Lubov the gentleman wanted a copy of the necklace for his daughter, as the original would be inherited by his daughter-in-law. Unfortunately the assistant was currently on National Service, so these were all the details Lubov could supply at the current time. Mr Samuels added he hoped the information might be of some use, and he looked forward to meeting Lady Anne on their travels in the future.

Anne read the letter to Charles, who had climbed off his painting stool and was stamping on the sandy soil to get his circulation going again.

'Shame about the assistant!' he said. 'Still, we know something now, don't we? Did your grandfather ever go down to London when you were at Holkham? Sounds like him, doesn't it? A daughter-in-law who will inherit the thing itself, and a daughter who won't?'

'Grandpa went once or twice,' Anne said, frowning at the neatly written page in front of her. 'And yes, I have two aunts, but neither of *them* would want a copy of the Coke necklace! It's a ridiculous idea.'

'Your father might ask them?' Charles suggested.

'He most certainly would not. As I said, there's no point. It's an obvious lie. Do think about it! They have jewellery of their own, and it would be ridiculous for them to wear a fake when my mother is likely to be at the same event wearing the original. People would think it most peculiar. And even if my grandfather had made a copy for one of them in 1943, what would it be doing in his pocket now in 1950? Added to which, if this story was true the original would still be in its case.'

Charles was clapping his arms around his body now. It felt strange to be holding a conversation with someone going through such an extended series of callisthenics.

'I see what you mean. I meant to ask you about the case.'

She sighed. 'It's in the safe and empty.'

'Has anything else gone missing?' he asked.

The idea was new to her, but now it seemed ridiculous she hadn't thought of it before. Anne shook her head. 'Not that I know of. If the Bible Picture Book or the Leonardo Codex were gone, Abner Mullins, our archivist, would be screaming blue murder. As would the British Museum.'

He paused suddenly in his jumping.

'What is it?' she asked.

'I was just thinking. Whoever took the original necklace and had the copy made – and perhaps that was your grandfather – they went to some trouble to cover their tracks, didn't they? A whole codex might be impossible to copy, but you have lots of other treasures at Holkham. Things not as grand as the Codex, or big as an Old Master painting, but still valuable. What if someone had taken a few pages of illustrated manuscript here and there, say? A couple of old coins? I know London was awash with all that sort of stuff during the war, what with refugees carrying all the valuable odds and ends they could manage. And thefts like that from the collection might not been noticed for years.'

Anne's eyes widened. 'Oh, Lord! You are right! Would people buy such things?'

He chortled into his muffler, wound up to his chin. 'Damn straight they would. There was a fellow at art school used to make fake medieval hymnals and sell them to Americans looking to pick up a bit of European culture. Only student in my year who could afford to eat. And rich people love collecting stuff. Especially the newly rich who don't just inherit a museum from their ancestors.'

'I suppose that's true.'

'And it's quite a museum you have. I read about the collection at college, your ancestor had a good eye. I suppose I shouldn't refer to things going missing as "thefts", should I? If it was your grandfather just selling a few things, trying to make ends meet, I suppose that's not theft at all. He had the right to sell if he wanted.'

'That's true too. Oh dear, I shall have to say something to Dad. Suggest he and Mr Mullins go through everything to check. We have to be sure, and it would be awful if we told the British Museum people we had things and then we found they'd been terribly damaged.' She thought of the groaning shelves in the classical and manuscript libraries, the great heavy volumes arranged in rows in the attic. 'What a job that will be!'

He gave his crooked smile. 'You can save that suggestion until after the funeral, can't you? Sufficient unto the day . . .'

'. . . is the evil thereof,' Anne finished. 'Yes, that's right. Oh, Grandpa!'

'You think it *was* him.'

'I don't know. Who else could it have been? But he loved

the collections at Holkham and was as fanatical about keeping the records in order as Mr Mullins is! Even if he did make a few sales, privately during the war, I would have sworn he'd have kept a careful record of them so as not to corrupt the archives. Honestly, he was as proud of those archives as of the artworks themselves. He would hate to sell though. Very few of the things the first Earl collected have been sold, you see. So it's rather special as a collection as well as the individual things within it.'

'Yes, I rather think that's why they got us to read about it,' Charles replied.

'But Grandpa had his secrets, certainly.' She leant against the trunk of one of the pine trees, caught a breath of its resinous scent and thought of playing in Donkey Wood with Johnnie, escaping the day to day of life at the house by diving into *Hotspur* magazine. Trying to catch the ghost of Lady Mary. 'The thing is, Charles, I know for a fact who took those photographs that were used to make the copies.'

'Who?'

'Me. Grandpa and I developed them together. It was the first film I did from beginning to end – he just supervised. Maybe that's why he suggested we take them. For this craftsman to work from, but he and Mr Mullins had me taking pictures of lots of things.'

'But even if he did, why did he have the fake in his pocket on the day he died? Your mother hadn't asked to wear it again, had she? Was there anything unusual that day?'

'No. That is . . . Well, he went round a few properties on the estate, and he'd had a meeting with the British Museum man the day before. Nothing out of the ordinary.' She paused, her throat tightening. 'But he did write down the name of a governess I had for a while. Mum thought she might have written to ask for a reference, but no sign of that has turned up in his correspondence.'

'What was her name?' He asked it so casually.

Anne hesitated for a second before saying it. 'Miss Lavender Crane.'

'Bit of a bully, was she?'

Anne nodded. 'Yes. And I haven't thought about her for a long time, not really, but now she keeps popping up in my head. She was foul.'

'A possible thief?' he suggested. He had picked up his palette again, hooking it over his thumb, and Anne thought of all the artists whose work filled Holkham, from Gainsborough to Reni to Rubens. He frowned at the painting and reached for his brush.

'I don't know . . . Perhaps. She did leave rather suddenly.'

Now he swung back towards her. 'Well, that's important, don't you think? Can you remember exactly when that was? Does it match the dates in the letter? Did this governess go down to London at all? Any men hanging around her? Lubov's customer was a man after all. You are trying to remember, Anne, aren't you?'

The sands seemed to shift under her feet, she felt a sharp angry pain behind her eyes and her palms and wrists seemed to burn. The world in front of her grew darker, narrowed. It was as if a sea fog, tinged black rather than grey, had roared up the beach and smothered them. Charles became indistinct, a vague shape lost in this sense of fear and confinement.

She had no idea how long it lasted. A minute, perhaps?

First she heard his voice, felt his hands on her shoulders. He had dropped the palette on the ground in his hurry to help her.

'Anne? Anne, do you need to sit down?'

The mist was gone, and what was left was his face, rather close. She could smell the cigarette smoke and turpentine impregnated into his clothes. She straightened up, shaking him off.

'Yes, I'm perfectly all right, Charles,' she said. She needed to be alone for a minute; his look of concern was embarrassing her. 'Many thanks for your help. I shall speak to my father about checking through the collection.'

Then she turned away and began to walk back towards the drive and the house.

'Good God, woman!' she heard him call out behind her. 'What the hell happened to you in that house?'

She raised her hand in farewell and kept walking. Nothing happened. Nothing at all. A foolish ghost quest. An unpleasant woman. Nothing worth talking about. Nothing that needed going over. Least said soonest mended.

She almost missed exchanging good mornings with Mrs Pullen, coming back from her cleaning hours at the Hall.

14.

'ANNE, DARLING, YOU haven't fallen in love with that painter, have you?' Carey asked.

The sisters were in Anne's room. Carey was sitting on the bed with a package containing their clothes for the funeral. Anne was at the window, staring out across the frost-laden park. It looked like an etching. First light, and the ice still spun in crazy patterns across the inside of the windows. She had breathed on it and was watching her breath dissolve the cobwebs and crackles, then rubbing away the moisture with her sleeve when Carey came in, and she hadn't yet moved away. Carey's question startled her.

'Oh, no! Of course not!'

'Thank goodness for that!' Carey said. 'Dad would go absolutely mad! And what a waste when you are just about to be launched on the world. I'm all for marrying for love, but it would be so much better to fall in love with someone suitable. I mean, if you did fall in love with a starving artist *after* you'd been to all the parties and dances that would be another thing.'

Anne left her post at the window and sat down on the bed next to her sister.

'I solemnly swear on the sisterhood I am not in love with Charles Elwood, nor do I have any intention of falling for anyone for a while yet. Dad wants me to marry one of his friends from the guards, but they are all at least forty. Though I'm sure they are very nice.'

Carey giggled. 'Well, if you have to choose between an ancient guard officer and a starving artistic type, I promise I shall support you running off to Bohemia.' She looked sideways at her sister again, her large blue eyes still drifting with concern. 'But you have been a bit strange since Grandpa died, Anne. That's why I asked about Elwood. Are you sure there's nothing you want to tell me?'

Anne looked down at her hands. There was a lot she'd like to tell her sister, but personally she didn't really believe that 'a trouble shared is a trouble halved'. It seemed to Anne that most of the time sharing troubles made them grow larger, and in strange and unpredictable ways.

'I am sure. I am a bit knocked sideways, I know. But I'll get over it. Best foot forward and all that. Come on, let's see what Mrs Greer has managed for us.'

Mrs Greer lived in Burnham Thorpe and was their mother's favourite local seamstress. Mrs Armstrong and Mrs Harbison could be trusted with basic sewing, sheets and under garments and Father's shirts at a push, but Mrs Greer was the person to go to when Elizabeth needed to dress her daughters with a handful of coupons and a stash of old material from the trunks in the attics.

Carey carefully undid the knots and wrapped the string around her fingers in a neat coil to use again, then unfolded the brown paper. Mrs Greer had done them proud. Two straight black skirts in good cloth, dyed to an inky black and the seams picked out in a satin that must have come from some of the Victorian mourning clothes their mother had unearthed. Each garment had a label, *Lady Carey,* or *Lady Anne,* in neat copperplate, pinned to it. There was a black jacket for each of them too, with a slightly nipped-in waist. Mrs Greer was obviously keeping up with the London fashions. The jackets and skirts were different for each sister. Longer, narrower lapels on Anne's jacket, a suggestion of a fishtail pleat on the back of Carey's skirt. Mrs Greer knew the sisters would not want to be dressed identically.

Carey tried hers on at once, shivering as she took off her sweater and shrugged on the jacket over her rather worn blouse. She looked stunning. The black jacket made a frame from her blonder hair and pale skin.

'I love Mrs Greer,' she said. Then kicked off her trousers and slipped into the skirt. 'Thank goodness – it is quite warm too.'

Anne tried on her jacket and skirt.

'I know one shouldn't say it, given what they are for, but, Anne, you do look amazing.'

Anne smiled. 'You do too. And I don't think Grandpa would mind. I mean, he'd shake his head and say we were vain and foolish girls, but he liked us to be well turned out, didn't he?'

Carey was already changing back into her work clothes and painting smock.

'Yes. And he was just as bad. Trimmed his moustache like it was an artwork every morning and before dinner if needed.' Carey glanced at her watch. 'Oh, damn. I have to get to the potting shed. They'll be firing the first piggy banks today.'

'Go! I'll put these in your room and tell Mum we shan't disgrace the family.'

'Angel!' Carey said, already half out of the door.

Anne had decided that the best way to talk to her father about the possibility of other missing items was through her mother. Elizabeth would know when and how to talk to her husband. She folded up the mourning clothes, dressed in her own 'about the house' outfit and went to deliver the sisters' verdict on Mrs Greer's work to her mother in her sitting room.

She found her mother wearing her own mourning clothes. Mrs Greer had slightly updated the suit she had worn for the funeral of the third Earl. Lady Leicester was now staring at her jewellery box brought up from the safe next to Shreeve's room. She had strings of pearls in both hands.

'What do you think?' she said as Anne came in. 'I don't want anything flashy, but then it *is* a public occasion, isn't it? And pearls always used to seem so modest and correct, but now there is a touch of the showgirl about them.'

'I think it's all about how you wear them, Mum. No one's going to mistake you for a Soho dancer.'

'I suppose so.' Elizabeth laughed a little sadly.

'I wanted to tell you that Mrs Greer has come up trumps for us. Carey and my clothes are perfect and fit beautifully as always.'

'Good. Anything else?'

Anne hesitated. Maybe this was the moment. 'Yes, there is. Just a thought I had.'

Anne didn't mention Charles Elwood, or the help she had asked of Mr Samuels. Instead she told her mother about the photographs she and her grandfather had taken during the war, and her conclusion that perhaps those were used to make the copy. Then, carefully, she offered up the suggestion that perhaps the contents of the house should be checked for other, smaller missing items.

Elizabeth sat down heavily in the chair at her dressing table, put her head in her hands and groaned.

'Heaven help us! Oh, Anne, you are quite right. I shall have to speak to your father. Why on earth didn't we think of that? Too busy and it's too ghastly to contemplate I suppose.'

She waved her hand at her own jewel boxes. 'Everything seems in order here, I'm glad to say.' Then she looked up sharply. 'Only these weren't at Holkham during the war! I had them in London when we got our marching orders for Cairo, so we just popped them into one of the security boxes in Coutts. Not that Tom would have swapped any of my jewels with fakes of course! He'd rather die. But then, I'd have said the same thing about the Coke necklace. Honestly, darling, my head is in a whirl. I keep thinking, about how queer Tom was when he said I couldn't wear it at Princess Elizabeth's wedding. He said he was sure your father would agree and said it in a rather *odd* way. I don't think your father gave two hoots. Said if that was what his father thought, then he didn't see the need to make a fuss. So, your grandfather knew it was fake then. I'm sure.'

'I wonder when Grandpa found out?' Anne said.

Elizabeth twisted round in her chair and crossed her legs, lithe as a child and just as unlikely to sit straight on any chair, at least when she was with her family.

'Well, either he knew all along, or perhaps he found out then. We received the invitation for the wedding and I probably asked about the necklace a day or two later. Gosh, it's so strange, isn't it? You don't think about a thing for years, then something happens and next thing you know you are picking over the past, trying to remember the expression on a person's face when they said something, or *exactly* what they said and half the time I don't know if it's a real memory or a kind of dream I'm just making up. Or if it's just a feeling that might have been a dream in the first place. Do you know what I mean?'

'I do,' Anne replied quietly.

Elizabeth pursed her lips briefly. 'Right then. I shan't tell your father you suggested looking for other things that might have gone missing. He won't like you even thinking that way. I shall wait until after the funeral, then mention it as if it's just occurred to me. I do think though, Anne, I might suggest you help Abner Mullins do some grand stock take of the house. You know the collection better than any of us other than him. You spent quite a lot of time going through things in the war with him, didn't you?'

Anne nodded, thinking of those precious hours stolen from her lessons with Miss Crane, but on days when she would be spending time with Abner Mullins her anger always seemed fiercer and more violent, as if intensified by being forced into a smaller number of hours.

'Your father has only a passing interest in it all. But even with you and Abner both at work it will take months and months.' She rapped her fingers on the top of the chair. 'Charles Elwood went to art college, didn't he? Did he study any art history?'

Anne remembered his remarks about the Holkham collection.

'I think so.'

'I might see if your father will allow him on the premises to help out. He'll probably make the servants swear an oath not to speak to him, in case they pick up communism from him like a bad cold.'

'Thanks, Mum.'

Her mother stood up and began putting away the jewels. 'You're a good girl, Anne. Now go along and talk to Mrs Warnes about the flowers again, will you? Remember we'll need at least two girls to make up the flower arrangements in the morning, and I think Cook has dragooned every female with a lick of sense within a five-mile radius to help with the cooking.'

Anne left her, pleased to have confided in her, her mind full of the scent of old books and the patient tutelage of Abner Mullins. She rubbed her wrists, then caught herself doing so and looked down. Clear pale skin. No visible marks at all. A door on the floor above closed and she jumped, her heart suddenly racing. *What happened to you in that house?* she heard Charles's voice say. *Are you sure there's nothing you want to tell me?* Carey's blue eyes looking sideways at her, full of love and concern. Anne went swiftly to her own room and sat on the edge of the bed and gave herself five minutes to cry quietly in privacy. But if she was crying for herself, or her grandfather, or the confusions that seemed to be curling round the house, she couldn't say.

15.

THE DAY OF the funeral was bright and cold, the ground heavy with frost. Lord Leicester ordered braziers lit in the tents for the tenants and estate workers. The fires in the state rooms had been burning since before dawn, and as Anne walked through them, checking the flowers were ready, the air was beginning to thaw.

How strange that it took a funeral for the house to awaken. There were so many people coming and going, fetching and carrying through the corridors, doing the final cleaning under the careful eye of Shreeve and Mrs Warnes, Holkham seemed more itself than it had since before the war.

The crowd of tenants had gathered on the lawns. Anne, Carey, and little Sarah, who was not sure exactly what was going on and was torn between excitement and sadness at the thought her grandfather was gone, had gathered with their parents in the chapel at first light to say prayers with the household. The late Earl's coffin had been placed in the chapel three days before. The lid was emblazoned with his name, the date of his birth and death and his long list of titles and honours as well as the family crest.

Lady Leicester, along with Carey and Anne, went to St Withburga's in the Bentley, while the funeral cortège, the Earl's coffin carried by eight gamekeepers wearing their bowler hats, came slowly behind them. Her father and her male cousins who were not on active duty followed behind the coffin on foot, and then behind them the other mourners. The aristocracy of England, a reduced and more threadbare band than their forebears, but still straight-backed, and eyes front.

At the lychgate, the vicar greeted the mourners, and the fourth Earl was carried up the sloping path into the church where he had been christened and married, and would now wait the second coming of his Lord among his ancestors and friends long gone.

Lord and Lady Leicester sat at the front of the church, while Anne and Carey were on the row behind with little Sarah between them. She remained solemn and quiet through the service, only looking around occasionally to check that her nanny was close by.

Anne sang the hymns quietly but was glad to be part of the songs offered up to her grandfather as the church swelled and warmed with the voices of his friends. Anne recognised among the baronets and earls the generals and colonels she had met during the war. Some had served with her grandfather in the Boer War, how lost in history that conflict seemed! Yet here were the men who had fought it. Others he had served alongside at Ypres, then the next generation, their sons who had survived the Second World War. Whatever the century had done to them, they raised their voices now and the sound was hopeful as well as sad, a giving of thanks to the Earl and to the God who had made them all.

Anne and Carey spent the reception after the service carrying messages between the kitchens, the state rooms and the marquees set on the front lawn. Once or twice she overheard tenants calling the occasion a 'decent showing'. High praise indeed. Most exchanged remarks with their neighbours about the Earl and the beautiful wreath the King and Queen had sent.

The photographer and reporter both behaved well, taking their photographs from a respectful distance, and wearing their Sunday best. The vicar had let them into the church for half an hour in the morning, so they could take pictures of the flowers and family monuments in the church itself.

It was only after the service that Anne noticed the photographer was a woman. It came as a surprise, yet women had become so many things during the war, some farm labourers like the land girls – she had a sudden memory of taking them soup and sandwiches while they worked, riding out in the pony cart with Mum after she and Dad came home. Others had moved to the city and become bus conductors and munitions workers. No wonder working in service had started to look a lot less appealing.

The woman photographer took pictures of the spread laid out for mourners in the tent, then disappeared up the avenue to take photographs of the house. Anne thought of the darkroom where she and her grandfather had worked together under the red glow of the lamp. She could hear the filing cabinets where they kept the papers and chemicals, the drawers where they stored the finished images, opening and closing with a swish and clang and she felt another burst of grief at their loss.

The guests began to depart and Anne took her place next to her mother and father, shaking hands and thanking people for coming. Little Sarah stood next to Carey. She was flagging a little, but Nanny was careful to keep an eye on her, so she shook hands and said thank you, and smiled like the rest of them, first to their fellow peers, then the tenants, then the workers, the order of precedence arranged and policed by the people themselves. The daily ladies and the house staff were already beginning to clear away. Anne remembered she needed to speak to Mrs Warnes about parcels for the families on the estate. She had seen Charles Elwood in the distance, but no sign of Johnnie Fuller. How long was it since Charles had told her he was missing? A few days at least. Strange; according to what Maria said Johnnie's disappearances normally lasted only one night. Two at most. If he still wasn't home, this was a much longer absence than usual. Perhaps he had abandoned Gina entirely? If so, they would have to see if they could take her on in the house again while one of the older women who lived in the alms-houses looked after the baby. She shook herself slightly. Her mind was running on and she'd rather forgotten where she was and what she was doing.

She was looking out over the north lawns, up towards the monument to Coke of Norfolk. She thought of the smug sheep and smiled.

'Lady Anne?'

She jumped and turned around, but it was only Shreeve approaching across the gravel driveway.

'Yes, Shreeve?

'Tea will be served in the long library at five o'clock.'

Anne glanced at her watch. Ten minutes. 'Thank you, Shreeve. I think that all went off well, don't you?'

'I do, Lady Anne. All very fitting.'

She nodded and was about to turn in to the house when she noticed a figure on a bicycle riding up the avenue from Holkham village towards them. 'Who is that?'

Shreeve peered, stretching his neck out like a turtle. 'I believe that is Mr Hudson.'

The landlord of the Victoria Hotel. He had only left the Hall an hour ago, yet here he was back again. He was in his shirtsleeves, Anne noticed, and rather red in the face.

'What on earth can he want now?'

'I shall enquire,' Shreeve said, a little darkly.

Anne shook her head. 'Don't worry, Shreeve, I'll speak to him. You don't want tea to be late.'

He bowed and returned to the house, and Anne walked across the drive and towards Mr Hudson. He was pedalling very fast, and when he did come to a halt next to her, it took him a moment to catch his breath. He was one of the 'grumblers' as her grandfather called them, the tenants who would make appointments to see Lord Leicester once a month to complain in vague terms about his lease, repairs needed on his property, or about the licensing laws, which he seemed to feel her grandfather, as Lord Lieutenant of Norfolk, could have rewritten at will. Her grandfather always gave him tea and half an hour and Mr Hudson went away content.

'A lynchpin of the community! And one of the best methods I have of knowing what troubles might be brewing,' her grandfather had said of him. 'He's policeman and weather vane, pressure gauge and a valuable asset. I don't mind some of his rough ways given the job he does here.'

'Mr Hudson, is everything all right?' Anne said with some concern as he bent over, drawing the cold air into his lungs.

'I tried to telephone, Lady Anne,' he managed first, with an expression of hurt.

'I'm so sorry, my father ordered all the phones disconnected today as a mark of respect.'

'Of course,' he panted. 'Yes. Quite proper.'

'It must be something urgent, to have you come out in this cold without your coat. Can I take a message to my father perhaps?'

'I'd have sent my boy with a note, but I'm a slow writer and I wanted to get word to you as quick as possible.' A new thought struck him, and he looked mildly panicked. 'Oh, what a shame it is you that saw me, Lady Anne, given as this affects you more closely than the rest of the family.'

'Please, Mr Hudson, you are frightening me. I am quite ready for whatever the news might be.' The people she loved most in the world were in the Hall, all heading towards the library for tea. Sarah was with Nanny.

'It's Johnnie Fuller, Lady Anne. The lad you used to play with.'

Anne blinked. 'I was just thinking of his wife a few moments ago, Mr Hudson. He was not at the funeral, I think.'

His pink face crumpled like damp linen. 'No, when we were coming to the service, we called on Mrs Fuller, my wife and myself. She said she'd had no word and didn't think bringing a baby along would be appropriate, so she stopped at home. Asked me to pass on her best wishes to His Lordship, which I did.' He hesitated.

'There is something more, Mr Hudson?'

He nodded. 'Yes, Lady Anne. My wife dropped round to Gina again just now while I took off my collar and got ready for opening. She took her a bit of pie and those venison puffs Mrs Hudson makes. Such a lovely spread and didn't seem fair her missing out just because she had the little one. Turns out while we were all here, poor Gina, Mrs Fuller that is, had a visit from the police!'

'Oh, dear!'

'Yes! It's an awful thing. Johnnie's not missing, he's *dead*.'

She should have seen it coming, should have sensed it from the distress on his face, but it was still a terrible shock. Another terrible shock.

'But . . . but how?'

He lifted his hands. 'My wife didn't get much sense out of her, but seems he headed out on a binge – he's barred at the moment from the Victoria and he must have ridden his bicycle into the ditch on the way back from whatever place would serve him Burnham Overy way! Been there for days, poor lad. One of the farmers spied him as he was cutting reeds before lunch today. Thought someone had dropped a coat at first, and then he finds Johnnie! He called the constable in Wells when he saw poor Johnnie was gone. Oh, he was a handful, but what a thing!'

Dead in a ditch. Anne felt as if she could see it. The darkness, Johnnie on his bicycle, the same one his brother had got him during the war, weaving his way home along the coast. Wouldn't take much, startled by an owl or deer in the moonlight, a jerk on the handlebars at the wrong place and he could go over into one of the ditches and be lost in the cold and the dry reeds would part and close over him. And those paths weren't much used this time of year.

'I'm ever so sorry to be the one to tell you, Lady Anne. But I thought you should all know at the Hall soon as possible and before the news comes in with the daily ladies in the morning. My wife would have come, but she's sitting with Mrs Fuller now.'

'That is very good of her. I shall make sure Gina's cousin, Maria, hears at once. No doubt Mrs Warnes will give her the day off so she can help with Gina and the baby. And I shall tell my father, naturally.'

His face still held a question, some mute appeal.

'I really am most grateful to you, Mr Hudson,' she managed, 'coming up to tell us yourself. It is very thoughtful. And thank your wife for us too.' She swallowed. What else? 'I shall call on Mrs Fuller myself tomorrow on behalf of the family.'

She had said the right thing; his expression settled back into one of gruff approval. 'Most generous of you, Lady Anne, especially given Johnnie's tales, but if you don't need anything else from me, I must get back. All the village will be in tonight what with the funeral and now this.'

'Of course. Thank you.'

She stepped back, and he clambered back onto his bicycle, starting off with a bit of a wobble, then stabilising as his momentum built. The deer, speckled in the last of the daylight, lifted their heads to watch him pass.

Johnnie dead? It seemed impossible. They had lost so many people to the horrors of war, to lose another man now to a stupid accident seemed like a cruel tragedy. She started walking back to the house, suddenly very angry with Johnnie. What a waste! He had made an awful mess of his life so far, but he had work and a wife who seemed to care for him and a child. So many men with as much and more to live for had died in the air, on land or at sea, but Johnnie – with all the advantages of youth and strength and free of the horrors that haunted other men – had driven into a ditch in a drunken stupor.

She pushed open the door to the house, walked through the lobby and the Marble Hall, her head down, jogged up the stairs and walked swiftly towards the Family Wing. She was five minutes late for tea. With luck her father would just stare at her coldly when she arrived, and she'd be able to explain. If she was unlucky, she'd have to wait until he had given her a rocket for her lateness. No time to change either. Should she tell Shreeve before going in? No. Tell her father first, then he'd ring for Shreeve and deliver the news himself, then Shreeve would manage its proper distribution round the household. She reached the door to the long library, breathed in and out, then pushed the door open and went in.

16.

1943

'AND HOW ARE Miss Anne' lessons coming along, Mr Mullins?' Mrs Warnes asked as she passed the archivist the plate of sliced ham. He took his modest serving, and it looked a little sad on the plate. 'I must say, you both seem to enjoy them. You have a spring in your step, the pair of you, when you've been working together all day.'

Abner smiled. It made him look much younger and Mrs Warnes wished he'd do it more often.

'Very well, thank you! We've talked about Lady Mary's engagement and wedding, and her stay here, and read some of the relevant documents.' He spoke with enthusiasm. 'We also got rather side-tracked into talking about her mother, the Duchess of Argyll, and her husband. Such an interesting story and that got us on to discussing the Jacobite rebellion and Lady Mary's father's role in suppressing it. Anne has a good head on her shoulders, no doubt of it, and takes these things a lot more seriously than many girls her age. We drew out the family tree.'

He spoke with almost parental pride.

'And what does Miss Crane do, while you and Anne are

researching?' Shreeve asked after his usual inspection of the cutlery.

'A very cultured lady,' Abner said. 'She has been taking the opportunity to make a study of some of the Old Master drawings. So she sits in the classical library with them, while Anne and I work together in the manuscript library.'

Mrs Warnes frowned slightly. 'I wouldn't want to speak out of turn, but Lavender did hint to me that Miss Anne fell behind in her schooling while in Scotland and has a lot of ground to make up.'

'I see no sign of that,' Abner replied firmly, shaking his head, 'however of course, Miss Crane is pedagogically trained, and I am not. Anne is a bright child and pays attention. She has a great deal more understanding than most children her age, in my estimation.'

Mrs Warnes was not sure what 'pedagogically trained' meant, but she assumed it had something to do with the certificate hanging on Lavender's wall so she contented herself with a noise of vague agreement. She enjoyed Lavender's company and the governess often popped down to her sitting room when they both had a free hour, bringing a magazine or a book she thought Mrs Warnes would like. She had a fund of interesting new conversation, having taught in London since the war began at a special school. So kind of her, working with those poor mites, when she with her certificate might work anywhere. Only from time to time Lavender said vaguely disapproving things about Miss Anne and Mrs Warnes did not like that. She was glad then to hear from Abner that the little girl was intelligent.

'Mr Shreeve,' Abner said, 'who was that man in airforce uniform I saw you speaking to yesterday afternoon as I was heading home? I think I noticed him at church.'

'That was Captain Horton,' Shreeve replied with a nod of approval. 'Mr Bartholomew introduced us. Apparently, he's been helping Mr Bartholomew come to some understanding with the Home Guard and the Royal Engineers about the number of heavy lorries going up and down the drive. A decent gentleman, I thought.'

'I am sure the Royal Engineers at least do their best to avoid unnecessary damage,' Mrs Warnes said firmly. The potato salad was very good, almost made up for the thin servings of ham. 'I hear they are planning to put on a little party for the local children in the old bowling alley.'

'Yes, at Christmas, before they light the tree,' Shreeve said. 'His Lordship seemed delighted at the idea. Of course, Lord and Lady Coke should be home by then too, and Miss Carey. I think it will be a celebration of homecoming, as well as of Christmas.'

'The reverend is teaching the village children the hymns already,' Ruby said. 'And there's talk of the Italian Prisoners of War doing a song or two. Not the Germans though, no one wants to hear them. It's not homecoming for everyone.'

Mrs Warnes wondered if Ruby was thinking of George Fuller. She felt disposed to be kind. 'Very true, Ruby. A lot more fighting still to be done and I feel for the lads who'll be doing it.'

'I'm not sure Miss Anne likes the new governess,' Ruby went on. 'She always seems so miserable when I take her their meals in the nursery – even when I know that Mrs Rowse has cooked one of her favourite things. Not at all the way she is when she's eating with His Lordship. She does like to watch him scrambling eggs on the silver burner! I think sometimes he orders them just because he knows she likes to watch. And she's terribly interested in Lady Mary, Mr Mullins. She's been asking for every story I could tell her about the times she's chased me down the corridors.'

Honestly these girls, give them an inch and they'll take a mile. 'Now, Ruby, Miss Crane is a qualified educationalist and Lady Coke selected her personally.'

'Lady Coke never met her, did she?' Ruby said, still pert.

'They corresponded, Ruby,' Mrs Warnes said, 'extensively. Now don't dawdle over your food and I want you to have everything ready for Mrs Pullen and Mrs Gray when they come in to do in the morning. No making them wait while you check the laundry marks this week! You'll have to help them get everything into the drying racks in the cellar as it is.'

Ruby got the hint this time. 'Yes, Mrs Warnes,' she said more quietly and turned her attention to her plate again.

'Christmas will be with us before we know it,' Shreeve pronounced. 'With a lot more people in the house, we shall all have to rearrange ourselves a little.'

Abner Mullins felt Shreeve's gaze. 'I promise I shall make arrangements so nothing will disturb Lord and Lady Coke's homecoming.'

Mrs Warnes was sorry for the man. 'I know you shall, Mr Mullins,' she said kindly. 'We all will.'

*

Anne hadn't realised how hard staying awake would be. Ruby came in to turn down her sheets and slip the wrapped stone hot water bottle into her bed at a quarter to eight, then supervised her as she brushed her teeth and her hair and said her prayers.

She had to be careful burrowing down between the sheets. They were icy cold, but the water bottle was scorching, and she could burn her bare feet on it if she was not careful as she pulled the sheets around her. She was allowed to read a while as Ruby tidied the room, and most nights she drifted into a strange dreaming state where the fairy tales she liked to read last thing got caught up with the happenings of the day. The witch in the story began to look like Miss Crane, and the path the lost child travelled twisted into a distorted version of Donkey Wood.

She would realise Ruby was gently lifting the book from her hands, then the darkness became complete. Next thing she knew the air was chill and damp with the morning and Ruby was opening the curtains. That could not happen tonight. With their plans in place, Johnnie had lent her his torch. It was rather heavy and awkward, and Anne suspected it had belonged to his father. She had smuggled it into her room before tea today and hid it under her old toys in the bottom of the dresser where no one was likely to look. Her new camera was on the shelf next to her story books and a rag doll that had belonged to her mother when she was a child.

While Ruby tidied, she closed her eyes, but rather than thinking of the story she had been reading she concentrated on her plan to find Lady Mary, plotting her route through the house. How did one address a ghost? With great respect, probably. And if the ghost was Lady Mary, probably as sympathetically as possible. Today had been a good day. She had spent a whole hour before lunch with Mr Mullins, examining Lady Mary's family tree and learning a little about what Norfolk and Holkham Hall had been like when she was alive. Most of it hadn't even been built then. Anne couldn't imagine Holkham only half there.

Miss Crane had seemed rather distracted at lunch. She produced a little book from her bag and started reading. Anne's grandfather would have disapproved, but it meant Anne was not expected to supply conversation and that was a relief. She only had to concentrate on eating in small mouthfuls and making no sound at all. Chewing had to be done very discreetly, that was why food needed to be cut up so small. The scrape of a knife, or even the clink of it being set down on the plate while Anne took a bite from her fork, drew dark looks, and too many dark looks would add up to a sudden explosion. Miss Crane would get up, and stand where Anne could not see her, and tell her to carry on eating. Then when the knife did finally once more make the tiniest clinking noise against the plate, she would pounce, grabbing Anne's wrist from behind, lifting and twisting it till the skin burned and bruised. Her book must have been very good today however, as Miss Crane had hardly looked up from her page, only slipping it into her bag when Ruby came to collect the plates, and Anne was dismissed to go for her walk.

She read again during tea. It was frightening still, always wondering if she was going to look up from her page. Anne had begun to notice the dark flash in her eyes that meant trouble was coming. Her pupils seemed to grow larger and blacker, and that tiny spot of colour would tinge her cheek under her powder.

Ruby turned off the light by her bed and left. As soon as Anne heard her footsteps retreat along the corridor, she sat up straight in bed and hugged her knees. Johnnie thought she should wait till midnight before looking for Lady Mary, because everyone knew that midnight was the time when ghosts were drifting around the place. Anne reminded him that Lady Mary did her shoving and whispering at any time of day. If she only drifted about in the middle of the night, they wouldn't even *know* they had a ghost as they were all in bed by eleven. She had to wait until Grandpa was likely to be in bed though. He liked to read and listen to the radio in the long library after supper, but sometimes he listened to the gramophone in the statue gallery. They had decided Anne should at least wait until half past ten then. Eleven would be better.

It was a shame that Lady Mary did not seem to appear much in the Chapel Wing where Anne's room and nursery were. Then Anne wouldn't have had to worry about Grandpa at all; but when she had written down all the times Ruby and Mrs Rowse had been shoved or whispered at, it looked as if she preferred the other end of the house, round the Family Wing and the Strangers Wing. Johnnie thought the fact that the Strangers Wing was shut up would probably make her more likely to be there than anywhere else. Anne wasn't quite convinced by his logic, but he was very sure, and she had to start somewhere.

She got out of bed and dressed quickly. It was far, far too cold to go wandering around the cellars in her night things. They had decided she should start in the cellars and work up through the house night by night. She agreed it would be easier to move around the cellars without being noticed, and of course, cellars were the sort of places ghosts liked to be, but the way Johnnie talked it was as if Anne was going to flush Lady Mary out like a beater driving partridge towards the guns. Again though, Anne thought as she pulled up her knee socks, she had to start somewhere. The house carpenter had his closest encounter with Lady Mary down there. That's what he had told Ruby, anyway. The longcase clock outside her room softly chimed ten o'clock.

She sat in the small armchair by the empty fire where the draughts did not reach and waited. When the clock chimed the half-hour she was struggling to stay awake. Better go now.

She lifted the camera from the shelf and hung it round her neck, then ferreted out the torch from the bottom drawer. The brass handles rattled as she released them and she froze. Of course no one would hear that, she told herself firmly.

She opened her door. Her room was at the top of the stairs above the chapel, so it was easy to find the first step in the gloom. She went down carefully. Miss Crane's bedroom was on this floor and Anne could feel her heart thudding faster knowing she was nearby. She imagined her lying on her bed with her arms by her side in the darkness, but with those strange dark eyes wide open. She pushed open the hidden door to the chapel gallery, then pulled it shut behind her. This time she did not just drop the little brass handle on the door, but lowered it, hardly breathing, so when she moved her hand away it swung, just a tiny bit, but did not click against the brass plate.

Anne was on surer ground now. No one slept near this staircase from the chapel landing to the ground floor and the cool stone steps would not creak or give her away. She was very careful to move softly, treading quietly, toes first. For a moment she wondered about going along the flagged corridors past the gun room and the smoking room corridor, and past Mrs Warnes's sitting room, but she might well be awake still. What would she say to Mrs Warnes or Mr Shreeve if they found her with her torch and camera creeping about at this time of night? It would take longer, but Anne had made her decision. She would take the stairs into the cellar here, at the bottom of the Chapel Wing, and travel from one side of the house to the other underground in a big 'U'.

She pulled open the door and turned on the torch. The flight was narrow and twisted at the bottom, with stone steps smoothed by the tread of servants coming and going. And Grandpa, of course, when he went down to his developing studio under the gun room. Anne climbed down, feeling the air grow colder and damper around her, then began to walk through the interconnecting chambers, swinging the beam of her torch in front of her. On each side of her the walls were lined with neatly stacked piles of wood, the logs, cut into points at their centre, quarters and eighths of whole tree trunks. She seemed to hear the distant thud and crack as the foresters swung the axes and split them. She and Johnnie sometimes watched the men cutting them from the slope above Longlands. On a still day you could see them from such a distance the sound took seconds to reach you, so the man would raise his axe, then you would hear the wood split at his last blow, like when the film and sound had got confused while she was watching a film in the cinema. Like another ghost.

The smell of the wood was comforting. She walked on from one little room to the next. Should she sing? Warn Lady Mary she was coming? Not yet. She wasn't on Lady Mary's side of the house yet. She must be near the old kitchen now, where the Royal Engineers had taken over some of the rooms; yes, she could see the bottom of the stairs that led up to that part of the house. A creak above and a splash of light coloured the shadows. She hid her torch under her cardigan and heard a man's voice saying something. Was he coming down? She heard the squeak of a willow basket, the clunk of logs bashing together. No, it was just someone helping himself from the basket at the top of the stairs. The door closed again, and the pale patch of light and the voice disappeared, leaving her in the dark with the glow of her torch showing a buttery yellow under her knitted cardigan. Now came the long corridor under the front of the house. It opened out into a much larger room. Not that Anne could see that right away, but at once the air felt colder and dryer. Anne swung the beam around the chamber and almost dropped her torch again. A great jumble of furniture, stacked almost to the roof, and in the middle of it, framed by table legs, was a huge collection of eyes, staring at her.

'Just animal heads, silly,' she said to herself firmly and raised the beam again. Half a dozen deer, or something like deer from abroad. They didn't have antlers, but each long elegant narrow face bore a pair of tall, slender twisting horns. They must have come from the old kitchen or other rooms the army was using like the furniture and were waiting here until the war was over and the soldiers had moved out and they could return to their places on the walls. She remembered them now, supervising the old kitchen and the vast range with its metal spit turned by a clockwork wheel. Mrs Rowse declared the new Esse Stove was much easier to manage. So Ruby said, anyway.

Now Anne was getting close to Lady Mary's favourite part of the house, under the statue gallery and closer to the Family and Strangers Wings. The scents in the air had subtly changed. She could not smell wood now, but instead she detected the musty, dust-laden smell of the wine cellar with its strange vinegary tang.

She decided to start under the Family Wing and shone her torch on her watch. After eleven. Grandpa and the servants would all be in bed. Even Mr Shreeve and Mrs Warnes in their rooms above her head shouldn't hear her if she kept reasonably quiet as the walls were thick, built to stand for centuries. She would ask Mr Mullins more about how the house had been built in the years after Lady Mary left. Her grandfather would like it if she knew more, and she did find it all very interesting. History was much more alive when you were living in the place it had happened.

'Hello?' she whispered into the darkness. Perhaps Lady Mary wouldn't want to be addressed so informally. And even if Lady Mary did appear, how would she point her torch and the camera at the same time? She and Johnnie hadn't discussed that in all their planning. Well, she would just have to work it out for herself.

She set the torch on a packing crate, so it cast its rather feeble glow over the edge of the chamber, and just penetrated through the arch into the next. The bottoms of the wine bottles in their wooden cradles reflected the light back, but the effect wasn't as alarming as the glass eyes of the deer skulls. Then she sat on the floor, cross-legged, with the camera on her lap, and set the aperture to its widest setting and the shutter speed to a full half-second. She'd never be able to hold it still enough like this. Stacked behind the crate were half a dozen wooden lids of wine boxes. She set one on her knees and put the camera on top of it. Better.

'Good evening, Lady Mary,' she said. 'I am Anne, oldest daughter of Lord and Lady Coke.' Lady Mary had once given her mother a shove when she was pregnant with Anne, so Ruby had said, but perhaps Anne shouldn't mention that. 'Though, maybe you know that. Anyway, I've been reading about your life with Mr Mullins. He's very nice and it was terribly interesting. I'm sorry you didn't have a nice time when you lived here and your mother the Duchess of Argyll, had to rescue you. There is a report about the court case between your husband and father in the archive upstairs. Mr Mullins showed me. Though he said he didn't know why you had to arrive in London in an old dress as there is an account book showing you had money for new clothes.' Did that sound rude? Anne tried something different. 'My father is a soldier, like your father, the Duke of Argyll. He's fighting the Germans in North Africa. Dad is, I mean. But it sounds as if your father was a very brave and important soldier too.'

Her voice echoed, a hollow, very lonely sound. It felt as if someone was listening, like the fizz in the air you could feel in the electricity-generating room. Anne sensed fear creeping up through her bones, like a chill coming up from the floor. She fought it away.

'Soon Mr Mullins is going to tell me all about your adventures in London. I'm looking forward to that. He has already told me that Horace Walpole dedicated a book to you. I'm going to read it.' Now to the main point. 'The thing is, I was hoping very much you might let me take your photograph? My friend Johnnie and I would like to send it to *Hotspur* magazine.'

She waited, tense as a hunting hound. Yes, she was sure she could feel someone listening now, like that presence in the corridor behind her in the library. A draught, a current of air, stirred the hair over her ear. Was there a whisper, a voice in it? A distant drip of water or was that a footstep? Did ghosts *have* feet? The fear was getting hard to keep down now. Breathing! She could definitely hear breathing. She pressed the button on the camera. The shutter clicked open and she held her breath until it snapped shut again. A shuffle in the dark! That was a definite noise that was not a draught or a drip and it was coming from the corner where her camera was pointing. Fear felt white and bright now. Anne wound on the film, her hand shaking, and clicked the button again, too terrified of what she might see to look up – the heavy, supernatural dread of it shivering through her bones.

The scuffle noise came again, and it felt much much closer, as if it was in the room with her now. She bit her lip and wound on the film and clicked the shutter one more time, not daring to look up, and she held as still as one of the statues in the Marble Hall until it flicked softly shut again. Something in the next-door room rattled, a thump and clatter of wood hitting the stone floor. Fear won. Anne grabbed the camera and torch and ran. The lid on her lap fell to the floor with a bang and echo like a thunderclap and the light of her torch bounced crazily round the walls. She had taken the wrong door in her panic! She was in the long corridor between the Family and Strangers Wings. It was damp and dripping and the rain had leached through the soil and made puddles along the length. The light caught on them, making strange patterns on the arched stonework over her head, and her running footsteps echoed back and forth until she felt as if she was in a storm of noise. Something was following her. Other steps, bouncing round the walls behind her! The tunnel twisted sharply as it entered the cellars under the Strangers Wing. She banged her shoulder, and the torch fell from her hands. It rolled across the floor and Anne saw a strange shape in its spinning beam, a pile or nest of crumpled linen or blankets, like an unmade camp bed. Her foot struck something hard and she fell heavily; her right hand flew up to protect the camera and the pain of the impact shot up through her left wrist and arm.

Someone, something, touched her shoulder.

She screamed, a kind of gulping groan, then grabbed up the torch and ran on. She was lost. Any door, any passage might lead to a dead end and that would mean turning around and going back towards whatever was chasing her, to whatever had touched her. Fear became panic; she had no idea how long she had been running now, or in what direction. A staircase! Yes, anything to take her upwards! She dashed up it and scrabbled at the door at the top. It stuck and she shoved it with her shoulder as hard as she could. Finally, the handle twisted, the door swung open and she fell over onto the cool stone flags of the ground-floor corridor. The torch banged and clattered and rolled as she spun round and kicked the door to the cellar closed, praying that whatever ghost or demon she had awoken down there would not be able to get through.

She lay on her back, lifted up on her elbows and stared. The round brass handle on the cellar door glinted in the reflected light from her torch. It began to turn.

'Miss Anne? My heart alive! What on *earth* are you up to?'

The handle went still. Mrs Warnes, her hair in curlers with a neat net over it, was standing at the door to her room to the left of the cellar steps. The light was on behind her, showing in its electric glow the corner of her armchair with the cushions her niece had embroidered. She was doing up the cord round her long flannel dressing gown. Anne jumped up and flung her arms around her, pressing her cheek into the pink material and sobbing with fright.

Mrs Warnes put her arm around her and Anne felt her other hand on the top of her head, smoothing her hair.

'There, there now, Miss Anne! Everything's all right now. You are quite safe with me.'

Anne clung on to her more tightly.

'Oh, you'll squeeze the life out of me, child.'

'Some disturbance, Mrs Warnes?' Anne recognised the voice of Mr Shreeve, but she didn't raise her head and she kept her eyes tight shut. Mrs Warnes smelt of talcum powder and for some reason that made Anne want to cry very much.

'Miss Anne out of bed and seems to have given herself a fright, Mr Shreeve,' she said, keeping her arm round Anne's shoulder. 'Were you down in the cellars, Miss Anne? I thought I heard the door shut.'

Anne made a muffled sound that Mrs Warnes took to be a 'yes'.

'I see.' Her voice was a bit heavy. 'Don't worry, Mr Shreeve. I'll get her back to bed and settled.'

'Thank you, Mrs Warnes,' Shreeve said, and Anne heard the door to his own rooms close.

'Now, Miss Anne, do stop squeezing so hard. There's nothing to be scared of now. Come into my sitting room and we'll get you cleaned up. We'll have a cup of milk and then get back to bed.'

Mrs Warnes was really very decent. She washed the scrapes on Anne's knees and hands and put iodine on them, and warmed milk for her over her own little grate. When Anne's mug was empty, Mrs Warnes held her hand as they walked back along the corridors to the Chapel Wing and up to Anne's room. She did not knock on Miss Crane's door, which Anne was very glad about, but she did take the torch and the camera away with her. Anne explained the torch was not hers and told her she had wanted to take a photograph of Lady Mary, but Mrs Warnes was firm.

'We shall make sure Johnnie Fuller gets his torch back, and I can understand you wanting a picture of Lady Mary,' she said, pulling the blankets round Anne and tucking them in. 'I'd even say it was a rather brave thing for a little girl to do. Still, I'll want to speak to His Lordship and it'll be up to him to give you the camera back. It's a dangerous thing, Miss Anne, creeping around the house so late. You might get an awful chill, and your clothes! There's a tear in your skirt *and* your cardigan.'

'I'm very sorry,' Anne said. 'I wasn't scared at first. Then I was.'

She felt very small all of a sudden.

'Well, that is how it tends to happen,' Mrs Warnes replied with a sigh.

'Thank you for looking after me,' Anne added and fought the impulse to start crying again.

'That's all right, my dear. Honestly, going down there in the middle of the night! I wouldn't have dared for all the tea in China. What an unusual child you are.'

'Unusual' wasn't as good as 'remarkable', but perhaps, Anne thought, it was better than 'ordinary'. Mrs Warnes put the torch in her pocket, picked up the camera and went to the door. Her finger touched the light switch.

'Mrs Warnes?'

'Yes, Miss Anne?'

'You will be careful with the camera, won't you? It's just, it's my absolute best thing.'

There was a smile in her voice as she answered. 'I promise, Miss Anne, I'll take very good care of it.' Then she switched out the light and closed the door behind her.

At first Anne was sure she wouldn't sleep at all. Now that the fear had retreated, she began to think through what had happened. She curled up under the tight blankets. The pain in her knee and hand had become a needly tingle. Perhaps she had managed it, maybe when the photographs were developed she'd see Lady Mary herself. She thought of that breathing scuffling presence in the dark. That clatter. Draughts didn't make things clatter. Of course, the box lid that she'd had on her knees had made a great noise when she jumped up, but there was something before that. It was what had made her jump up. She thought of the glass eyes, the bottles. That nest of linen and blankets. Or was that the ghost? Could it have been Lady Mary's silk gown? Even if she went to London in rags after she was rescued from Holkham, she was wearing very nice clothes in the portrait Mr Mullins had showed her, and a lot of them. No. In her memory it looked like blankets more than silk. Then she remembered that touch, heavy and real on her arm, and shuddered.

But what would her grandfather say? Would he be angry with her, or think she had been brave like Mrs Warnes did? And worse than all that, what would Miss Crane say? And Ruby would have to mend the tear in her skirt and she had got mud all over her socks when she ran through the puddles in the corridor. Perhaps *Hotspur* would do a drawing of her, like the maid in the copy Johnnie had been reading. She imagined it, her with her camera and torch in the wine cellar with Lady Mary's ghost rising imperious in the beam of the torch. It made her feel slightly less small, and on that thought she finally fell asleep.

17.

The summons came just after breakfast. Miss Crane had heard nothing of the adventures of the night before, Anne guessed. She did not notice the iodine-stained scrape on her knee and when Anne nibbled her toast as quietly as possible – porridge was much easier to eat in silence, but Anne loved toast, which made the times it arrived on her breakfast tray very difficult – she kept her hand angled away from Miss Crane so she wouldn't see her grazed palm.

Ruby came to collect the tray. She gave Anne a significant look, then addressed Miss Crane.

'Miss Crane, ma'am, His Lordship apologises for the interruption, but he'd like to see you and Miss Anne in the long library now please, before lessons.'

On the long walk to the Family Wing Miss Crane moved stiffly. She hissed at Anne as they went.

'I hope Lord Leicester isn't displeased with you, Anne. I should be sorry to have to tell him what a poor student you are. I have of course been trying to protect you, and not complain about how hard it is to teach anything to such a stupid, clumsy little girl. What have you said to him about our lessons? Tell me!'

Anne looked at the long red and yellow carpets at her feet. Miss Crane liked walking through the state rooms, even if they were all under sheets and everyone else used the ground-floor corridors. She lifted her chin and caught sight of the van Dyck portrait of a man on horseback.

'Nothing, Miss Crane. We talk about music and photographs and things.'

That was true; at least Grandpa had asked once or twice about lessons and Anne had told him she was learning to write neatly and about the counties of England. He had nodded in an approving way, and then they talked about other things while Anne tried very hard to forget Miss Crane for as many minutes as she could.

Lord Leicester did not invite them to sit down when they came into the library. Mrs Warnes was there already, looking a lot neater and not quite as friendly as the night before.

'Now, Anne, what's this about creeping round the cellars in the middle of the night?' Lord Leicester began.

Anne felt Miss Crane stiffen then relax next to her as she tried to find an answer.

'I was trying to take a photograph of Lady Mary's ghost, Grandpa,' she said. 'I am sorry I got scared and disturbed Mrs Warnes.'

'And made a mess of your skirt and shoes, I hear,' Lord Leicester said sternly, but Anne thought he didn't sound very cross. 'Well, did you get one? A photograph?'

'I'm not sure. I hope so.'

'I suppose we shall see in the developing room. I might

have a little time later today as it happens.' He sounded rather excited, but then caught himself and frowned again. 'But Anne, you cannot go running around the house in the middle of the night. It's dangerous. Mrs Warnes tells me you apologised very nicely last night, but I want you to do so again. In front of me.'

Anne stood very straight and looked at the housekeeper.

'I really am very sorry, Mrs Warnes, for the trouble. I promise not to do it again.'

'Thank you, Miss Anne,' she replied.

Lord Leicester dismissed Mrs Warnes with his thanks, and as she passed Anne, she put her hand on her shoulder and squeezed it gently, which made Anne feel a lot better. When the door had closed behind her Lord Leicester nodded towards Anne's camera, which was sitting next to him on the sofa.

'Very well. You may have your camera back. But no more shenanigans, Anne, if you please.'

'Yes, Grandpa,' she said and went to pick it up.

'Ghost hunting, eh?' he said. 'I shall look forward to hearing more about it.'

She beamed at him, then remembered she was still officially in trouble and tried to make her face more serious again. But she felt brave enough to ask now.

'Grandpa, none of the soldiers sleep in the cellar, do they?'

'Certainly not! Why do you ask?'

'It's just as I was running away, I thought I saw a sort of bed, like a nest, under the Strangers Wing. I don't remember seeing anything like that before the war.'

Her grandfather frowned.

'But I was quite scared and dropped the torch for a moment, so I might have been confused.'

'Quite likely,' he said, picking up his newspaper and snapping it open. 'I shall have a look later. But no more wandering around the cellars, Anne, day or night, am I understood?'

'Yes, Grandpa.'

'Off you go then. Apologies for disturbing your lessons this morning, Miss Crane.'

'Not at all, Lord Leicester,' Miss Crane said in her nice voice.

They left the room, then Miss Crane stopped on the landing. 'Wait here a moment, Anne,' she said, then knocked softly on the door they had just come through and went back into the library.

Anne hoped she was not going to tell her grandfather about what a bad student she was after all. Mostly though she was just delighted Grandpa hadn't been cross, and to have her camera back. She checked it over very carefully. It had survived the night's adventures without any visible damage. Perhaps after lunch she would use up the rest of her roll of film taking pictures of the statues in the conservatory, then see if Grandfather had meant it about developing the film.

Miss Crane returned from the library and led her back to the Chapel Wing for lessons. She seemed to be in a good mood. She only sniffed and rolled her eyes at Anne's written lines and marked her sheet of maths problems with smooth even ticks.

After lunch Anne took careful pictures of the statues in the conservatory, watching how the light fell across their smooth stone bodies, dressed in the deep shadows of the plants still growing there, and then found Lord Leicester out in the estate offices and told him her first roll was ready to develop. He got up at once and suggested they go to the darkroom straight away.

When he pushed open the door to Mr Bartholomew's office to say he was leaving, Anne noticed that Captain Horton was there. Grandpa had obviously met him before. They both wished them success in the darkroom, and Captain Horton said it so kindly, Anne thought he must not have been told as yet what an embarrassment she was.

Once in the darkroom Lord Leicester seemed to move very slowly, and take twice as long as usual to prepare the chemical baths to develop the negatives. Her toes kept wriggling in her shoes with impatience. He noticed.

'Now, Anne. When things are most urgent you have to move carefully, you know. You must concentrate. Now, fill that bottle with clean water and let's see, shall we?'

He asked if she'd like to try the important bit, taking the film off its roll and putting it in a lightproof container for its first baths of chemicals, but it was a fiddly process done in a black box with rubber light seals you squeezed your hands through, and Anne said she'd rather he did it this time. He seemed to approve of her decision and for the next few minutes they worked in silence, punctuated only by the Earl's request that she hand him this bottle or that. Then the negatives were hung up to dry from a clothes peg. Anne was practically dancing with excitement now, but the Earl was firm. Setting the timer again and making her recite the Kings and Queens of England and Great Britain in order until it tinged. Then he unhooked the strip and cut it carefully into short lengths and set it on the light box. He bent over it with his magnifying glass.

'You've done nicely with the statues, Anne. And these ones of Johnnie are very good. I think later this week we might try and get some pictures of the Coke necklace. We can discuss the best way to light them so the reflections don't obscure the detail. Archives need clear detail, not art.' He looked at her sideways, his smile warm and teasing. 'But perhaps those aren't the photographs you are most interested in?'

He moved the magnifier thing along the strip and made a noise, a short 'hum', which he made when he was interested in something, or impressed.

'I think you might have got something, my dear.'

'Really, Grandpa?' Anne felt such a thrill of victory and excitement, she lifted up onto her tiptoes and squeezed her fists together.

'Yes, this last one of the three in the cellar. Perhaps. Let's make a print and get a proper look, shall we?'

Somehow it felt very important not to look until the print was in the developing bath, thinking if she did, it might spoil. Leicester moved to one side slightly as he used his wooden tongs to push the print into the liquid. Anne crowded up next to him. First in the red glow of the darkroom safe light she saw the deep black shadows on the right of the image, out of range of the torch beam, then the texture of the floor and the arch with the winking bottles, then the inky blackness of the room beyond and there, towards the top of the doorway that linked the two spaces was a shape, a blur of movement, subtle greys showing the outline of *something,* a dress or a cloak and above it a pale twist, hair perhaps framing the smudge of a face.

'Too much to expect her to hold still, but Anne, I rather think you got her!' Leicester said. 'Well done.'

'May I take it down to the village to show Johnnie?' Anne asked.

He glanced at his watch. 'You may, but you'll have to be quick about it. Don't be late for tea. And well done, Anne.'

She was very quick, speeding down the avenue and shooting through the side gate like a racing driver, and calling for Johnnie while she was still pedalling up the slope to the wood. He was there, with his comic and wrapped up in layers of knitted scarfs, his back against a tree trunk.

She jumped off her bicycle, letting it fall to the ground, and drew out the precious print from her bag.

'Johnnie! I got it! Last night in the cellars I took the photograph and Grandpa and I just developed it and look!'

He took the print from her without saying anything, then instead of congratulating her and getting excited, he wrinkled his nose.

'This could be anything!'

'It's Lady Mary!' Anne insisted. 'You can see her face, almost, and that must be her dress. I know it was her because I heard her moving about before I took the picture. Who else could it be?'

'Might not be anyone at all! Honestly, Anne, I don't know why you are getting so excited. *Hotspur* would never print anything like that.'

Anne flushed. 'Why are you being so beastly? Grandpa said he thinks I got her. He was really pleased!'

'Oh, well, if Grandpa says! I can't believe you have that new camera and a haunted house and that's all you can come up with. Anyway, who cares about ghosts? Ghosts are silly. There is a war on, you know.'

'Yes, I do know there is a war on *actually*! But we planned how to take this picture of Lady Mary together, and now I've got it you're being horrible. What's the matter with you?'

'It's a terrible picture and I've been waiting here for hours because I have something really important to tell you. Last night while you were playing in the house, I was watching for spies and I saw lights by the lake. I think maybe there are spies sending messages about the defences round Holkham and that's much more important than ghosts.'

'I wasn't playing! And those lights were probably just the Home Guard doing exercises and how could you see the lake? Johnnie, did you climb over the wall? That's really dangerous! What if the guards saw you and shot you? They might think you were an escaped prisoner or a poacher!'

'I'm too good at hiding for them to see me. And it wasn't the Home Guard. They're always in bigger groups. And I'll go where I like.'

That was so silly, Anne just laughed. His face turned beetroot.

'I shall! Anne, there are important things happening at the Hall and you just don't understand them!'

Then he turned away and stomped back down the hill leaving Anne looking after him in rage and confusion. When she got home, she found prints of all the photographs she had taken in a neat pile on her dressing table. The ones of Johnnie were very good. Her grandfather had included another print of her ghost photograph too. He had laid tissue paper between each print, and on top of the pile was a note in his handwriting. *Good work, Anne!* She felt a bubble of pride and she no longer minded about Johnnie being a jealous beast at all.

Shreeve went down to the cellars with Lord Leicester after tea. There was no sign of Anne's adventures that either man could see, and no sign of any nest under the Strangers Wing.

Lord Leicester pronounced himself satisfied, then looked upwards.

'I hate to think what's happening in that wing with no one to look after it, Shreeve.'

'Yes, my lord.' Shreeve did not say anything further. There was no need. The difficulty in finding, keeping and paying for sufficient staff in the house was a problem they had discussed often enough in the past. He hoped the end of the war might improve the situation, but was afraid, as he had told Mrs Warnes more than once, that the problems of staffing a home like Holkham would continue. He blamed motorcars. Young people racing around the place. At least one knew where trains were going, but in cars they could end up anywhere, and the young people got far too used to being forever on the move. He had been conducting a pointed but subtle vendetta against Smith, the chauffeur, as a result of this conviction for a decade. Smith did not appear to have noticed.

'You know, I've had reports that the Italian POWs working

the harvest this year really put their backs into it,' Lord Leicester said. 'I wonder if any of them might like to stay on after the war.'

'Not in the house, surely, my lord?' Shreeve asked, rather shocked.

Leicester chuckled and put his hand on the cool brick wall next to him, feeling for signs of crumbling or collapse.

'No, no. Estate work. But I did wonder if some of them might have sisters who could be trained up as housemaids. Dear old Italy will be in a bit of a state for a while when this is all over, and a few of their young people might be willing to try their luck over here.'

Foreign maids were a different thing altogether. You could not turn a peasant into a footman, the training needed to start when they were young, but girls were different, used to looking after their family homes and putting on a good show for their neighbours.

'Shall I put the suggestion to Mrs Warnes? Even if the war lasts a while yet, it might be a good idea to let her prepare herself.'

'Hmmm?' His Lordship's study of the pointing had become absorbing. 'Yes, please do, Shreeve. So this is where Anne said Lady Mary touched her! I shall send a copy of the photograph down to the servants' hall. I was rather impressed.'

'I think we should all be very curious to see it. We are all fond of Miss Anne.'

'Yes, yes. Lady Mary can be a nuisance. Once a week I hear her whispering and turn a corner and nothing is there. Have you heard her, Shreeve?'

Personally, Shreeve thought that was more likely to be Ruby, talking to herself as she went about her work and then making herself scarce when she heard Lord Leicester approach.

'Not that I'm aware of, my lord.'

'Well, the foundations still seem solid, and the Royal Engineers haven't set up a distillery down here, so I shall be grateful. In fairness, I should be grateful to Lady Mary too. If she'd consummated the marriage and given her husband an heir, I'd just be an obscure cousin of the family, playing my violin in tea rooms. Who knows whose dinner you'd be serving then, Shreeve.'

Shreeve looked around carefully. Yes, all neat and tidy.

'I am sure we are all very happy as we are, my lord,' he said, and meant it.

'Oh, and could you please tell Ruby Miss Crane has volunteered to put Anne to bed from now on. It makes more sense, given how much Ruby has to do, and with Miss Crane sleeping in the Chapel Wing.'

'Certainly, my lord.' It was a very sensible idea, not usually part of a governess's role, but these were unusual times. It reflected well on Miss Crane, Shreeve thought.

18.

Then evening came. Ruby was in a bit of a mood when she collected the supper things, but Anne didn't think much of it, given how busy she always was. When the door opened again at bedtime, however, it was Miss Crane, not Ruby, standing in the doorway.

Anne was shocked into speechlessness at seeing her. She had her hand on her hip, and her eyes had that dark flashing quality that made Anne's stomach tighten.

'After your disgraceful behaviour last night, Lord Leicester and I have agreed it would be best if I put you to bed from now on, Anne,' she said in a purr.

Anne's heart started racing. There were so many things she might get wrong at bedtime. Things she had never thought about before. She had already brushed her hair, washed her face and done her teeth. Had she done those things incorrectly? Miss Crane came in and shut the door behind her.

'Stand up when I come into the room!'

Anne got up quickly from her chair and Miss Crane grabbed hold of her shoulder. Her fingers always seemed to know exactly where to squeeze and pinch to make it hurt as much as possible.

'Open your mouth.'

Anne did.

Miss Crane dragged her towards the light of the bedside lamp and pulled Anne's upper lip up with her free thumb and forefinger pushing her head sideways at the same time. It twisted and stung terribly.

'Good enough, I suppose,' she said. 'Did you just try to bite me? You did, didn't you, you nasty little creature!'

She released Anne's lip, and Anne's hand flew up to cover the new hurt.

'I didn't, Miss Crane! I swear.'

'Like a little rat!' Miss Crane said. 'Get into bed. Lie down on your back.'

Anne got into bed. No mention of hair-brushing and that twist to her lip had hurt, but she seemed to have passed the inspection. Miss Crane pulled open the top drawer of Anne's dresser and took something out. Anne couldn't see what it was. The sheets were damp and cold, no stone hot water bottle this evening.

'Give me your hands.'

'I don't understand.'

Miss Crane sighed, sharp and angry. She grabbed Anne's wrists, holding them together tightly in one hand and wrapping them round and together with a pair of Anne's winter stockings, then knotting them. Anne squeaked as the fabric bit into her flesh.

'Be quiet!' Miss Crane said. She was breathing heavily now. She pulled Anne's bound wrists over her head and leant over her. Her wrists were jerked back. Instinctively she tried to pull away, but Miss Crane yanked on the stockings and Anne's shoulder blades squeezed together painfully. Her necklace tapped Anne's forehead, a chilly and metallic touch like a drip of water. Anne bit her lip and breathed through her nose, a sweet smoky scent of Miss Crane's perfume, just below it the animal tang of sweat. What was she doing? Miss Crane stood up, and Anne tried to move. She couldn't. Miss Crane had tied the stockings through the metal bars at the head of the bed. The stockings pressed into the bruises on her wrists. Anne tried to pull again.

'You won't go wandering round the Hall *now*, I think,' Miss Crane said as she smoothed her hair back from her flushed face.

'I'll stay in my room, I promise,' Anne said. 'Please, Miss Crane, it hurts!'

'*Please, Miss Crane, it hurts,*' Miss Crane mimicked in a high whining little girl voice. 'You can't be trusted, Anne. Lady Coke was quite right. You've been spoiled in Scotland. We must take further measures to make you fit for society. It's shameful. I do pity your poor parents.'

Anne wriggled against the bonds. 'Please!' An idea struck her. 'Please, Miss Crane, I need to say my prayers.'

Miss Crane's lip curled. 'Baby Jesus doesn't listen to nasty little girls like you, Anne. If you struggle it will only hurt more.'

Then she turned off the light and left Anne alone in the dark.

*

So bedtime became another time to be dreaded. No matter how good she was during the day, or how quick in her lessons, the same thing happened night after night. Then each morning, while it was still dark, Miss Crane would come into Anne's room in her dressing gown with her hair falling around her shoulders and untie her, complaining Anne's wriggling had made the knots tight and difficult to undo. Then she would put the stockings back into the drawer and leave.

For an hour Anne could curl up and fall into a sleep of exhaustion, her hands tucked under her armpits, trying to get them warm. Then Ruby would come in, bright and cheerful as ever, to open the curtains and do the picking up she used to do at bedtime.

Miss Crane had seemed to spread through Holkham like an ink stain on linen. Anne had not realised how lucky she was only seeing her in the schoolroom or nursery. Now she seemed to be everywhere. Wrapped up in her long coat reading in the shell grotto in the pleasure gardens near the stable yard and estate offices, or appearing behind her suddenly when she was absorbed taking photographs in the state rooms with a pinch, or placing her hand on Anne's head in what looked like a gesture of affection, but twisting her hair between her fingers till the pain made Anne whimper, and hissing horrors as she did. Sometimes she wouldn't touch Anne at all, only taking a half-step towards her, then looking pleased when Anne flinched before gliding away again. Anne saw her talking to Abner Mullins, to Mr Shreeve, to the military men who came and went around the house and grounds, and they all beamed at her, and she at them.

The only time Anne felt happy was when she was developing her photographs with her grandfather. It took, rather deliciously, her entire attention. Her mind cleared and she sank into the task at hand. In the minutes when they were waiting for the chemicals to do their work, her grandfather would talk to her about art and music, and Anne, free of the terror of Miss Crane's slaps and pinches, could enjoy listening to what he said.

Mr Shreeve and Mrs Warnes both told her they thought her photograph of Lady Mary was very impressive, and Ruby said she had shrieked when she saw it. This made it much easier to dismiss Johnnie's comments as nothing but jealousy. When she asked about sending the picture to *Hotspur* magazine however, her grandfather shook his head.

'No, Anne. I'm afraid that won't do. Lady Mary is part of the family, and we do not talk to the press about the family. It's one of those rules which does not come with an exception, even for your photograph. You may write up a report, however, for the archives. An essay on Lady Mary. We can include a photograph of the pastel portraits of her and her husband, and your picture from the cellars. That will do.'

He sensed her disappointment. 'Now, Anne, a lady doesn't go seeking publicity, you know. It is occasionally thrust upon one. And think how glad your father and mother will be to see it when they come home.'

One morning, as Anne lay slightly stupefied in her bed, lifeless as a rag doll, Ruby frowned and touched her forehead, brushing a curl of her hair off her face.

'You aren't ill, are you, Miss Anne? You've been looking a bit peaky.'

Anne felt too miserable to speak.

'I'll have a word with Cook,' Ruby went on. 'Maybe there will be a sausage at tea. That's something to look forward to, isn't it?'

Anne agreed that it was. Ruby lifted off the blankets. 'Come on now, time to get up and ready for the day.'

Anne's legs felt like lead as she swung them over the edge of the bed.

'That's the way! And Miss Anne, if you see Johnnie today, be nice to him. His ma's a bit unwell. Got the bus into King's Lynn for tests yesterday, so he might be fretting.'

'I shall, Ruby,' Anne said. She hadn't seen Johnnie since he was so mean about her photograph. She remembered the pictures she had taken of him. That would make a fine peace offering, and perhaps his mum would like it too. It was a good idea. Now she had that to look forward to, perhaps getting through her lessons and meals with Miss Crane would be a little easier. She chose the one of Johnnie with his bicycle and put it ready to take to the village after lunch.

19.

1950

Anne woke early on the day after her grandfather's funeral, and realised she had slept again with her wrists crossed above her head. It happened from time to time. Her first thoughts were of Johnnie Fuller. Her mum and dad and Carey had been shocked by the news of his death, and, like Anne, a little angry and disappointed too.

'I suppose Ruby will come to his funeral,' Carey said after Shreeve had been told the news and left to inform Maria and the rest of the household. 'I know it's an awful thing to say, but I will look forward to seeing her again. I thought she was lovely when she worked here.'

'Yes, she was a dear,' Elizabeth replied. 'I was sorry to see her go when she married, but she got the better brother no doubt. She sent a lovely letter about Tom, and all that time her brother-in-law was dead and she knew nothing about it. You were fond of her too, Anne, weren't you?'

'Yes, I was,' Anne said. 'I even tried to embroider a set of handkerchiefs for her when she and George got married. They weren't good, but she seemed very pleased with them.'

What would Ruby remember about Holkham during the war? Anne thought. Her duties had taken her all over the house, and at all hours. Would she have noticed something about the necklace? Perhaps, given she was no longer living in Holkham, she would feel freer to discuss what she had seen too. Though she and George would probably be worrying too much about Gina and her child to want to think much about the past. Sarah was brought in by her nanny to spend an hour with the family, and they spoke about other subjects..

There was no reason at all to walk to the end of Lady Anne's Drive before going back to Holkham village and visiting Gina, but Anne did anyway. She and Carey had played down here with Johnnie. Still, she knew she was really looking for Charles. Although talking to him was often upsetting, after each conversation she felt as if a key had turned in the depths of her mind. A click of wheels like the combination on a safe – of course she'd think of a safe – and she felt, maybe, if she kept talking to Charles a moment would come when she'd be able to look inside and find – what? An answer, an understanding of what had happened during those cold months of 1943 that were still so clouded and cobwebbed and smothered over with strange voices in dark corridors.

He was there. She saw his car first, then him, hunched in front of his easel and staring. He heard her coming and turned, smiling crookedly over his shoulder.

'I'm beginning to think Monet had the right idea, you know. When he was painting his haystacks he used to have half a dozen easels set up, each with a different canvas on it, and he'd move between them as the light changed. It's always so different!'

'I didn't know that about Monet,' she said. 'Our landscape collection stops dead at about 1775.'

'Locals weren't keen on him. Resented him painting their haystacks, like tribes now who think a camera might capture their souls. Or maybe they just thought painting wasn't proper work. When they spotted him at his canvas, they'd tear down the stack and rebuild it somewhere else, just to show him.'

'At least the locals can't do that to you.'

'One of the reasons I'm grateful to your family for letting me paint here. I've waved your note at half a dozen game-keepers already. They do seem to like coming as close as they can to shoot rabbits when I'm at work.' He noticed the basket over the crook of her arm. 'You look like Little Red Riding Hood.'

'I'm not wearing red.'

'Little Brown Duffle Coat doesn't sound so good.'

'It's a few things for Gina Fuller, I'm on my way to visit her. Have you heard about Johnnie?'

He immediately got up from his stool and began to pack away his kit. 'I have. I was in the Nelson when the news arrived. Never seen the inhabitants of Burnham Thorpe so ready to talk, first about the details of the funeral, and then about Johnnie when they heard the news come in. Mr Armstrong even bought me a pint.'

Anne said nothing, just twitched the gingham cloth covering the basket. Two loaves of bread, a jar of honey and half a pound cake, some bacon and a dozen eggs as well as fresh milk.

'May I come with you?' Charles asked suddenly. 'I'm sorry – that's why I'm packing up – to come with you, but perhaps that's not the done thing. I want to let Mrs Fuller know I have the car, you see, so I could offer to drive her about to arrange things. That might be helpful if she has to visit the police or wants to see where it happened. Don't you agree?'

She looked up from the basket again.

'Yes, I'm sure that would be helpful, and of course we can go together. I imagine there will be a lot of visits today.'

He drove her back up the avenue, and then they walked together through the village, past the reading room with its twisted Tudor-style chimneys and the Ancient House to a row of modest cottages on the edge of Donkey Wood.

Anne knocked, and they heard movement inside. Anne frowned over her shoulder at Charles until he took off his cap.

The door was opened by Maria, rather than Gina. She was flushed and her lips were tightly pursed.

'Miss Anne!' She shook her head. 'Lady Anne. Come in, please. Gina is in the parlour with the baby. Oh, I should have come here before. I do not think she has done a stroke of housework since Johnnie bicycled away. And her trained at Holkham! Please, do not tell Mrs Warnes what a state the cottage is in, she would be so ashamed. I want it to be in order before she comes to visit. She was not sure we Italian girls could be trained up to English standards when we arrived and if she comes here now, she will think she was right all along!'

Anne could not see much of the cottage at the moment,

but it looked perfectly tidy to her. A little dusty in the corners perhaps.

'I'm sure it's not half as bad as you think, Maria,' Anne said, 'and you've all been working so hard to have the house ready for Grandfather's funeral yesterday.'

Maria still looked pained, but noticed Charles for the first time. She looked at him, a little frown between her dark, finely arched brows.

'This is Charles Elwood, one of our tenants and an artist. He has a car, and is offering to take Gina around if that might be helpful, or run any errands.'

Her face cleared. 'Ah, yes! I think, yes it would. There are errands. Johnnie's brother George cannot come for two days, and there are so many things to be done. Please. Come in.'

She stood aside and Anne walked past her through the narrow corridor and into the parlour, a small pleasant room, full of light, gently filtered by the trees, and warmer than any part of Holkham. Gina was sitting in an armchair by the fire, a grey knitted shawl wrapped around her shoulders. Her black hair was pulled back severely from her face and tied in a bun at the nape of her neck. She stood up unsteadily as Anne came in.

'Gina, I'm so desperately sorry.' Anne put out her hands and Gina took them. She was a little older than Johnnie, Anne remembered, but when she worked at the Hall she had been undeniably beautiful, huge eyes and a Mediterranean bronze to her skin. Slim and however hard she worked at her duties, her scent was always lavender.

'Like Tuscany just walked in with the tea tray,' her

grandfather had said at the end of her first month, early in 1946. 'A joy to have around the place.'

Not that Mrs Warnes would have put up with her if she was wasn't a good worker too. Gina had been trained to wait at table and helped Anne and Carey to dress when they were home from school. The senior staff debated whether she should be groomed for a position as a lady's maid or a housekeeper. Then she took up with Johnnie. When it became clear she was pregnant, Lord Leicester insisted Johnnie did the right thing and married her. He arranged a modest pay rise for Johnnie, and gave them the cottage, but they had missed her at the house.

Marriage and motherhood had changed her, taken the shine out of her eyes and aged her skin. Anne was shocked to see her looking so old. But, she reminded herself, her baby was still young, just six months, and she was grieving for her husband. Perhaps the effects of that were temporary, not the inevitable decline in her looks a woman faces in her twenties.

'Thank you for coming, Lady Anne,' Gina said, then sat down again in the armchair and began to cry into her handkerchief. Maria took over the duties of hostess, showing Anne into the other armchair by the fire. Johnnie's chair, Anne presumed. She could smell hair lotion and tobacco coming off the upholstery, and Maria fetched a pair of sturdy-looking dining chairs from under the window for Charles and herself.

A squall from a bassinet against the other wall showed where the baby was. Gina looked over. A tiny fist raised above the woven edge was all Anne could see of the child, but Gina did not move to comfort him. On the wall over the cradle hung an engraving of an Italian hillside, and a few family pictures. Gina and Johnnie's wedding outside the Registry Office, and another showing Ruby and George at St Withburga's church door, and, Anne noticed, the photograph she had taken of Johnnie with his bike. His delight and pride shone out of the frame. Anne couldn't look at it.

'I shall fetch tea,' Maria said, then scooped an angry bundle of cloth from the cradle and held the baby to her chest. 'Come help me make the tea, Pietro.' The noise of crying quieted.

Gina wiped her eyes, then looked up. 'He is a good little baby. But I am so tired. I can't remember when I last fed him, one hour to the next. He gets angry with me.'

'I'm sure it must be very hard,' Anne said. Then she introduced Charles and his offer.

'Thank you. Yes. The police have his bicycle. And I must get his suit to the undertaker.'

'I'll be happy to take those clothes to him, and collect the bicycle,' Charles said quietly. She smiled at him briefly, then looked away again.

'How much do funerals in England cost, Lady Anne? Maria does not know and we spent all my savings on things for the baby.'

'I haven't the faintest idea, I'm afraid,' Anne replied. She wanted to say the estate would pay for it, but she didn't dare. She thought most of the villagers paid for funeral insurance, a couple of pennies a week to ensure they avoided a pauper's grave, but Johnnie did not seem the kind of person who would have insurance. 'This is such a terrible shock, Gina. You must have been worried sick and now this – the worst news possible. I am so sorry. Please don't worry about the funeral, I'm sure something can be worked out.'

Gina shrugged and turned to stare into the fire. 'I thought he had got some money then run away and taken it with him. I thought so many bad things about him these last days. I thought he'd gone and I will not be able to marry again for many years, and I read in a magazine about getting a divorce for . . . desertion. But it seemed to take a very long time and much money. Better that he is dead. But who will marry me now? A foreigner with another man's child. There are hardly any men left in England.'

Anne did not know what to say. Selling pottery, school, her months at finishing school in London or time spent learning how to run a household had taught her a lot of things, but she felt like she was floundering across a minefield now. Not that Gina seemed to expect a reply, but someone had to say something. She cast a rather desperate glance in Charles's direction.

'Surely it is too soon to think about any of those things now, Mrs Fuller,' he said. He managed to make it sound warm and comforting, then added something in Italian, his condolences, Anne guessed.

Gina brightened slightly and looked at him. 'You speak Italian? From the war?'

'*Un poco.*' Then he switched back to English, perhaps for Anne's benefit. 'I am sorry your husband had given you reason to think so poorly of him.'

Gina nodded. 'Perhaps it is easier to be angry! He was a sweet, funny boy before we married. Always telling tall stories and boasting. He said his brother was going to get him a job in Norwich, selling cars with him. That we would drive around Wells in a fancy car, better than a Bentley. Then when we got married, I found his brother had not heard about this plan. George does not own the car selling place, only works there. He said in maybe a year, if Johnnie studied numbers and cars and engines, he could try for work there. But Johnnie did not like to study. He liked to make plans in the pub, then go to work sick and smelly.'

'His brother and Ruby were his only family, I think,' Anne said.

'Yes. His mother died two years ago, so he was an orphan. Like me. But he did not want to make a family with me, not in truth. Just plans over pints.'

Maria came back and settled the baby back into his cot, then went out and came back with the tea tray. Charles got to his feet to help her with it and for a while the talk disappeared into a fog of filling and handing out cups and bread and butter. Gina lapsed back into silence, and Maria put her cup and slice next to her on a side table, but she made no move to take it.

The baby began to fuss again, and Maria started to stand with a sigh, but Charles got up and fetched the child himself, sitting him on his knee and bouncing him up and down while looking into his face and talking quiet nonsense. The infant stopped crying and looked first surprised, then delighted. He gave a breathy giggle and Gina smiled again. This time it transformed her face, and she became rather lovely. Charles realised the women were all looking at him.

'I'm the oldest of five,' he said by way of explanation.

'Before I went to war, I spent half my time playing nursemaid.'

'Your mother?' Gina asked, still in that transformed state.

'She was in service, then took in sewing and laundry after she married,' he said. The Italian girls nodded approvingly. Anne remembered her basket.

'Oh, Maria – just a few things from the Hall.'

Maria took the basket and lifted the cloth. 'So very kind. I thank you.' Then she was up on her feet again and carrying it off to the kitchen.

'Mr Elwood, the police,' Gina said. 'When you collect the bicycle, ask them if he had money, please. I need it.'

'I shall make sure,' he said and she relaxed a little.

'Gina, do you know where Johnnie was before his accident?' Anne asked.

Gina shook her head. 'We had a fight. We always had fights. I was very ashamed because Mr Hudson brought him home in the evening, right to my door, holding onto his collar like he was a bad puppy to be carried by his neck, not a man. Said he could not drink at the Victoria till Lady Day. He had spent all his money, and I needed money for food. But he spends it then shouts he cannot go to work on only bread and margarine, but how am I supposed to buy bacon and dripping with no money!

'I tell him this, and then Mrs Gower,' she nodded to the shared wall, 'she hits on the wall with her stick. And Johnnie shouts he has to think, and he goes out and when he comes back he smells of smoke and whisky, and I know he's been eating rabbit over a fire in the wood with that simple gamekeeper man who does not speak. So he has meat in his belly and his clothes all foul. And I am afraid to tell him what I think because of Mrs Gower and her stick – bang, bang, bang on the wall. So I do not speak to him, do not look at him and he sleeps like a dog in front of the fire.

'Next morning he does not go to work. I wake up to make him his tea and he is having a bath. A bath! Johnnie! He sits at that table and writes a letter. Then he puts on his best clothes and goes, but not to work. He says he has a big plan and when he is done Lord Leicester will give him enough money to learn numbers in Norwich and he will hire his brother and he goes. And he never comes back.'

'He went to see my grandfather?' Anne said, startled.

'I do not know where he went. He went, he never came back.'

Charles was continuing gossiping, nonsense conversations with the baby all this time, but it seemed he had been listening attentively.

'But he had no money to go drinking with when he left.'

She shrugged again. 'He got some money, somehow. Maybe he begged from His Lordship. Maybe he stole it from the gamekeeper or made a bet.'

Maria had come back into the room and set the empty basket at Anne's side. She also carried a wrapped bundle of clothes with the address of the local undertaker's written on it in neat capitals. This she set on the table next to Charles's empty tea cup.

'When was that, Gina?' Anne asked.

Gina put her hands out towards her child, and Charles passed the infant across to her. She settled the infant in her arms, and looked down at him, utterly absorbed, it seemed, in his soft features, and stroking his cheek with her forefinger. She was as lovely as ever, really, Anne saw, it was just a different type of lovely.

'The day before His Lordship died,' she said. 'I woke up the next day and Johnnie was not here, but the sun was shining so I sat on the bench outside for a little while so Pietro could have fresh air. Then Mrs Gower walked up the path and said Lord Leicester had fallen, badly, down the cellar stairs and was maybe dead and we were very sad.' She looked up. 'He will be hungry soon, I must feed him, Lady Anne.'

'Of course,' Anne said, getting up and picking up the empty basket. Charles gathered up the parcel of clothes and promised to deliver them and collect the bicycle, as Maria showed them out of the house.

They didn't say anything until they reached Charles's car. The village was quiet.

'What do you think of that?' Charles asked at last.

'You don't think Johnnie's accident and my grandfather's fall can be connected in some way, do you?' Anne asked. It seemed so ridiculous. 'It must be a coincidence!'

'I have no idea. But perhaps if you are not busy you might come with me on my errands this morning? The police will hand over Johnnie's possessions to you far more easily than they will to me anyway.'

She nodded. 'Yes, I shall call the house from the telephone box and let them know.'

'Tell them you won't be home for lunch,' Charles said. 'I can't help feeling we shall have a lot to talk about.'

20.

WELLS-NEXT-THE-SEA WAS ONLY a few minutes' drive away. Charles manoeuvred his car along the narrow Georgian streets leading up from the quayside and parked in the shadow of the church. The town still had a wintery, locked-down feel to it but by the summer it would fill with tourists and day-trippers ready to enjoy the long sandy beaches and eat whelks from paper cones within hours of arriving on the quayside. Anne wondered if Charles would paint them, the holiday crowds, when they arrived, fooling around on the boating lake in brightly painted rowing boats, or the children at play among the dunes. Perhaps those simple summer pleasures would seem rather trivial to him.

The officer at the front desk of the police station, a boy hardly older than Anne with a rather thin moustache, recognised her at once. He was very happy to accept her word that they were there on behalf of Gina Fuller and promised to fetch Johnnie's personal effects immediately.

The sergeant heard the voices in the front office and came out to greet them himself.

'I hear Lord Leicester had a proper send-off, Lady Anne,'

he said after they had exchanged greetings. 'I hope the gentlemen of the press did not give you any trouble?'

He said it in a tone that made Anne's brain rattle with a warning signal. Yes, Dad had said a couple of local constables had been asked to park at the north and south gates to keep away unsavoury types and uninvited press men.

'No, no trouble at all. The two who came behaved terribly well. Thank you so much for your help, and could you pass on the Earl's sincere thanks to your men? It is such a relief not to have to worry about such things on a difficult day.'

She had pitched it right. The sergeant looked pleased and flattered.

'This is such a terrible thing about Johnnie Fuller,' she went on. 'We have just come from visiting his widow.' She found she had to introduce Charles again, artist and tenant, generously offering to run errands for the widow in his car while everyone one at Holkham was still at sixes and sevens after the death in their own family.

'Don't trust Lady Leicester's Mini Morris after your mishap on the way home?' the sergeant asked. 'Well, of course Mr Elwood will have more time than you at the moment Lady Anne, as all he has to do is paint every day.'

'Indeed,' Anne said. Such a useful word, not really a yes or a no. 'I wanted to come and collect Johnnie's belongings for his wife in person, and there are so many other little arrangements.' Not that she could think of anything at the moment; she hurried on, 'but as you say, I am often needed at Holkham.'

'Such a fine place,' the sergeant said. 'I remember fondly being in that temple house when I was in the Home Guard.

I remember you too, Lady Anne, little thing as you were then always running around. Looking for ghosts, I heard tell! Got yourself into some scrapes, didn't you?'

He did look familiar.

'I suppose I did,' she managed. 'I haven't seen Mr Ketteringham for some time, I hope he is well.'

The sergeant nodded. 'He is! Still hasn't got around to retiring. He was with me the day we found you in the Ice House. You'd got yourself locked in, if you remember, and were rather knocked up afterwards.'

The Ice House. Yes. The memory came back to her, or rather little pieces of it did, like a jigsaw that did not seem to fit together. She had been ill, just before Mum and Dad came home.

'I was, and I'm very glad you found me.' She was guessing now, just trying to make her way through the conversation. It was like floundering through thorn bushes, bits of memories all twisted with forgetfulness snagging on her mind.

Charles must have sensed something. 'I imagine I'll be surplus to requirements, Sergeant, after Mr Fuller's brother arrives from Norwich. He was in the Scots Guards, like myself, during the war, wasn't he?'

The sergeant's attention swivelled mercifully away from her.

'That's right, sir.' So Charles was 'sir' now; the elocution lessons had paid off. That and the fact he was standing next to Lady Anne. 'Excellent young man, George Fuller. We were sad to lose him to the big city, but it seems the war has shaken up all the young people. You're not from these parts, are you?'

'No, I came to paint. I'm a Yorkshireman originally.'

The sergeant approved. If one was not fortunate enough to be from Norfolk, Yorkshire was an acceptable alternative.

'Yes. George took after his mother's side of the family. All good workers and respectable people. Johnnie was more like his father. I had a few run-ins with him in my youth, I can tell you.'

Anne still felt muffled and strange as if everything was happening at a slight distance from her.

'Lady Anne did not want to press Mrs Fuller, naturally,' Charles went on, 'but we are still a little unclear as to what happened. Would you be kind enough to share any details that we might pass on to the family? And of course, Lady Anne and Johnnie were such close friends in their youth.'

'Yes, he made sure everyone knew that,' the sergeant muttered. Outside a man on a bicycle called a greeting to the grocer arranging his goods outside his shop. The light filtering in to the front office of the police station through the smeared plate windows caught the dust motes in the air; a faint smell of beeswax rose from the polished counter where the constable had settled again on his high stool and was filling in reports, a parcel of Johnnie's belongings on the counter top next to him. His pen tapped on the ink well. It seemed strange to discuss such a thing as death, in these gentle surroundings.

The sergeant accepted this request as proper. 'Naturally, sir, naturally. Johnnie had been barred from the Victoria after making a bit of a fool of himself the day previous. He'd been taking a while to settle into his responsibilities, it seems. As a result of our enquiries, we found he'd been drinking at one of the fishermen's establishments he was known to frequent in Burnham Overy Staithe. I've had my eye on the landlord there a while. Not one who likes to cooperate with the civil authorities, but he did say that Johnnie had been in that evening and seemed mighty pleased with himself. Made a bit of a show of buying his first round with a five-pound note. The landlord remembered that clear enough. Not often he has a customer with one of them in his pocket. Johnnie stayed till he could hardly stand, then set off home on his bicycle. He rode right off the coastal path, hit his head on the way and . . .' He lifted his palms.

'Did he drown?' Anne asked.

The sergeant looked uncomfortable and looked sideways at Charles, as if either asking permission to answer, or seeking to find a way to avoid doing so.

'No. Might have been the cold, Lady Anne, and that crack to his head. Not enough to kill him in Dr Cox's opinion, but enough to make him woozy. No water in his lungs however, Dr Cox said. Between that knock on the head and the booze he most likely passed out where he lay and the cold got him. Cause of death is heart failure. Same thing what kills us all in the end.' He paused, then added, 'He was probably too tight to know anything about it, Lady Anne. Doc said by the looks of him, bruises on his arms and side, he'd probably already fallen off the bike once or twice on the way.'

'No sign of any other vehicle involved though, Sergeant?' Charles asked.

He thrust out his chin and shook his head. 'No room for a car to get down that path, sir.'

They were unlikely to learn anything further. The constable and Charles loaded the bicycle into the back of the car. Anne looked at it, remembered how it used to gleam when it was new and freshly painted. Sitting in the passenger seat, Anne checked Johnnie's belongings, to see if the money was there. The package contained a cheap watch and a clean handkerchief, a tobacco pouch and cigarette papers, a penknife and a coil of string, and yes, a wallet with a pair of grubby ten-shilling notes folded carefully into quarters and a few coins, all the change that remained from his five-pound note. They delivered the clothes to the undertaker.

'Shall we go and see for ourselves?' Anne asked as she got back into the car again.

Charles looked at her sideways. She sighed. She did have these strange unexplainable moments of panic sometimes, but she was not *delicate*. She decided that sideways glance had suggested he could not quite bring himself to share his thoughts.

'Just because the sergeant called you "sir" and acted like you were somehow my chaperone, does not mean you are, Charles,' she said, staring out of the windscreen. 'I want to see where Johnnie died and have a very close look at that bicycle too. Then I want very much to know how Johnnie got that five-pound note before he rode into a ditch. I think we should go to the pub he was drinking at and speak to the landlord ourselves. And it would probably do no harm to find out what the fracas was about that got Johnnie thrown out of the Victoria too.'

He pressed the heels of his hands onto the top of the steering wheel for a moment, then turned the ignition key and put the car into gear, shoving the gear stick fiercely, and took the road back towards Holkham.

'There has to be a limit, Anne. Fine, I will take you to where Johnnie died and we can take a look at the bicycle, but we should be bloody careful that no one sees you. As for wandering into pubs asking for the details of his last conversations, well you will leave that to me.'

'Why should I leave it to you?'

'For goodness' sake, you are daughter of the Earl of Leicester! You cannot be seen haranguing local publicans for details of the last few hours of Johnnie Fuller. It's not fitting and if you stop and think for one minute, you'll see that.'

'Why on earth should you care about what is "fitting"? And why shouldn't I see where he died? Why should we be secretive about it?'

'Lady Anne Coke, just about to start her first season as a debutante, mooning around over the place a boy like Johnnie Fuller died? You don't think that would start people talking?' He sounded quite angry now. 'What duke will marry you, if he thinks he's the second choice to your first love who shovelled clay in the brickworks?'

Anne was so surprised she laughed out loud. 'Don't be so ridiculous! Nobody would possibly think there was ever anything between Johnnie and me! We played together for a while when we were children. I hardly saw him after I went to school.'

He was silent for a second, and Anne became curious – he was picking his words carefully again. 'Anne, I don't think you realise sometimes . . . You know I think the English class system is a pernicious load of nonsense, a terrible lie that some people have the right, just by accident of birth, to have authority over others.'

'Yes, you've made that perfectly clear.'

'I have. But it exists, and while it does, a lot of people gain a great deal of pride from being associated with you and your family by having, or pretending to have, some intimacy with Holkham. How many people see your photograph in the London magazines? You're not even out in society yet, and I recognised you.'

Anne thought of the photographer at the funeral, the man who had come to Holkham a few months ago to write a feature on the pottery for *Tatler*.

'Yes, I do understand that. The photographers can be a bit wearing, but we have certain duties in the community – we act as figureheads. But what has that got to do with Johnnie?'

'Look, the sergeant hinted at it. And I heard the same stories in the Nelson the night of your grandfather's funeral when the story got out Johnnie Fuller had been found dead in a ditch. He boasted about knowing you, Anne. And more than that, he always suggested you and he had some sort of . . . childish love affair. That even when he courted Gina and got married, it was only because he couldn't be with you, his true love.'

Anne felt her eyes grow hot. Not with shame, or love for Johnnie, but with a deep sense of disappointment and with it a hurt and grief that were utterly unfamiliar. She had been betrayed.

'How utterly rotten of him,' she said, her voice very small. She remembered now Mr Hudson had said something about

Johnnie's tales. 'We were children! There was never anything of that sort . . . how *could* he pretend that there was. And what a terrible, terrible thing to do to Gina.'

Charles sighed, and let the silence unroll between them for a little while before he said anything else.

'I can't say I've formed a very good impression of Johnnie Fuller,' he said at last. 'He seems like a stupid boy, too stupid to understand he was lucky to have been too young to serve and forever trying to make up for it. Perhaps he knew he was lying, perhaps he even talked himself into believing you cared more about him than you did. Whatever the case, it was his way of stealing a little bit of the glamour that surrounds you. Borrowing it maybe. Perhaps that made his life easier. And it sounds like he was a bit of a dreamer – with his plans for a car dealership in Norwich and all that.'

Anne was aware of a great feeling of sadness.

'No one believed him, did they?'

He snorted. 'Not for a second. The people round here knew him and know you. But if you were seen apparently on some pilgrimage to where he died, they might start to wonder.'

'I see,' she said. 'How absolutely horrid.'

'I'm sorry I snapped.'

Anne lifted her chin. 'I think I'm rather getting used to you snapping at me.'

'I deserved that. Well, let us see what we can find out while making sure we keep your reputation as pristine as possible. Leave the pubs to me.'

They reached the spot where Johnnie had been found, and the sergeant had been quite right, there was no tell-tale clue the local constabulary had missed to indicate foul play or accident and the bicycle was just a bicycle, a little dirty and rusted round the spokes, but if dents told a story about how Johnnie had died and why, it was not a story Anne or Charles could read.

21.

THEY PICNICKED IN Charles's car, looking over Holkham beach, on sandwiches Charles had bought from the Victoria. He had managed to get some information too. The reason Johnnie had been barred and carried home the night before he disappeared had been because he was bothering a customer. Mr Hudson had been light on the detail but said the customer had been up at the Hall that day and had stopped in for a bite and a beer before heading back to London.

'That must have been the British Museum man,' Anne said. 'He comes quite often. I shall speak to him next time he visits. I can probably do that without risking my reputation.'

She chewed on her rather limp sandwich and watched the patterns of clouds over the sea.

'Charles, do you really think Johnnie's death and my grandfather's are connected?'

Charles had brought a bottle of beer from the Victoria to go with his sandwich, while Anne had opted for lemonade. It sloshed in the bottle as he drank, then he wiped his mouth with the back of his hand.

'I think so, but it's hard to say how it all joins up. It is like laying down the first marks on a canvas. You start to see an outline, but you are a long way off a finished picture.'

'I can't even see the outline,' Anne said. She opened the door and twisted round to brush the crumbs from her skirt.

'Yes, you do. Just say it out loud, Anne.'

She stared down at her shoes, the sand and dry pine needles that formed the ground at the end of the track, and tried to pull her thoughts into order.

'Very well, I'll try. Johnnie goes to the Victoria, as he often does, and has too much to drink. He comes home and has a fight with Gina, then goes off to sit in the wood with one of his cronies for a while. So far nothing unusual. In the morning though, rather than going to work, he decides to go and see my grandfather and writes him a note. Sounds like he has realised something after his night in the pub and thinks he'll get a reward for it. Perhaps he does. My grandfather did carry a few five-pound notes with him. I've seen him give them to workers he likes when he learns it's their birthday or some such. Certainly, by the end of the day Johnnie is in funds again and off he goes and gets so drunk he rides into a ditch. Poor Gina thinks he's run away. That same night my grandfather decides to put the fake necklace in his pocket and is walking round the house with it. At some time after supper he falls on the cellar steps. So, if Johnnie did go and see Grandpa, what did he say that earned him a five-pound note? That the necklace was a fake?' She leant forward, her elbow resting on her knee and her chin in her hand. 'No, Grandpa knew it was a fake already! He told my mother she couldn't wear it two years ago. He may have had it made himself. And anyway, how would Johnnie know the necklace was a fake? He never even saw it and one thing I'm sure of is that it wasn't Johnnie who went to London to get that copy made.'

Anne could hear Charles drumming his fingers on the steering wheel. 'Putting the fake in his pocket wasn't the only unusual thing your grandfather did that day.'

She spun around. 'No, you are right! He wrote down the name of my old governess! Do you think Johnny might have said something about her? He was keeping watch on the house then. Looking for spies, he said. Might he have seen her doing something unusual?'

'Can we walk? I think better when I walk,' Charles said.

He got out of the car and she did the same. They took the path out of the pines towards the dunes. The wind stirred the sand at their feet. The barbed wire still showed on the edge of the dunes, wrapped around poles and almost rusted away. Anne shielded her eyes, trying to remember it as it had been during the war.

'I think there is a taxi cab under there,' she said, pointing to a steep-sided dune to the east. 'I wonder if it will be there forever.'

'Anne,' he said, too lost in his own thoughts to hear her. 'I think whatever Johnnie saw, when he told your grandfather about it, the Earl realised it meant that Lavender Crane may have stolen the necklace and had it replaced with the fake. Then perhaps that revelation caused these accidents. Johnnie seems to have been the sort who would be ready to drink himself silly when he had a five-pound note, and if your grandfather was distracted, perhaps having learnt via Johnnie that Lavender Crane may have stolen the Coke necklace, he might well have fallen.'

'I think that makes sense,' she replied, taking in a long breath of the salty air. The wind twitched at the edge of her headscarf and she tucked it back into place. Sea and sky had taken on a wintery glower today and spring seemed a long way off. 'But what about the man who had the fake necklace made in London? Charles shook his head. 'He could be anyone – an accomplice of Lavender Crane's to whom she sent the photographs.'

Anne sighed. 'Would that be the end of it then?'

'I suppose so, in so far as any story is really finished. I thought perhaps your grandfather fetched the fake necklace to hand to the police, along with Johnnie's testimony, all ready to set them after Lavender Crane, wherever she may be. I'd give my eye-teeth to know exactly what Johnnie said. Do you think your father might want to pursue Miss Crane if she was involved in the theft of the necklace? There must be some way of finding her.'

'Oh, it's still too cold to just stand on the beach. Let's go back and take the path through the woods.' He agreed, and they climbed back up to the shelter of the trees, then began walking slowly east. 'I think my father would want to go after her if we knew what Johnnie had said. But there is no sign of the note Johnnie wrote, Dad would have said if something like that had turned up. Dad won't go to the authorities when all we can say is we think Johnnie might have said something about my old governess. We are simply guessing.'

Charles hunched his shoulders. 'You are right, but perhaps

we still have a chance to find out more. You can talk to this British Museum man when he comes again, and what about George Fuller's wife, Ruby? I got the impression she was in service at Holkham?'

Anne smiled. 'That's right. She looked after me a lot of the time. I was wondering about talking to her, but I can't bombard her with questions at a family funeral.'

'You'll find the right time to talk to her, Anne. I think you are rather good at that. Now let's get you back to the car before you go blue.'

They turned, and now the wind was at their backs Anne could lift her eyes. The sun was settling low in the sky and she began to walk faster, worried about missing tea as well as lunch.

'By the way, Charles, my father might be in touch. Mum agrees we'll have to go through the contents of the house to make sure nothing else is unaccounted for, and you may be dragooned in to help. It will at least be slightly warmer than painting here. Can you give me a lift back to the house?'

'You shall all have me tugging my forelock before the tenancy is over, won't you?'

'Ten minutes with Mum and Carey and you'll be so charmed you'll be singing the praises of the English aristocracy,' she promised.

He looked struck. 'I shall be barred from the avant garde art scene in London forever if that happens.'

The man from the British Museum called at Holkham only two days later. As soon as Anne learnt that he was in the house, she went to find him and discovered him at work in the classical library.

He looked up as Anne came in and stood up. Tall, a loose-limbed man and in his mid-thirties Anne guessed. He had a heavy head of blond curling hair and his eyes were a startling light blue.

'Lady Anne,' he said, coming around the table and putting out his hand. 'Mr Mullins told me the volume I'm working on was a favourite of yours during the war. My name is Carstairs.'

She glanced down at the Holkham Bible Picture Book. 'Indeed it was, but I looked on it with the eye of a child, rather than a connoisseur. I loved how it told so much of the story of the flood or whatever in one picture.' He looked familiar. His handshake was loose and silky. 'I am sorry, but haven't we met before? Didn't you visit during the war?'

He smiled at her and the skin at the corners of his eyes creased. 'I did have that lucky chance a few times when my war work brought me here. I play the viola. I think your grandfather and I played for you once.'

The memory came back, glowing with warmth.

'Yes! Twice in fact! I was allowed to attend when you and Grandpa played for the Italian prisoners, and yes, you both played for the household just before Christmas during the last year of the war, after Mum and Dad had come home. I thought you were marvellous.'

He shook his head. 'I was just trying to keep up with Lord Leicester, he was an excellent musician. I was very sorry to hear of his death.'

'Thank you. Do please sit down, I am very sorry to disturb

you but I have a rather delicate question for you, Mr Carstairs. You visited my grandfather the day before he died, I believe?'

Anne perched on one of the dining chairs and wondered how on earth to go on.

Carstairs looked kind, but somewhat bemused. 'I'm happy to be of service to you in any way I can,' he said, 'but I am somewhat at a loss as to what your question might be.' He paused. 'I did see your grandfather the previous day. As I told Lord Leicester this morning when I arrived, he seemed in good health and good spirits at that time. You had, I think, already left on your sales trip.'

'Yes, it must seem rather strange, and I'm afraid it's only going to get stranger. After you left the house, I think you stopped in at the Victoria?'

He nodded. 'I did. Mr Hudson knows how to keep his beer. I decided to pop in and write up a few notes while they were fresh in my mind. Mr Hudson had heard your grandfather and me play together too so once the notes were done, he and I had a pint and talked about music, and the war and how long it will take us to recover from it. Almost five years now, and that's still all any of us can talk about.'

'And something happened, I think,' Anne said carefully.

Carstairs frowned. 'Yes, there was a young man who had been drinking too hard and fast during the early part of the evening who got very loud. He irritated me I'm afraid, and I cut him down on a couple of strong opinions he was expressing. He did not take it well. Mr Hudson stepped in very quickly, barred the boy and marched him off home. When he came back we finished our pints, made various remarks on young men who haven't learnt to take their drink and shook hands. Then I motored back to London. I haven't given the matter another thought.' He shifted a little uncomfortably in his chair. 'The young man was not threatening or abusive, Lady Anne. It would be a shame to make more of it than it was. I hope he woke up with a sore head and has held off the beer a bit since.'

Anne looked down at the polished surface of the dining table on which the books were arranged. Its warm mirror-like gloss seemed to absorb, soften and reflect the chocolate browns of the books surrounding them.

'His name was Johnnie Fuller. I'm afraid he's dead. He got very drunk again only a day later and disappeared. He was found in a ditch on the day of Grandpa's funeral.'

Carstairs looked shocked. 'I am so very sorry to hear that.'

'Yes. Mr Carstairs, I know this will sound very inconsequential, but you would be doing me a great kindness if you could give me an answer. What exactly were you talking about? What did Johnnie say?'

He sat back in his chair and stared into the air above her, frowning with concentration.

'What was it exactly? Oh, yes, Mr Hudson and I had been discussing the beach and what a slow and painful business it is gradually getting rid of all the military rubbish strewn around the place. Even with the mines cleared, all that barbed wire and detritus from the practice bombings remains. Not to mention the concrete pillboxes. I said, I thought, that from what I learnt after the war Hitler had always planned on invading along the south coast, so we had despoiled the beaches for nothing. We couldn't have known that, naturally – wastage is part of war and such things are necessary evils. That was our broader point, I believe. I think that was when this young man, Fuller, intervened. He said the defences had been vital and started talking about spies being landed up and down this part of the coast, enemy agents scattered among the populace and all that bunkum. I wondered if he'd been in the Home Guard, but he seemed too young even for that.'

'Was it bunkum?' Anne asked. 'There were so many stories about Nazi spies in the comics and story papers. I remember reading them.'

He shook his head. 'We had to stay vigilant, of course, so those sorts of stories were never officially discouraged and we were all certainly very aware of the dangers in the first year or so. By the middle of 1942 though, we were confident that Hitler's attempts to set up an intelligence network in Britain had been an abject failure. You must remember, Lady Anne, Hitler never expected to be at war with the British. He was quite certain we would be his allies, not his enemies. No, the Soviets had an excellent intelligence network in England, sometimes I'm concerned they still do. The Germans did not.'

'You are quite certain?'

'I am. The few there were rounded up in the first months. One man shot himself. After that, nothing. No, it was code-breaking and interception of international communications that kept us awake at night. And though of course I can only ask you to take my word for it, be assured, I am in a position to know.'

He spoke with quiet confidence, and she did believe him.

'So, you were not looking for spies when you came to visit my grandfather?'

'No. I had some business with a few of the German pilots you had on the estate, following up reports on their information. Captain Horton had sent us some interesting tit-bits. But that was all about building up a picture of the state of morale in Germany as we began planning for D-Day. There were no German spies at liberty, and we had those people we thought likely to be Nazi sympathisers among our own population under very strict guard.'

'But Johnnie disagreed?'

'He was proclaiming loudly that spies were hiding round every hedgerow at the time, and that if loyal British citizens and official spy catchers hadn't been on the lookout, D-Day would have failed! Perhaps I didn't explain the situation as calmly and fully as I have to you, but I made it clear he was talking rubbish. He took it as a very personal slight.'

Anne sighed. 'Johnnie and I were friends as children. We read all those magazines and talked ourselves into all sorts of excitements. But I didn't think he really believed it then, or believed it still.'

'You have grown up a great deal since we last met, Lady Anne,' Carstairs said. 'Johnnie Fuller looked to me like the kind of lad who had got stuck somewhere along the line.'

'I think you are right. Thank you so much for telling me.'

She stood up and Carstairs got to his feet again. 'I take it you are not going to tell me why this is important to you?'

'I'm terribly sorry, but I'd rather not just now. I do apologise for disturbing you.'

'Not at all.' He reached into his jacket pocket and produced a card from his wallet. 'If I can be of any help in the future, Lady Anne, do let me know.'

Anne thanked him and left him to his work. She retreated to her room and curled up in the armchair by the empty grate, one of her shawls wrapped round her to keep off the worst of the cold. Spies. Certainly she and Johnnie had talked a lot about them, revving each other up discussing which of the servants or gamekeepers might be Nazis passing secret messages to the prisoners, and Johnnie had been very sure of himself in 1943, but to be spouting that sort of nonsense now? It was very strange. But that conversation had got him thinking, and that thinking had sent him to her grandfather the next day in his good suit. How she wished she could see that note he wrote to her grandfather!

22.

Anne's father read the lesson at Johnnie's funeral and the whole family joined Gina and the rest of Holkham village in the Reading Rooms afterwards. Mrs Warnes had obviously helped with the food. From the scraps of conversation Anne overheard, the general consensus seemed to be that while the late Earl's funeral rites had been fitting, Johnnie Fuller had got a better send-off than he deserved.

George Fuller looked handsome and serious and Anne thought her father enjoyed talking to him. Carey and Anne were both very pleased to see Ruby again. Motherhood suited her, and she had grown into a smart and sensible-looking woman. She looked prosperous too, without any showiness, and the party from Holkham, from Mrs Warnes to Elizabeth, looked at her with mingled admiration and pride.

Anne did not have a chance to speak to her for some time, but when Ruby said her two boys needed to have a run round the green before they drove back to Norwich, Anne took the chance to go with her. The children were six and four, lively and robust little boys who quickly invented some game, a little like football, to entertain themselves on the grass while Ruby and Anne watched over them.

'It is so nice to see you, Lady Anne,' Ruby said once the boys had settled into their game. 'You've turned into quite a beauty. I've got my scissors ready, and shall cut out all the pictures that they publish for your season and put them in my scrap book. When will you be presented at court?'

Anne watched the boys tumbling over each other on the grass, obvious to the chill in the air. 'Not until May, which seems like a long way off when the weather is like it is today. You're looking very well, Ruby.'

'Thank you. I must say, George is a good provider as my mother would have said. I'm not sure if he'd be a good salesman if he sold refrigerators, but he loves cars. You should have heard him bending Lord Leicester's ear about the latest American models just now. Even at his brother's funeral! Not that they've been close since the war. We hoped he'd settle a bit when he got married, but no such luck. Still, I'm glad to say we'll be able to look after Gina. We have a nice little house of our own and it has central heating if you'd believe such a thing, if she wants to stay with us.'

'That sounds glorious!' Anne said heartily.

Ruby chuckled. 'Holkham still chilly, is it? And does Lord Coke, sorry, Lord Leicester still insist on keeping the windows open at night?'

'Fresh air is vital!' Anne said. 'Yes, he does. Though Carey and I close them again the second he goes to bed.'

'George Junior! Do not be rough with your brother!'

'But Mum . . .'

'You do not want me to come over there, George.'

The games resumed at a slightly more subdued level. 'I am a very lucky woman, Lady Anne, but I do miss you all up at the house, I really do.'

'Do call me Anne, Ruby.'

She smiled sideways. 'Well, that's very nice of you and so I shall. But perhaps not in front of Lord Leicester.'

Something about her smile brought the past flooding back again, but this time Anne didn't feel panicky or unwell. Even in her smart black pillbox hat with her face delicately powdered, Ruby was still Ruby, a friend when Anne had really needed one.

'Ruby, do you remember my governess, Lavender Crane?'

'Oh, her!' Ruby said, her voice rich with dislike. 'It was a happy day when she packed her bags and left.'

'I thought everyone liked her,' Anne said, confused. She sat down on the iron bench on the edge of the green and Ruby sat next to her. The air felt damp with coming rain.

'They did at first, Anne. She knew how to flatter people. I think that Mr Shreeve and Mrs Warnes started to go off her when she seemed to lord it over them and throw her weight around. Of course, they didn't like that one bit. As for me, I never liked her. More than that, I thought *you* didn't like her either and then when you got sick . . .'

'You know, it's the strangest thing, Ruby, but I can hardly remember that. The sergeant at Wells used to be in the Home Guard and mentioned something about the Ice House and me being unwell afterwards, but it's all very confused in my mind.'

Ruby patted her hand. 'That'll be Bill Coogan. I'm not surprised. You'd been in a funny way for a while, insisting someone was living in the cellar. His Lordship had to take you down to look before you'd be still about it. Then you got shut in the Ice House and when we got you out you were properly ill and in quite a state. Nervous exhaustion, the doctor said. So I took charge of you, moved back into the maid's room next to yourself. Miss Crane was gone before you were fit to have lessons again.'

Anne shook her head. 'I don't remember insisting someone was in the cellar. I remember thinking I had seen some blankets down there, but that's all.'

'Oh, you were very sure, but I think you were on your way to being ill by then anyway.'

George Junior seemed to have declared victory; the boys were now fighter planes engaged in some vicious dogfight. The sound effects were terrific.

The memory came back like an echo. Yes, she had asked her grandfather to check again. Johnnie and she were convinced it was important, but when they had explored the cellars together before going to the darkroom one day, there was nothing to be found. Just the furniture, and animal heads and wine and wood. But suddenly she could see that bed again and it *was* a bed, not just a pile of blankets or a trick of the light. A little bed, with a small metal trunk beside it like a bedside table. Anne had fallen over the trunk as she fled Lady Mary's ghost.

'Ruby,' she said slowly, '*was* someone living in the cellars?'

Ruby watched her boys in silence for a while before replying. 'I was never sure. And I didn't want to know, not really. So we put anything we saw or heard down to Lady Mary and got on with things. You'll find this out some day,

Anne, but the things we will do for our children when they are hurt. You can't ever believe it till you have a kiddie of your own. But there we are, I have nothing else to say about that.'

'Ruby,' Anne asked carefully, 'why was it you who looked after me when I got ill? You had so many duties in the house – why didn't they ask Miss Crane to look after me?'

'Oh, Miss Anne, your memory has been playing tricks on you! Though it was a nasty fever you had. From the moment you were fetched out of the Ice House you screamed blue murder whenever Miss Crane came into the room. You said she was Lady Mary come to kill you. Broke our hearts, it did. Of course I looked after you.'

Anne put her hand over Ruby's. 'Thank you.'

'Happy to do it,' Ruby said. 'You had me and that funny rag doll. I think the Italian prisoners made it for you. Then of course your mother and father and Carey arrived and we had a happy Christmas in the end.'

The doll! Yes, she remembered it now. Where on earth was it and where had she got it from? The door opened behind them and Charles Elwood emerged from the reading room, pulling on his overcoat.

'Lady Anne, I think Lord Leicester is ready to leave. And I have been recruited by Mr Mullins. We shall be cataloguing together.'

Anne managed to say something suitable, then kissed Ruby's cheek and went back inside the reading room to make the formal farewells with her family.

23.

1943

JOHNNIE WAS INSIDE one of their redoubts, a rough teepee of fallen branches, when Anne arrived. He stuck his head out of the opening when he heard her coming and she caught his quick bright smile of pleasure before he quickly adopted a look of vague unconcern.

'Oh, hello, Anne. How are you?'

She got off her bike and rested it against a tree at the side of the clearing.

'Fine, thank you.'

There was a slightly awkward silence, then Johnnie said with enthusiasm, 'I've got a new *Hotspur* magazine! Do you want to see it?' Then he added a bit more plaintively. 'I've been bringing it with me for days in case you wanted to read it.'

That made Anne feel a lot better.

'Sorry. I've been taking lots of photographs and developing them with Grandpa.' She took the carefully wrapped package from the basket of her bicycle. She had found a bit of card in the schoolroom to keep it straight. 'I brought you this.'

Johnnie took it and unwrapped it, and when he saw the image of himself and his bike his smile was huge.

'Gosh, that's splendid! Thank you! The bike looks really good, doesn't it?'

She nodded and a little of the misery of the last days and nights retreated under the force of his pleasure.

'You are very good at photographs, Anne. I'm sorry if I was rude about your ghost picture. I suppose I thought it would look like one of the pictures in the magazine.' He ran on. 'And I didn't want you to be upset when they said they wouldn't print it.'

Anne didn't think that last bit was true, but he had apologised, which was difficult for boys.

'That's OK. Grandpa says I'm not allowed to send things to *Hotspur* about Lady Mary anyway, which is a shame, because I know a lot about her now. Mrs Warnes said she liked the photograph, and so did Ruby. Mr Mullins is going to help me make a report about Lady Mary, then we can show Mum and Dad when they come home. And Mr Mullins can put it in the archives.'

She sat down on one of the large flat stones they had dragged into the clearing to serve as a chair. 'It's not as good as *Hotspur* though.'

'Still,' Johnnie said encouragingly, 'it's pretty good.'

He rewrapped the photograph with a great deal of care and slid it into his satchel.

'So what was it like looking for Lady Mary?'

She told him all about it, and he said she'd been very brave, and anyone would have got scared meeting a ghost like that. Even him.

'That bed you saw, Anne,' he said, after they'd been through the details a few times. 'Do you think maybe Lady Mary led you to it?'

Anne frowned, and poked at the soft mulch of the ground with the tip of her shoe.

'Grandpa went down and checked. He told me when we were taking pictures of the Coke necklace. He said I must have imagined it.'

'But that was the next day,' Johnnie insisted. 'Someone could have hidden it again by then. I bet it's all connected!' He started talking very quickly. 'Those lights and everything I've been seeing late at night in the park. What if there is a spy in Holkham, taking notes of all the defences to tell Hitler, and Lady Mary chased you towards where he was sleeping so you could raise the alarm. Just because she's a ghost doesn't mean she's not a patriot!'

Anne considered. It made a lot of sense. Lady Mary probably knew a lot about what was happening in the house. Yes, she was mostly just a bit mean with the shoving and whispering, but what if she had seen spies in the house and was trying to warn them?

'Poor Lady Mary!' she said. 'Wouldn't it be terrible if you knew there were spies in the house and you couldn't warn anyone about them?'

'Exactly!' Johnnie said with great enthusiasm. 'So she chased you down there so you could see for yourself, but of course the spy must have been watching you too, so he cleared it all away. Maybe that explains the lights I saw. He might have been throwing things in the lake, or burying them so Lord Leicester and the soldiers couldn't find them.'

It sounded like Johnnie had been over the wall again when he shouldn't have been. Anne really wanted to be sure he didn't get shot, or into trouble, but then this was obviously very important too.

'I shall tell Grandpa and ask him to have another proper search. Maybe the Royal Engineers will want to help him.'

'Yes, that's a good idea,' Johnnie said. 'Is it true that they are going to hold a party at Holkham at Christmas? The vicar said something about it to Mum.'

'Yes, I think they are.'

'I hope they have proper games,' Johnnie said. 'With prizes. A shooting gallery would be amazing.'

That did sound fun. Her mother and father would be home by then. When Anne thought of her parents now, they seemed strange and fuzzy. She wasn't sure if she was remembering them, or the photographs of them in silver frames from the long library. She hoped she would be able to prove to them she didn't need to be tied up at night any more. Her feelings became strange and tight and confused. Best to think about the spy.

'Johnnie, if the spy is still at Holkham and sending messages to Hitler, do you think he'd do it from the house, or from the beach?'

He considered. 'I think they have spies in boats just offshore to collect the messages. You can't really see the sea from the house, can you?'

'The trees are in the way, mostly,' Anne said. 'Unless you go up to the Ice House or the obelisk, and I don't think a spy would go up to the obelisk, because that is right next to the temple and that's always full of the Home Guard.'

'The Ice House would make a good spy base,' he said thoughtfully. 'You should check that. I'll keep an eye on the beach.'

'There are minefields!' she said.

'Not at the bottom of the drive, and you can see for miles from there if you just go to the edge of the trees.'

'Did you get your torch back?'

'Yes, Mrs Warnes brought it round.'

'She wasn't cross about you lending it to me, was she?'

'No. She was pretty decent. Just said you wouldn't need it again.' Did Mrs Warnes know Anne was being tied up to her bed? The humiliation of the idea made her blush. 'She and Mum had a long chat, but they were mostly talking about my brother George and the war and stuff. We got a letter from him last week.'

The afternoon unwound. Anne helped repair the redoubt, until they were confident it wouldn't let in much rain, and they even dug a small channel round the edge on the inside to let the water that did get in run away and for a while Anne was almost as free as she was when she was with Grandpa.

Lord Leicester was sceptical about the idea Lady Mary had been trying to tell them about a spy in the cellars, but that Sunday after lunch he took Anne round the cellars one more time with Shreeve following them. There was no sign of the bed, or of any other secret spy equipment. Anne was disappointed; Johnnie had convinced her Lady Mary had been trying to tell them something.

'I can understand your logic, Anne,' her grandfather said

kindly, holding her hand while they examined the piles of furniture moved from the rooms the Royal Engineers were using. 'But remember the cellars aren't deserted! Shreeve has to come here to fetch the wine, and a lot of the time Christopher and Smith are down here fetching wood and stoking the boilers. If someone was living down here, you would know about it, Shreeve, wouldn't you?'

Shreeve nodded. 'I would. I shall stay vigilant, Miss Anne, but I promise you to the best of my knowledge there are no German spies in the cellar. No one in fact who poses any danger to you, the family, or the country.'

Anne had to be content with that.

Johnnie was not free to play every afternoon. On Tuesdays and Thursdays after school he went to Wells and helped his mum in the tea shop. Anne had taken all the photographs she could in the house, so, hoping it was too cold for Miss Crane to be reading there, she went to the pleasure gardens near the stable yard.

She liked the gargoyles by the pond. One sat in a block of stone, heavy with ivy, his chin in his hands as if he was looking out of the window of an old castle. Above him another had his mouth open, as if he was waiting for snow-flakes to drop on his tongue, and they were all surrounded with ferns of different greens, some dazzling and some dark. Anne approached and bobbed a curtsey to them, then she saw a movement near the shell grotto. Miss Crane was here, but she was not alone. Mrs Warnes was with her and they seemed to be arguing about something, or at least, Mrs Warnes was talking very fast. Miss Crane was just smiling. Anne turned away, feeling she was seeing something she shouldn't, and hurried back into the stable yard. A horn beeped and she turned round. One of the Royal Engineers' great trucks, so big and heavy they looked like tanks, was nosing away from its parking spot along the wall and she was in the way. She jumped, not sure which way she should go, and caught a glimpse of a rather annoyed-looking soldier in a peaked cap at the steering wheel.

'Anne!' Captain Horton was coming out of the estate office. 'Come over here!'

She did and they watched together as the great truck turned out and along the avenue towards Holkham village and the beach. It made the ground shake. The soldier raised his hand as he passed, and Anne waved shyly back.

'You have to have your wits about you here,' Horton said. 'I'm sure no one would want to stop you playing in the pleasure gardens, but you will be careful around the yard, won't you?'

She nodded mutely and looked over her shoulder. She hoped Miss Crane hadn't seen her getting in the way.

An officer who had been supervising the loading of the truck came towards them, tucking his clipboard under his arm.

'Afternoon, Horton!' he said, then added to Anne. 'Hope you didn't get a fright there, Miss Coke.'

He had such a friendly air about him Anne felt immediately better. 'No, I'm sorry, I didn't mean to get in the way.' Then, thinking of Johnnie, she added, 'Is it true you are going to have a party at Christmas? My friend in the village thinks it sounds smashing.'

'I am glad to hear that! Yes, Lord Leicester thinks it is a

viable plan, and we do want to try to be good tenants. Now, what entertainment do you think we should have?'

'Johnnie wants a shooting gallery, but I'm not sure about that.' Anne searched her mind for distant memories of funfairs. 'Perhaps we could have darts?'

'Very good! I think we can manage that. Do children still like pin the tail on the donkey?'

Anne nodded. 'But perhaps we could pin the tail on Hitler instead.'

He laughed. 'Yes, that sounds more fun. I have a rather good artist in my squad. We'll get him to draw a Hitler we'll all want to pin things to.'

He nodded to Horton and made to move away.

'Lieutenant!' Anne said.

'Yes, Miss Coke?'

'Lieutenant, do you think there are any spies at Holkham? My friend says he's seen strange lights and . . .' She tailed off, feeling a bit foolish, but to his credit the lieutenant didn't roll his eyes at Captain Horton, but looked serious.

'We all keep an eye out, of course, but I think not. I think your friend is just seeing the various training exercises we run. And of course the men at the battle camp are quite often sent to the beach for night training. That might well look like spies, but it is just our men practising. Will you warn your friend to be careful? Only I think we'll be seeing more bombing practice along the beaches, night and day. The RAF keep us informed, don't you, Horton?'

'We try,' Horton agreed.

'Anyway, do warn him to be careful.'

Now his eyes flicked away from her and he touched the

edge of his cap, Anne looked round and saw Miss Crane, watching them in her cat-like way. At least she couldn't pinch her when she was with Horton and the lieutenant.

The adults exchanged good days, and comments on the increasing cold of the weather.

'Don't be late for tea, Anne,' Miss Crane said. 'And make sure you have a proper walk.'

Then she walked away. The two men watched her.

Anne returned to the gargoyles and the shell house, tracing the patterns set into the stone of the little gazebo and wondering if they meant anything.

Miss Crane must have seen something. That night when she bound Anne up to the bed and slapped her legs for wriggling, even though Anne was trying very, very hard to be still, she told her stories of rats running around the pleasure gardens, big fat ones waiting behind the ferns and in the ivy that surrounded the gargoyles, watching for a chance to bite her with their sharp yellow teeth, and she nipped the flesh under Anne's arms with her fingernails to show her how it would feel. Like a plague, they infested her dreams with their yellow eyes and their slippery, sharp teeth and she couldn't fight them off because her hands were tied.

24.

Anne had said she'd investigate the Ice House, so she did even though her legs felt very heavy as she climbed the slope towards it. It was a strange, thatched building. The gable end with the door in it was high, built in soft red bricks, then it had a long, low body where the thatch swooped down almost to the ground, and an extra cone at the end that looked like a neat, pointed haystack. It was very old. It stood a little way from the avenue, flanked by high trees that looked like bony, bare guardians in the wintery afternoon. Anne was sorry they didn't use it any more. It must have been rather wonderful watching the men cut huge slabs of ice from the lake and drag them up here. They were then stored between layers of straw so the house could use it all summer. Ices! Her stomach rumbled. Her skirts were getting loose, and she was hungry all the time, but eating with Miss Crane was such a torture she couldn't finish the food on her plate. She thought of the fruit they used to get from the gardens; of course that was when there were boys enough to stoke the fires that warmed the hollow walls. She had the vaguest memory of what a peach tasted like. Peaches and ice cream. Cake with fruit jam between the layers. All gone because of Hitler. If she could catch his spy it would serve him right.

She reached the Ice House. The door was wood, but very heavy looking and it looked even more like a witch's cottage now she was close up. She hadn't heard of Lady Mary's ghost appearing up here, but then hardly anyone came this way, so perhaps no one would notice if she did.

A wood pigeon cooed nearby, then took off from the roof of the house with a muscular beating of wings. Anne jumped. There was nothing to be frightened of, she was just going to have a look inside and see if the spy was there, but the day suddenly seemed duller and more watchful and the naked trees rattled their branches. She heard a whisper. Lady Mary *was* here! No, Anne could hear sentences, and Ruby said you could never work out exactly what Lady Mary was saying to you, not more than a word or two at a time.

'They are terrified I'll give them away . . . come and go as I like.'

Anne recognised Miss Crane's voice, much worse than Lady Mary.

Anne flattened herself against the wall, then looked round the edge. She could see Miss Crane's long coat, the shine of the handbag over her arm, up at the other end of the Ice House, the haystack end. Then Miss Crane turned round and saw her.

'Stay there, Anne,' she said and walked towards her, dark flashes in her eyes.

'Are you spying on me, Anne?'

'No, Miss Crane!'

'I think you were. Nasty sneaky little girl that you are. And a liar too.'

'I didn't want to see you,' Anne said. 'I just wanted to see in the Ice House.'

Suddenly Miss Crane smiled, such a lovely warm smile that lit up her eyes, and Anne felt a burst of relief. Had Miss Crane decided to stop being cruel?

'Oh, in that case! Shall we look together?' She twisted the heavy latch on the wooden door and wrenched it open. Then she stood aside a bit to let Anne look. A great draught of cool damp air rushed out to greet them, but Anne couldn't see much. An earth floor, scattered with damp thatch, then darkness beyond, where the pit was.

'No handle on the inside of the door, I see,' Miss Crane said. 'Perhaps it wasn't *just* an Ice House.'

Anne couldn't see the pit. She was a bit curious to see how deep it was, but the Ice House was very dark and she didn't like the smell.

'I bet this is where they kept Lady Mary,' Miss Crane said. 'I'm quite sure of it. She was probably here when her mother found her, with the rats chewing her fingers and nesting in her dress.'

'That's not true,' Anne said. 'She complained about lots of things in her letters. She would hardly miss it out if they locked her in the Ice House.'

'She didn't want anyone to know what a wicked woman she really was. Only the very worst people would be shut up in here.'

Anne felt a burst of frustration. Miss Crane was making something up, and about her family. Anne had read Lady

Mary's letters and about the court case when she separated from her husband. She was, for once, on solid ground and she knew it.

She turned and looked at Miss Crane.

'That's just a silly lie.'

Miss Crane's face transformed. Even when she was angry, or taking pleasure in hurting Anne in some way, she was still pretty; now though her face seemed to distort, stretched and twisted with rage as if in a funfair mirror.

She grabbed Anne's arm, forcing it high behind her back, and pushed her through the arched doorway. The smell of damp and rot clogged Anne's nostrils.

'What did you say to me, you little bitch?' Miss Crane hissed. Anne let out a yelp of agony – something was wrong with her arm beyond ordinary hurt – but she couldn't say anything. Then Miss Crane threw Anne forward. She fell heavily onto the floor and her head hit something hard. The pain changed and flowed sickly through her, arm to head and head to arm, and everything spun. She turned on her side and Miss Crane kicked her in the stomach. She couldn't breathe or cry out, she just let out a grunt, then the door to the Ice House slammed shut and she was in darkness.

Anne struggled to her knees and half crawled, half dragged herself to the door. There was no handle, Miss Crane had said. She beat on it with her fist, feeling sick and swimmy.

'Miss Crane! Let me out! Let me out! I'm sorry,' she shouted. Miss Crane must be there, waiting to open the door. She beat on the solid wood again. It didn't move. She would be good. She wouldn't complain. Something squeaked in the darkness. She felt a movement against her leg and panic overwhelmed her. She was in the cellars again. Hands reached out for her, the dead animals were rising up, pressing closer to her. She felt the nightmare touch of Lady Mary's rotten clothes and the dark damp smell of the old thatch filled her nostrils. Her chest tightened until she couldn't breathe. She was alone with the witches and rats from her story book, all creeping towards her in the dark, whispering. She screamed and she couldn't stop.

Lieutenant Ketteringham wrote up his latest report sitting in the main room of the temple and read it through with a sense of frustration. The invasion of France was coming, and he wanted very much to be part of it. When he returned from Dunkirk, pulled out of the shallow water by a Harwich fishing boat and leaving the horror of that beach behind him, taking this role had seemed both necessary and useful. The Home Guard were decent chaps, and using them as cover to set up an auxiliary unit to fight behind the lines after Germany invaded was a good idea. For most of the following year while the Battle of Britain was fought overhead, it had felt urgent. Ketteringham had been certain it was only a matter of time, and not much time, till the Nazis made it over the Channel. He was prepared, mentally and physically, to live wild and, for as long as he survived, use guerrilla tactics to disrupt and delay their inevitable advance across England. Then the news came, impossible to comprehend for any student of history, that Hitler had broken his non-aggression pact with Stalin and invaded the Soviet Union. The imminent *likelihood* of invasion became a *possibility*, and as the fortunes of war turned against the madman in Berlin from North Africa to Stalingrad, and the Americans and Japanese got involved, the fact he had weapons in secret stashes across the Holkham estate and a dozen well-trained men to use them became unimportant.

He added his usual request to be transferred to frontline duties. He had no hope or expectation it would be granted. No doubt he'd be sucked in to whatever misinformation campaigns the clever bods in London were dreaming up now to cover the allied invasion of Europe when it came. Many areas on the coast were being primed to fake movements of men and large-scale construction works that were simply theatrics, to confuse any aerial reconnaissance the Germans managed. Carstairs had hinted as much on his last visit. All vital work of course, but he had never thought the shots he had fired in that panicked, desperate retreat to the beach might have been his last in this war.

He checked the diary for the upcoming week. The usual weapons training and patrols. Horton had been in a number of early morning training runs for bombers and fighters along the beach, breaking in the next generation of flyers who could then be shipped off to do their part.

He got up and went out into the sharp winter air and walked to the obelisk so he could enjoy an unobstructed view of Holkham Hall. Very lovely it looked too in the pale winter sun. He glanced at his watch. He would be able to finish the rest of the paperwork on his desk in the next hour or two, then bicycle back to his digs in Wells.

He returned to the temple and worked away studiously, then tidied away his work, put on his bicycle clips and shrugged on his overcoat before fetching his bike from the back of the temple. Strange building to spend a war in, but there you go. A pheasant chuckled in the woods behind him and he turned towards the noise, and caught a glimpse of the lake. It would do no harm to walk his bicycle along that open stretch of grass rather than take the avenue. He ambled down the track and, not far from the Ice House, met Bill Coogan, the local constable and mainstay of the Home Guard, coming the other way. Poor Bill, at least Ketteringham had got to do *some* fighting. Bill was in a protected profession, like the doctors and dentists who made up the rest of the auxiliary unit. He spent his days on the lookout for black marketeers and the illegal drinking and prostitution that flared round the American air bases.

'Evening, Bill,' Ketteringham said.

'All in order, John?' Bill asked.

'Yes, yes,' Ketteringham said absently. 'Everything seems present and correct so far. No sign any of the locals have stumbled across the caches, and all the guns are in good condition. However, I'd like to complete the full audit before the ground freezes solid.'

Bill frowned. 'Did you hear something?'

Ketteringham shook his head. 'Just the birds.' Then he did hear something. A rattle and bump coming from the Ice House.

The men exchanged looks. Ketteringham leant his bicycle against a tree and without saying anything further, they walked slightly uphill towards the thatched building. As they approached, the door rattled again. Ketteringham lifted the latch and pulled open the door and found himself looking down at a child, covered in mud and blood and rotten straw, her eyes swollen with weeping.

'Oh my goodness!' Bill exclaimed. Ketteringham always felt a bit baffled by children, but Bill, father of three, seemed to know exactly what to do.

He crouched down and put one large heavy hand on the girl's shoulder and smoothed away her hair with the other, looking for the wound.

'What happened to you, my treasure?' he said.

The child didn't reply, but immediately collapsed against him in a swoon. He caught her, and lifted her up in his arms. At last Ketteringham recognised her.

'Is that the Earl's granddaughter?'

'It is – Miss Anne. Can you see if she is still bleeding?'

'I don't think so, but that's a nasty bump!' Ketteringham replied. He examined the child as she lay across Bill's knees and against his chest like a Christ in a pietà, then hissed with surprise. 'But her shoulder is dislocated. Poor child must be in agony!'

'What do we do?' Bill said. 'It'll take the doctor a while to get out here.'

'I can do it. It'll hurt the poor mite though.'

'Best now. Longer it isn't done, the worse it'll be,' Bill spoke firmly, then addressing the swooning child went on, 'Now, lovely girl, your shoulder is hurt. My friend John is going to fix it, but it'll hurt something fierce for a second while he does it.'

The child turned her head towards Bill's tunic and Ketteringham thought he saw her jaw tense.

'Good girl,' he said. 'I'll be as quick as I can.'

He nodded to Bill, and Ketteringham braced himself. It was brutal and quick. He felt the sickening pop as the child's shoulder realigned, and released her wrist. Her body shook, but she didn't cry out.

'That's got it.'

'You are a very brave lass!' Bill said to her. 'We will tell your grandfather how brave you have been! I've never seen the like, have you seen the like, John?'

'I have not,' Ketteringham said. He still felt a bit sick. Handling a child like that, even to help her, disgusted him. 'Remarkably brave. Now, let's get her back to the Hall.'

25.

IT WAS DARK by the time the men carrying Anne reached the terrace, but as they approached, a girl in a maid's uniform opened the door of the Chapel Wing. Her hands flew up to her face when she saw them.

'Ruby!' Ketteringham said. 'Miss Anne has had an accident and got shut in the Ice House. Where should we take her?'

'Oh, Miss Anne! I've been looking for her since tea!' She hurried over to them and put her hand on the child's head. 'She's warm! Oh, her poor head! Up to bed at once.'

Ketteringham put out his arms. 'Bill, give her to me. You've carried her all this way.'

Bill surrendered her reluctantly and Ketteringham felt her slight weight against him. He put his arms under her, and her head flopped against his shoulder. 'Lead the way, Ruby.'

They climbed to the top of the wing, Bill walking anxiously behind him as if afraid Ketteringham would drop the child while Ruby trotted ahead. Ketteringham could feel the child's forehead against his neck, hot as Hades, but the rest of her body was as cold as ice. The room Ruby led them to was chilly, but at least there was a bed in it. Ketteringham set his burden down and Ruby crouched by the bed, her eyes wide with distress as she examined the state of the little girl.

'Shall I run down and find Mr Shreeve and Mrs Warnes, Ruby?' Bill said.

'They're at their supper in the steward's room. Do you know where to find it?' Ruby replied. She was pulling off the child's shoes. Bill shook his head. He grabbed a shawl from the end of the bed and put it round the little girl's shoulders.

'I know it,' Ketteringham said. Lord Leicester had given him and Carstairs a tour of the place when they came to the Hall to discuss the auxiliary unit. 'Bill, you stay here. Tell Ruby about the girl's arm.'

He set off down the stairs again at a fast trot and went through the state rooms. A few lights burned softly to light the way, but he was in too much of a hurry to admire the treasures around him. He was so fixed on his direction he almost ran into the archivist, Mullins, talking to that rather elegant governess in the shadows.

'Ketteringham?' Mullins said in surprise.

'Miss Anne has had an accident,' he said over his shoulder, then hurried on. Bloody woman should have been looking after the child, shouldn't she?

He jogged down the stairs of the Marble Hall, then round to the steward's room on the ground floor and told the senior staff what he knew. Shreeve left to inform Lord Leicester at once while the cook gasped and Mrs Warnes announced she would ring the doctor in Wells.

'Tell him she has a high fever, and that she dislocated her shoulder. I put it back in, but her arm should go in a sling.'

'Yes, Lieutenant,' she said and left the room. Strange how this small thing had shaken him. It was something about the wild look in the child's eyes when they found her, then the way she didn't cry out when he dealt with her arm. It felt wrong somehow, terribly wrong.

'She's awfully dirty,' he said to the cook. 'She was shut in the Ice House. Is there anything I can take to help Ruby clean her up? And her head was bleeding.'

Mrs Rowse seemed delighted to have a purpose and within a very few minutes Ketteringham was on his way back to Anne's room with a kettle of water and bottles of iodine and tinctures.

'Mrs Warnes is calling the doctor,' he told them. They had got the child undressed and into bed. Her damp and muddy clothes were piled on the floor. Ruby pounced on the hot water and strips of linen and began to clean her face and hands.

'Lieutenant?' Bill said, touching his cheek and then pointing at the mirror. Ketteringham checked. He'd got a smear of the child's blood on his cheek. He cursed and bent down so he could see himself properly, wiping it off with his handkerchief.

The door opened and he turned, expecting to see Lord Leicester. It was the elegant governess.

'Oh my goodness! Anne, dear!' she said, crossing the room towards the bed. 'We've been so worried.'

The child's reaction was immediate. She scrambled backwards on the pillow, staring at the governess, and screamed.

'Go away! Go away! You're evil!'

'Why, Anne! What are you saying? It's me! Miss Crane!'

She put her hand out towards the child, and the little girl squeaked and drew herself up into a foetal position. 'Make her go away!' she screamed.

The governess looked angry. 'Now, Anne. Don't be silly.'

Idiotic female. Ketteringham might not have any children but he knew what was required now at least.

'Miss Crane, the child has had a bad fright and isn't well. I think it best if you leave her alone.'

'She is my responsibility,' she said, looking down her nose at him. He resisted the temptation to ask why in that case it was the maid who had been looking for Anne while she skulked in the state rooms with the archivist.

'Ruby can look after her, I'm sure.'

He felt her assessing gaze, the look of a person sizing up an opponent's strength and deciding on a course of action.

He had put that child through agony, and had just wiped her blood from his cheek. He'd defend her to the death now. The governess must have seen something of that determination on his face. She blinked, then turned on her heel and left them.

Ruby was crouching by the bed, smoothing the child's hair. 'Were you ghost hunting, Miss Anne? Did you think that was Lady Mary?'

She looked sideways at Bill, who only shrugged. 'First thing she's said, poor mite, since we found her. She's terrified no doubt, can't say why. It's a ghostly witchy-looking spot though, the Ice House.'

'It is that. Well, I'll not leave her tonight,' Ruby said firmly. 'And if I can't sit with her, I'm sure Mrs Warnes wouldn't mind taking her supper up here, and if Miss Crane doesn't like that, she can jolly well lump it.'

Mr Mullins waited for news of Anne in the steward's room with Mrs Rowse, the cook. She had plenty to be doing, people needed to be fed, and they'd need feeding again in the morning, but she didn't seem to mind Mullins sitting in her kitchen chair trying to read the newspaper while they waited for news of Miss Anne. Abner couldn't face going home yet. He didn't want to be alone with his own thoughts.

News arrived with the form of Ruby, who swept in with a storm of words. Miss Anne should have broth, the doctor had said, and Ruby wanted to take it up to her straight away.

Mrs Rowse told her to sit down while she warmed it up and Abner poured the girl a cup of tea from the pot. Once she realised she'd have to wait ten minutes, Ruby flopped down. Mrs Rowse didn't tell her to take her elbows off the table, a remarkable concession, which underlined how shaken up they all were.

Abner waited till Ruby had recovered enough to take some swallows of tea.

'How is Anne?' he asked.

'Poor thing is in a dreadful way.' Ruby sounded angry. 'I thought she were dead when I saw those two Home Guards fellows carrying her across the lawn. My heart stopped in my chest. I was ever so glad they were there. Can you imagine if they hadn't found her? It getting dark and none of us knowing where she might be. She could have been there all night!'

She told them about Miss Crane coming in and Anne

behaving the way she did and how Lieutenant Ketteringham sent Miss Crane off again.

'Mrs Warnes has promised she won't leave Anne till I get back. She brought the doctor up herself. Walked him from the front door.'

'Why did Anne react like that to Miss Crane?' Mullins asked.

'She's had a bump on the head, and Lord knows how long she was in there in the cold and her arm all injured! She's covered in bruises and scrapes! I think perhaps she was still looking for ghosts, or spies, and now she thinks Miss Crane is Lady Mary come to get her. Honestly, only thing I can think of,' Ruby said in a rush. 'I've never seen a child behave like that. Went from being mute to a wild animal, then she wouldn't say a word after, but she was shaking like a leaf.'

'Lady Mary does look very tall and elegant, doesn't she?' Mrs Rowse said as her spoon rattled in the saucepan. 'Miss Crane has the same build. Not like me or you or Mrs Warnes, Ruby.'

'I had no idea Anne was so *frightened* of Lady Mary,' Mr Mullins said and refilled Ruby's tea cup. 'She seemed just excited and curious about her when we worked together.'

Ruby nodded. 'I'd say the same, Mr Mullins, I would. But then think of her in the Ice House hurt and afraid. That might change it, if she thought Lady Mary was there in the dark, spooking at her.' That would alter things, Abner thought. 'His Lordship came in while the doctor was having a look at her,' Ruby went on. 'Doctor says she might have picked up a fever or infection and got exhaustion. Now

His Lordship's giving the doctor and the Home Guard gentlemen a sherry in the long library. Is that broth ready yet?'

'Five more minutes, Ruby,' Mrs Rowse said patiently. 'You sit there and draw breath. You'll be no good to Miss Anne if you are as riled up as she is.'

Ruby was about to protest, then stopped herself. 'You're right, I suppose. Me heart is hammering now.'

'Possibly to make up for when it stopped before,' Mrs Rowse said quietly and Mullins smiled briefly to himself.

'Do you think,' he said tentatively, 'I should call in to Mrs Pullen's house on my way home and ask her to come in early tomorrow? If Ruby is going to be looking after Anne, perhaps she would be helpful.'

'A very good idea,' Mrs Rowse said. She took a bowl out of the range where it had been warming and set it on a tray. 'I'm sure Mrs Warnes would agree with me. That lad Mr Shreeve has had polishing the silver will bring you up your tea and slice in the morning, Ruby. You tell him what Miss Anne needs and he can fetch that up to you with Miss Crane's tea.'

She poured the contents of the pan into the bowl and covered it as quick as she could to try to keep the heat in. Ruby downed the rest of her tea and spun round to take it.

'You just stay with Miss Anne, my girl. We'll all run around you for a day or two.'

Mrs Warnes waited and watched while Ruby tried to coax the child into taking her broth. She had heard about how Anne had reacted when Miss Crane came in the room, and she had noticed too the look of inchoate fear in the child's eyes when she had opened the door herself to lead in the doctor. It worried her.

Even with Ruby's tender care, the little girl didn't take much of the broth, but once she had, she seemed to fall asleep and Ruby shared her theory that Lady Mary's ghost and Miss Crane had got mixed up in Anne's bruised head. It made sense to Mrs Warnes.

She took the tray back to the kitchen, then went upstairs again to speak to Lord Leicester. The doctor and the two Home Guard officers were still there. Good. They stood up as she came in, and once she had refused the sherry Lord Leicester offered her, she came straight to the point.

'I think, my lord, it would be a good idea if Ruby were to be put in charge of the sickroom until Miss Anne recovers. Miss Anne seems to have got Miss Crane mixed up with Lady Mary in her head, and is afraid of her. She seems quite comfortable with Ruby however. Miss Crane is a governess, not a nursemaid and I wondered if the doctor would agree with me, the best thing is for Anne to be kept calm at the moment and that means leaving her in Ruby's care.'

They all looked towards the doctor. He was an elderly gentleman who had returned to the local practice again so the man who had taken over from him could train for the front, so he had known the family for many years.

'Yes, Mrs Warnes,' he said, his voice quite high and thin like well-washed linen. 'I agree most heartily. Bumps on the head are funny things, and nature is a much better healer than modern medicine at such times. Anne should not get excited at all for a week or two, and if she's scrambled up a ghost and her governess, I think it only sensible she be allowed to gather her wits in her own time. Keep the governess out of it.'

Lord Leicester frowned. Mrs Warnes was afraid he'd protest; they all knew how over-worked Ruby was, and it would seem perverse to him to have Miss Crane sitting around doing nothing. It was the policeman who spoke up.

'My lord, that little girl hardly made a sound when John reset her arm. Bravest thing I've seen in a long time. I saw that, and I saw how downright terrified of Miss Crane she was too. Her fear of this Miss Crane might be just a fancy, but it's real.'

Mrs Warnes smiled at him gratefully.

Leicester lifted his hands, resigned. 'Mrs Warnes, I shall not interfere with your domestic arrangements. Do whatever you think is best.'

'Thank you, my lord,' she said.

'How is Anne now?' Leicester asked.

'She took some of the broth, and when I left she had fallen asleep.'

He looked relieved. 'I had a fall hunting once,' he said, musingly. 'Cracked my skull open and I couldn't think straight for a week. My head unscrambled in the end though.'

'I'm sure all she needs is a little rest,' the doctor said.

'Excellent. Well, I shall come and see her again in the morning. Do give Ruby my thanks, and Mrs Warnes, if there is any change during the night, anything at all, you'll see I'm fetched at once, won't you?'

'Of course, my lord,' she said and withdrew. She would fetch a few of Ruby's things from her room in the Family

Wing and take them over. They could make her up a little cot in Anne's bedroom. She had a sudden image of the lurcher her father had owned when she was growing up who lay across the threshold of her room like a guardian every night. Now, why would she think of that?

26.

1950

THE DAY AFTER Johnnie's funeral Anne spent the morning in the potting shed. Carey was delighted with how the piggy banks had come out and Anne was more convinced than ever she would find a market for them on her sales trips or at the trade fairs. There were a few coming up over the spring and each would be full of shopkeepers, and department store buyers examining the output of the Holkham pottery alongside wares from Dalton and Staffordshire and selecting lines for their summer customers.

'Carey and I will have to manage without you at most of the fairs, Anne,' her mother said, smiling at one of the piggy banks. Carey had painted them with long eyelashes, which gave them an insouciant expression.

'Because of my season?' Anne replied.

'Yes, of course,' Elizabeth replied. She was sitting at her desk in the office area they shared away from the mess of the pottery itself, a pencil behind her ear. She must have caught something in Anne's voice.

'It's all rather nerve-racking, darling, but I promise you'll have a splendid time and I know your father worries, but

I think we'll be able to do something wonderful for your dance in June. He and Shreeve were examining the champagne stores and came out looking very happy.'

Carey had come in from the pottery and was leaning against the door. Somehow the spots of paint on her cheek made her look even more glamorous than usual.

'Did Grandpa put down a stash of Pol Roger for my coming out too?' she asked a little plaintively.

'Of course he did, Carey,' Elizabeth replied. 'Anne's is the 1932 vintage, and yours is the 1935. Good thing neither of you were born in 1934 or Winston would have requisitioned the lot for the war effort. Anyway, the important thing is we'll have buckets of it for Anne's dance.' She took the pencil from behind her ear and made a note, then pointed it at Anne. 'And I've been meaning to tell you, I had a letter from Tommy Kinsman's manager. They'll be happy to play. We'll put them in the long gallery.'

Carey didn't say anything, as she stamped off back to her painting.

'I am pleased, but I shan't know anyone, Mum.'

'Your father *is* keeping the guest list strictly controlled,' she said with the hint of a smile. 'I think you can expect a lot of his army friends in the crowd. But your cousins will come, and you have to start somewhere. Chin up, darling! You'll get into the swing of it eventually and the parties and nightclubs in London will be great fun. Until then, just keep smiling.'

Anne had to be content with that and turned her attention to the pile of correspondence that had built up since Grandpa died. Some of the shop owners she knew had sent condolence letters to the pottery. She answered them with her thanks for their good wishes, and told them to look out for her mother, Carey and the piggy banks at the trade fairs.

After lunch Carey wanted to get straight back to her painting, but Anne needed to stretch her legs. It seemed inevitable, after talking to Ruby, that her walk took her up the avenue towards the Ice House. It made her feel a little queasy, looking at it now. The memories of being locked in there were still a bit murky and disjointed, but talking to Ruby had sorted those last weeks before Miss Crane disappeared into some sort of order and new recollections kept popping up to fill in the gaps.

Captain Horton was talking to one of the gamekeepers on the edge of the wood. He waved to Anne, and then they both disappeared in the direction of the temple. Anne put her hand on the red brick wall of the Ice House, then took a deep breath and opened the door.

She was not sure what she was expecting to see. It was a simple chamber, the afternoon sun reaching in through holes in the thatch. The musty cold of the air brought back a memory of the fear she had felt in here, but she didn't wobble this time. It was just a memory of the fear, not the fear itself.

Had she really confused Lady Mary with Miss Crane as Ruby had said? Perhaps. No sign of any spies or ghosts in here now. That felt like a comfort.

She closed the door and stepped outside again. Horton was coming down the path towards her.

'Lady Anne? Are you going back to the house? Would you like some company?'

'Yes, thank you, Captain Horton.'

They strolled slowly down the slope. 'I hope we'll have an early spring,' Horton said. 'At least two of our older tenants have sworn to me by a certain pattern of moss on their apple tree, this year is going to be an excellent growing season.'

'I do hope they are right,' Anne replied. The great fountain in front of the Hall, St George and the Dragon in all its chiselled glory, reared up before them. She and Carey had swum there last year.

'Do you think we'll be able to use the beach this summer?' she asked. 'I remember Grandpa saying you were still fighting with the War Office about the clean-up. Has there been any progress?'

'I doubt it will be this year,' he said with a sigh. 'Every time I think we are close, one of the Royal Engineers throws up some difficulty. Also Shreeve and Mullins have a lot to say about how we open up the old kitchen and manage repairs in Strangers Wing.'

'What does that have to do with the beach?' Anne asked.

'Oh, it's all bound together in Holkham's compensation claim,' he said with a shrug. 'We all have to present a united front and I've been in consultation with the gardeners and gamekeepers about the warrens near the beach and the replanting of the dunes. Honestly, Lady Anne, one person makes an objection and the whole plan unravels. It makes dealing with the tenants look like a straightforward pleasure. What were you doing at the Ice House, by the way?'

'Oh.' Anne laughed, a little embarrassed. 'I remembered

Johnnie Fuller and I thought there were spies living there at some point.'

'Ah, yes! I remember your spy hunt. Well, no sign of spies or ghosts now. We repointed the brickwork last summer and will redo the thatch when the weather clears up. We want to make it all look smart for your dance.'

Anne nodded, and they spoke on indifferent subjects until their ways parted, Anne going into the house from the terrace, and Captain Horton walking briskly through the chill air back to the estate office in the stable yard.

Mr Shreeve had his base of operations in the butler's pantry. Before the war, it was from here he would coordinate the battalion of indoor staff, teach the young men to wait at table and pay their wages, offer guidance or reprimands as needed. Now he polished the silver there himself in his heavy apron and wearing cotton gloves, ready to strip them away the moment the bell rang to tell him the family needed him. The door was open and he looked up over the top of his half-moon glasses when he sensed Anne pausing in the doorway.

'Good afternoon, Lady Anne. Is there anything you need?'

'No, thank you, Shreeve. Actually, there is something I want to ask you.'

He invited her in and, once she had taken a seat at his table, he removed his polishing gloves and sat down himself.

'I've been thinking a lot about 1943,' Anne said carefully, 'when I was here with Grandpa before Mum and Dad came back.'

'Ah, yes! It cheered His Lordship up a lot having you here. He did enjoy working in the darkroom with you. We were worried when you were ill, of course,' he added. 'Ruby, Mrs Fuller now, has turned out very well, hasn't she? And her two boys the picture of health, I thought. Though such a shame about Johnnie.'

'Yes, it is. And you are right, they are lovely boys.' Best just to get it over with, like ripping off a sticking plaster. 'Do you remember when we went down into the cellars because I thought Lady Mary had led me to a spy?'

Did she imagine it, or did his expression become more guarded? 'I do, Lady Anne. I hope we put your mind at ease.'

Anne shook her head. 'Oh, I thought there were spies around for some time after that, I'm afraid.'

He leant back in his chair and tented his fingertips. 'I often think how everyone who lives in a house such as Holkham always lives with the sensation of being watched. All of us going about our business rather on top of each other, coming and going. Do you think that might have been part of it, Lady Anne?'

'I'm sure it was, but, Mr Shreeve, *was* there someone living in secret in the cellars in 1943? I'm sorry, my mind keeps going back over it and I rather think there might have been.'

He looked sideways, considering. One of the gas heaters Lord Leicester had bought was burning on a low flame in front of the empty grate, but the room felt rather cold all of a sudden.

'We have served your family for many years, Lady Anne. Mrs Warnes, Mrs Rowse, Mr Mullins and myself. I hope we have earned your trust.'

'Oh, Shreeve, of course you have!' Anne said, her eyes feeling quite hot. 'That's what's making me unhappy, you see. I am certain that all of you would lay down your lives for us, but I have this odd feeling that I knew something I shouldn't have known and it's making me feel as if I'm a little mad.'

He recognised the sincerity and looked mollified.

'Well now, that's a handsome thing to say and we would. But, I wouldn't be where I am today, Lady Anne, if I didn't know how to keep secrets on behalf of others, I'm sure you understand that.'

'I do, Mr Shreeve.' Funny how she was addressing him as she had done when she was a child again. It felt correct somehow.

'Good. But I don't like the idea of you being troubled by something that happened so long ago, or fretting about your mind playing tricks on you. There was a lad who found refuge here for a while. We took pity on him and fed him and kept him out of the way. After you had your accident in the Ice House, I decided we had to inform Lord Leicester.'

'What did Grandfather say?'

Shreeve shook his head. 'He was angry with us, but he understood. The lad was gone before your parents came home. Arrangements were made. Papers procured in London.'

'Who was it, Mr Shreeve?'

He just shook his head in reply. Anne got to her feet and looked around the tidy, comfortable room.

'You don't have children yourself, do you, Mr Shreeve?'

'No, I was born to be a bachelor, Lady Anne. But I have four nephews and two nieces. All excellent young men and women. My sister's eldest boy just became valet to the Duke of Devonshire.'

'You must be very proud of him,' Anne said. 'Thank you for telling me. I think if Grandpa decided not to mention this . . . old story to my parents, then neither shall I.'

'Whatever you think best, Lady Anne.'

She left and turned in the doorway to see him putting his cotton gloves back on and beginning work on one of the silver chafing dishes. Grandpa had used it to cook eggs, and now her father did and it remained as bright as the day the first Earl had bought it nearly two hundred years ago, under the care of Shreeve, and the care of the stewards and butlers who had come before him.

27.

When Charles Elwood arrived at the house on the following Monday morning to start helping Mr Mullins and Anne in the library, he was wearing a knitted tie and a rather threadbare jacket.

'Don't laugh at me, Anne,' he said as she came down the steps in the Marble Hall to greet him. 'I had an image of my mother's face if she saw me arriving at the home of the Earl of Leicester in my usual painting gear, and I'm afraid I just couldn't bear it.'

'I promise faithfully I won't laugh at you, Charles. Does your mother approve of your painting career? I've never asked. Do come with me. Mr Mullins is in the classical library waiting for us.'

'She doesn't really understand painting,' he said as he followed her slowly up the stairs, craning his neck to look at the statues as they peered round the columns to look at him. 'But she knows I love it, so she does try to be pleased. I did write and tell her that I was going to be doing a bit of work in the archives here. She'll understand that. I promise you, everyone in her street will have heard all about it by now.'

He paused in the salon and Anne stopped and waited. He was staring at the Rubens, *Flight into Egypt*, life-sized figures of the Holy Family looking like Dutch peasantry on an outing along the Rhine, in spite of the palm tree appearing between the beech trees above them.

'Your mouth is open, Charles.'

'Now you *are* laughing at me. I'm sorry, it's just rather wonderful to see this in the flesh. Reproductions really can't capture it.' He walked towards it and bent forward to study the brushwork. 'He really was a master.'

'Not like your style of painting, is it?'

'Not a bit. And painting like this today would be like walking around London in Elizabethan costume, but he was an absolute master. How wonderful to grow up under his eye.'

'I always liked the donkey best,' Anne said lightly. 'Mr Mullins has given us tasks, you know. He and I will begin to work through the manuscripts, from the most valuable to the least, then on to the early printed books but I believe you are to check the portfolios of Old Master drawings first.'

She had expected him to be pleased, but he looked pained.

'I don't want to dawdle when your father is paying for my time, so I will try and be efficient, but I don't know if I *can* just quickly tick through a list of drawings by a bunch of sixteenth-century masters, only glancing at each one. It's like asking a starving man to work in a chocolate factory and not eat anything.'

He had come to a halt again, this time in the drawing room, staring up at the Gainsborough portrait of Coke of Norfolk.

'Good morning, Elwood.' Anne's father was coming through from the Family Wing and had obviously heard that last remark. 'You'll have an hour for lunch, and I'm sure we can trust you not to get grease stains on the drawings if you want to study them. And as long as you are out of the house before eight in the evening, I have no objection to you staying late. You may look at them at your leisure.'

Charles turned round. 'Thank you, Lord Leicester. That would be marvellous.'

Anne tried not to smile. He sounded much more like a BBC announcer when speaking to her father.

Leicester looked him over. 'Glad to have your help. Anne says we can rely on your discretion?'

'You can,' Charles said firmly.

Leicester made a humpfing noise, just like Grandpa had done when he saw something he approved of or that interested him. 'I'll see you at lunch, Anne,' he said, then strode off. Charles watched him go, looking slightly baffled.

'Did you know you aristocrats have a certain gravity to you?' he said. She assumed the question was rhetorical and he went on, 'I am a committed democratic socialist.'

'You have mentioned that.'

'Hang on, I'm making a point. I am a committed democratic socialist and I don't think any of these titles or inherited riches make your father any better than the rest of us, but I swear to God, when he speaks to me, I feel the accumulated pressure of a thousand years of obedient peasanthood blood surging through my veins and want to pay a kind of fascinated homage. It was all I could do not to bow!'

Now Anne did laugh. 'I assure you we are very human. Now do come on, Mr Mullins is waiting for us.'

Abner seemed to have aged since her grandfather's funeral. When they arrived in the classical library, he did not exude his usual air of calm, but seemed nervous and fretful.

'Lady Anne,' he said as they settled around the table. 'Your father took me into his confidence about the Coke necklace last night.'

'I suppose he had to,' Anne said. 'He'd want you to know why we are having to go through this process. I assume he told you Carey doesn't know anything about it, and he hasn't mentioned anything to the senior staff?'

'Yes, yes,' Abner said. 'Lady Carey's piggy banks have turned out rather well, haven't they?' he added with a nervous smile.

'They have,' Anne replied encouragingly.

Charles took his seat at the table. 'I would imagine as a historian, Mr Mullins, the idea of keeping secrets is very unpleasant.'

'Indeed!' he said. 'I've always loathed keeping secrets, though of course I quite understand Lord Leicester's reasoning, and at times one has to.'

'Let's not think about the secrecy or any ghastly scandal for now,' Anne said firmly. 'Our job is just to see if there have been any other losses. We can worry about everything else later.'

Mr Mullins nodded his agreement.

'I have told Charles he is to go through the drawings; do you still think that is the best idea?'

'Yes, I don't think I'll be able to sleep until I know they are all there. Each one is a masterpiece. I went through the coin and medal collection last night after I spoke to your father, Lady Anne. I am delighted to say I am quite certain everything is in order.'

'You must have been up all night! Charles, you must finish the portfolios of drawings today so Mr Mullins can rest.'

'I shall,' Charles said. 'I would feel just the same, Mr Mullins.'

A thought struck Anne. 'Mr Mullins, where were the coins and medals during the war?'

'At the British Museum for safe keeping,' he said, 'along with some other valuables. Your grandfather and I sent a consignment down to them in 1939. Some I brought back up from London when it was clear the danger of an invasion was past. For one thing Lord Leicester felt they were more at risk in London from the bombing than they were here, and for another I feel he suspected the British Museum would never give them back if they stayed there too long.'

They arranged themselves around the table and began work. The Bible Picture Book had been seen by Carstairs only a few days before. Anne's first task then was to go through the Leonardo Codex in case any pages were missing, checking each one against the description in Abner's records. She licked her finger to turn one of the sheets and caught the sound of a horrified gasp from Mr Mullins. She looked up guiltily and wiped her fingers on her handkerchief.

'Did you do that,' Mr Mullins asked faintly, 'when you aired the book during the war? Lick your fingers to turn the pages, I mean?'

'I'm rather afraid I did. I don't think I ever made the ink run or anything though,' she added cheerfully.

'Good,' Abner said in the same faint tones. 'Please don't tell anyone you did that.'

Anne lowered her eyes demurely and went on turning the pages. It was like seeing an old friend after years apart. She could almost feel her grandfather and Leonardo looking over her shoulder again. She didn't really need the descriptions, she knew these pages too well, but she dutifully ticked off each line of description with her pencil. It was quiet, peaceful work and every sheet was as it should be. Anne had lunch with her family, then rejoined them in the library. Just after tea, Charles announced that the Old Master drawings were all present and correct and they heaved a communal sigh of relief. She left Charles going through them again at a steady pace at the end of the day. Tomorrow he would join them on turning page after page of manuscripts.

Anne had promised to show Charles her ghost report from the war. She found it the next day, neatly boxed away with the other papers from 1943 in the upper attic while she was looking for the last condition reports on the shelf full of manuscripts that would occupy them for the rest of the week. She was touched to see that Abner Mullins had put one of his official paper labels on it. *Report on the Life and Afterlife of Lady Mary Coke, née Campbell by the Honourable Miss Anne Coke.* She lifted it out of the box and set it aside to take downstairs. Below it was a folder labelled *Staff 1943*. She picked it up and leafed through the pages, not knowing what she was looking for until she found it.

A letter to her grandfather from Lavender Crane. It was dated December 3rd 1943.

Dear Lord Leicester, it read, *I regret that a family emergency means I shall have to leave your employment sooner and more suddenly than I would have wished.* Anne seemed to hear her voice, the nice voice she used when other people were around that had a low film-star purr to it. *Of course in the circumstances, I do not expect payment for my services for November, but I ask that my trunks be sent to my previous employer in London. They will be happy to store them until I can arrange collection. Yours sincerely, Lavender Crane.*

It was typed, even the signature. Another hand, Mr Bartholomew's, she thought, had written an address on the page of a children's home in Kentish Town. Then in her grandfather's writing was one word. *Sent!* One could almost hear him adding 'and good riddance'.

Anne got out her notebook and wrote down the date, and after a second's thought, the address of the school in Kentish Town too. It did read like a running away letter. Strange Miss Crane didn't just write down the address of her previous employer, instead of putting Grandpa and Mr Bartholomew to all the extra trouble of finding it out. She replaced the file in the box, gathered up the ghost report and necessary paperwork, and went back down to the classical library.

They all stayed in the library for lunch that day, and Maria brought them sandwiches. They asked after Gina and the baby and learnt she was going to live in Norwich with George and Ruby, for the time being at least. They sent their best wishes and Maria promised to pass them on.

Charles was impressed by the ghost dossier.

'All Lady Anne's work,' Mr Mullins said. 'We should send you to university and you can become a historian.'

She laughed. 'I don't think Dad would approve, and I'm not sure I'd really like it that much either, university women are so ferociously clever, and just ferocious some of the time.'

'How many have you met?' Charles said dryly.

'I admit, I'm mostly thinking of a dragon who taught me history when I boarded at the House of Citizenship after the war. I had a very nice time working with you,' she added, smiling at Abner.

'I am glad,' Abner replied.

'Here is the ghost photograph!' Charles said gleefully. 'I can see why your grandfather was impressed.' He turned his head sideways. 'And why Johnnie wasn't. Bit disappointing if you were imagining one of those floating apparitions in a long frock with a skull for a face. Might just be a smear on the lens.'

'I'm glad Johnnie didn't say he was expecting anything like *that*!' Anne said. 'I'd have never dared go down to the cellar with that idea in my mind. And it can't have been a smear on the lens, because the other frames were quite clear.'

Charles turned the page to read Anne's careful paragraph about Lady Mary's burial in the Campbell family tomb in Westminster. She had stuck in a postcard showing the memorial.

'Lucky to have had this to hand,' Charles said, tapping it.

Anne tidied the lunch things back onto the tray. 'Yes, Mr Mullins very kindly got it for me on one of his trips.'

She became aware that Charles was looking at her sideways.

Did he think it might have been Abner who had arranged for the fake to be made and brought back to Holkham? She shook her head. No, not Abner. Though perhaps he might have done, if he had thought he was acting on Grandpa's instructions. However if that was the case Abner would have said so as soon as her father had told him about the Coke necklace! She put the idea out her mind, and the afternoon and then the week smoothly unrolled without them finding anything amiss.

28.

THE FIRST TIME Anne's tally of pages did not match the number on the condition report, she was sure she had miscounted. Then she thought perhaps the original archivist had made a mistake. At last she found it, a certain give between two pages that was not consistent with the way the rest of this hand written manuscript, bound in the eighteenth century by her ancestor, felt in her hands. A minute examination discovered a sliver of exposed glue on the binding, like a fine, silver scar. The Bible had been owned by the anti-pope, Clement VII, and now one of its pages, filled with delicate drawings, portraits, flights of whimsy and decoration by a devoted scribe more than six hundred years ago, was gone.

Her voice, when she called Mr Mullins over to check, came out as a bit of a squeak. Mr Mullins checked her tally, then, when she pointed out the gap and the description, his face fell. He sat down very heavily.

'Oh dear. Oh my goodness. I had begun to think there were no losses to be found.'

Charles found the next, again a single page gone from a

Latin manuscript on architecture. Whoever had done it had not been so careful this time. The page had been razored out of the volume, leaving its stump. By the end of the month, Abner's list of losses had eight entries on it and there were still hundreds of volumes to check. They worked on. From time to time they came across extra odds and ends, notes and addendums from past archivists and Cokes tucked between the pages, including odd folded pages of sheet music and occasional correspondence addressed to Anne's grandfather.

The losses they uncovered convinced Anne of one thing: it was not her grandfather who had taken these pages. She could, at a stretch, imagine him selling or pawning the Coke necklace during the war, but he would never, she was sure, vandalise these books. As a historian and a scholar he would sell an entire volume, preserving its integrity, rather than chop it about like this.

Anne had thought the damage Miss Crane had done during her stay in Holkham had been restricted to her, but had she managed to damage the library too? Anne remembered her, drifting around the place while she worked with Mr Mullins, and tried to think if she'd been carrying a purse or a bag, anything in which she could have smuggled out the stolen sheets. Some of them were huge! No memory presented itself.

Abner hoped they would be finished shortly before Anne's dance. The weather improved and the days lengthened. Charles began to spend his lunch hours in the gardens painting and returned to the beach as the evenings lengthened.

Anne's studious hours in the library were increasingly disrupted by the needs of the season. The week before she was due to be presented at court she went down to London for a final fitting for the dress she would wear for the presentation itself, with its wide skirts and nipped-in waist, and a rather glorious white evening dress for some of the dances she was going to. The dressmaker promised to make the final alterations and send them to her grandmother's London flat. Anne had travelled alone down to London, but she had no wish to linger. She would be seeing quite enough of the city in the weeks to come. She went to Charing Cross Road to pick up an armful of art books for Carey, and was ready to head for the station when she thought of the home Miss Lavender Crane had taught in before coming to Holkham and took out her notebook. The address was not far away.

Before she could think about it too much and lose her nerve, she hailed a taxi and within ten minutes, she found herself outside a red-brick Victorian building and stepped out onto the pavement.

'Shall I wait for you, miss?' the driver said.

Anne looked around her. Moving between Holkham and the smarter parts of London, she had not quite taken in how war-scarred the city still was. The street on which she stood looked like a mouth full of decayed teeth. She could see building work going on at the top of the road, but the school was surrounded by empty lots. Most of the rubble had been cleared, or piled at the corners, but the violence and suddenness with which the houses had been destroyed was in no doubt. Behind her was a long row of small terraced houses, but the windows were boarded up with rough planking, regularly stencilled with warnings the structure was unsafe. A group of children who had turned one of the partially cleared plots into a playground looked at her curiously.

She would rather like the cabman to stay, she thought, as she had no idea how far she would have to walk to find another taxi, or in which direction she should go. She looked at the stock of coins in her purse.

'I shan't charge for the wait, miss,' he said. 'Not if you mean to be less than an hour. I was about to have my lunch break and a sandwich.'

'That's awfully kind of you. If you don't mind?'

'Pleasure, miss.'

Thus reassured she turned back towards the school. She couldn't run away now.

She walked into the narrow yard and up the steps to the main entrance, expecting something rather grim. Miss Crane had told her she'd end up in an institution like this once, a place for the simple-minded. When had that been? Another memory, shaking loose like plaster from a bomb-damaged house. No matter. Anne had been deemed worthy of a presentation at court and a grand dance at Holkham. Still, she was glad the taxi was there to take her away again. Then she pushed open the door. The lobby area was a pleasant surprise. It was large and airy and a stained-glass window patterned the scrubbed tiled floor with pools of colour. The smell was of over-cooked vegetables and disinfectant, but the walls were painted a pale blue, studded with paintings of modern-looking landscapes. The first sound she heard was that of a child laughing. She was about to announce herself to the nurse on duty at the front desk, whose head was bent over a pile of paperwork, when a thin woman, her dark hair shot through with grey and wearing a wool suit the colour of heather, came out from a side corridor, saw Anne and put out her hand.

For a second her heart stopped and she felt ill, but no, a moment told her this was not Miss Lavender Crane. This woman's face was rounder, plainer and unpowdered.

'Good afternoon!' she said. 'Can I help you? I am Mrs Penrose, superintendent here. Are you visiting one of the children?'

Anne shook her outstretched hand. 'I'm so sorry to bother you. No, it might seem odd but I have a question about one of your former members of staff. My name is Anne Coke.'

Mrs Penrose seemed to accept that. 'I only took charge here quite recently, but I will certainly help if I can. Nurse Hutt, could you ask someone to bring us some tea in my office?'

The office was as pleasant as the lobby and Mrs Penrose's walls were decorated with strange, but very brightly coloured artworks, full of complicated twisting patterns and forests of faces.

'They were painted by some of our children,' Mrs Penrose said with a smile, seeing the direction of Anne's gaze. 'I think they are rather wonderful. Before I arrived they used to destroy everything the children made. Now, who is it you wish to enquire about?'

'Miss Lavender Crane,' Anne said. 'She was my governess at Holkham Hall for a little while during the war and I would like to know what happened to her after she left us.'

'Holkham Hall. You are the daughter of the Earl of

Leicester.' It was a statement, not a question, though Anne nodded anyway. 'Were you fond of her?'

'I'm afraid not.'

Tea was brought in. Mrs Penrose poured and handed Anne her cup before speaking again.

'I am very sorry to say institutions such as this one have not always served the children within them well,' she said carefully. 'When I arrived here too many people on staff had been taught to behave towards our children with a callousness that often tipped into cruelty. The best people left, the worst revelled in the situation. I think this is a very different place now.'

'I'm sure it is.' Anne hesitated. 'Did she come back to work here again after her time in Holkham? Do you know where she is?'

Absolutely not,' Mrs Penrose said and her cheeks flushed red. 'If I saw her on the street, let alone in this building, I would have her arrested at once.' She controlled herself with a visible effort. 'My apologies, Lady Anne. I never met Lavender Crane. The older children did tell me about her however. She is a monster to them, and some still have nightmares. There were others who worked here who were almost as bad, but theirs was a type of brutish indifference that the children are only too used to. Crane was poisonous as well as cruel. They still expect her to appear from under their beds in the middle of the night. She used to tie them up!' She shuddered. 'I am an educated woman, Lady Anne. I am a pacifist and a Christian but I think I would shoot that woman dead if I had the chance, and I wouldn't lose a wink of sleep over it. I am so very, very sorry you had to endure her.'

Anne had known for years it wasn't her fault, had known almost since the day her mother and father returned from Egypt that Miss Crane had told her nothing but lies and her mother would rather die than see her daughter subjected to Miss Crane's 'methods', but it was a wonderful relief to hear it said out loud. She couldn't speak for a second, and she felt Mrs Penrose take her hand and squeeze it.

'Now,' Mrs Penrose said more softly, 'why are you thinking of her, and what can I do?'

Anne swallowed, then explained that Miss Crane had left Holkham very suddenly in early December 1943. She added she had recently come across a note asking for Miss Crane's luggage to be sent to the school and it had made her wonder where her old governess was now.

'Are you worried about her turning up now you are coming out into society? You are debutante of the year, I think? I saw your picture on the front of *Tatler* – it's a lovely portrait.'

'The photographers are very good,' Anne murmured.

'I can see how it might make you worried. Yes, her luggage was delivered here, but it was never collected,' Mrs Penrose said with a sigh. 'According to our files, after she left here to become your governess at Holkham, the institution had no further communication with her. At some point her luggage arrived with a note saying it was to wait for collection.' She sipped her tea and stared up at one of the strange swirling pictures on the wall. 'This building has a lot of old rooms in the cellar used for storage and clearing them out took an age. By the time I stumbled across her trunks, I had heard all I needed to about Miss Crane. I went through them of course, to see if there was a forwarding address, but there was nothing but clothes and a few books. They mostly seemed to be about Brazil. No papers or anything like that.' She shook her head. 'I wouldn't admit it to just anyone, Lady Anne, but God forgive me, I had it all burned. Stood over the incinerator and watched it go up in flames. An awful thing to do given the rationing, but I couldn't bear the idea some of our children might see anything belonging to her. I treated every scrap like it was cursed.'

Anne had an image of the flames eating up those neat twinsets and narrow skirts. 'I am sure that was the right thing to do. Thank you for telling me and speaking so honestly about it. I know it sounds awful, but I feel almost better for knowing it was not just me she treated in that way. I suppose I've always worried she saw something terrible in me that made it happen.'

'It was not you, Lady Anne.'

They finished their tea, and Anne pressed a five-pound note into Mrs Penrose's hands for the school before she returned to the cab. She had been planning to spend it on new stockings and powder, but she could manage with what she had.

For a while, on the cab ride to the station and the train to Holkham, Anne thought only of Mrs Penrose and the children with gratitude and relief. Then she began to think about what had happened. Miss Crane had abandoned all her worldly possessions at Holkham, other than what she could carry in an overnight case. Asked for it to be sent on, then failed to collect it. Why? Because she was on the run with the Coke necklace in her pocket?

Her father had sent the car to wait for her at the station.

She would talk to Charles in the morning while they worked on the manuscripts and tell him what she had learnt. Perhaps it would confirm his theory she had made off with the diamonds and the pages from the manuscripts at the Hall and simply disappeared. Strange though, that she had done her thieving with such subtlety then left in a rather suspicious manner.

The hedgerows were thick with Queen Anne's lace, spotted with yellow buttercups, and the soft spring air carried its scent of musty honey through the open windows. She thought of Mrs Penrose, who had never even met Lavender Crane, burning her clothes trying to lift her curse from that institution. Judging from what little Anne had seen of the place, she'd been successful. Perhaps Anne could find a way to do the same.

29.

ALL AT ONCE, the dance was less than a week away. Anne worked in the library, confident they would be finished with their stock-taking in the next day or so. Miss Crane seemed to have left the printed manuscripts alone and it was a week since they had added anything to the list of losses – more than a dozen pages in total. It might not seem a great deal out of the thousands of pages in the library, but each meant a unique volume had been damaged and lost some of its meaning for current and future historians.

Thinking of the dance, the great mountains of food being prepared, the lists of guests invited, and just wanting to get this final bit of the job done made it hard to concentrate. Anne could have missed the note entirely. Her tally of the pages, lifting a corner of the book and flicking through rapidly, had come out correctly, but the way the last leaves fell between her fingers stopped her, and made her push aside her tally sheet and look again.

A single page of cheap writing paper between the marbled end papers. The side she was looking at was blank. She pulled it out and turned it over.

'Charles?'

He looked up swiftly, catching the note of alarm in her voice.

'What is it, Anne?'

She pointed at the page. 'Charles, I think it is the note Johnnie wrote to my grandfather!'

The shock and surprise of it made it hard to read for a second. Charles came round the table at a gallop and leant over her shoulder. Johnnie's handwriting was remarkably neat; he had written in soft pencil, but his hand was perfectly legible. Charles read it out loud.

'My Lord, A funny thing happened in the Victoria last night and it set me thinking about something I saw in December 1943 when Ma was first ill and I was spending time on the beach looking for spies. You remember Anne and I were always patrolling to keep Holkham safe from Hitler! Well, I saw a thing there I always thought was a spy being caught and I was proud to keep the secret what with George off fighting. Made me think I was helping. Anyhow, now I think that it wasn't a spy being caught at all but something much worse and which might be a danger now, as the man what told me she was a spy and going to be handed over to Churchill still works very close with you in the house. It was Miss Anne's governess, I mean, the person I thought was a spy. Maybe I should have told Anne I'd seen her getting bundled off between the dunes on the beach, where they had them taxi cabs for bombing. I thought the

spy catchers were there and they took her away. He said he was going up to the Hall to tell you straight away, and I should get home so as not to interfere. When Anne just said she'd left, I thought it was you, my lord, who had told her that, you see? So I thought you and me had the secret together and it made me proud. Now I am thinking I was wrong. I've asked Mrs Pullen to give you this note and I shall wait out of the way in the conservatory in hope you'll have a minute. Or tell Shreeve when I should come back. Yours sincerely Johnnie Fuller.'

'Good heavens!' Anne said as he finished. 'What on earth do you make of that?'

'You'll have to give me a minute,' Charles said, sitting down next to her and still staring at the note. 'Johnnie had a bit of a stream of consciousness thing going, didn't he? It's like reading a Norfolk version of James Joyce.'

'He didn't remember Miss Crane's name,' Anne said.

'Yes, I suppose that's why your grandfather wrote it in his diary. It's the sort of thing I do when I've remembered something and don't want to forget it.'

'So Johnnie saw her *fighting* with someone on the beach,' Anne said, 'and then this person bundled her off for the spy catchers to take away. What can that mean?'

'It sounds to me like he saw someone he knew fighting with Miss Crane, and then, I think whoever it was must have spotted Johnnie watching, don't you think?'

'Yes, perhaps Johnnie made a noise or called out,' Anne said, trying to see it in her mind's eye. 'Then this man spots Johnnie and comes over and feeds him this story about Miss Crane being a spy and how they've caught her. He tells Johnnie he's off to inform Grandpa and that it's important Johnnie keeps quiet. No wonder Johnnie was proud.' Anne was staring at the note still. 'That is a cool customer! He must have known Johnnie and I were mad about spies. I mean, everyone did, I told lots of people I thought Lady Mary was trying to tell us something and was always asking if there were spies about – the staff, the Royal Engineers, the Home Guard too. I bet whoever it was made a big show of telling Johnnie how clever he was to be on the lookout and thanking him for his help. His head would be far too swollen with pride to think straight.'

'But what happened to Miss Crane if she didn't run off with the diamonds and whoever her lover was, and wasn't spirited away by spy catchers?' Charles said. 'Where is she now?'

Anne sat bolt upright. The idea that had tortured her for years, which she had tried to tell herself was just childish nonsense, might actually be true. What if Miss Lavender Crane had never left Holkham at all?

'I'm going to the beach,' she said and stood up.

'Anne!' Charles protested. 'Think for a second, please.'

'No, Charles, stay or come as you want, but I'm going there right this minute.'

She walked out of the library; Charles snatched up his jacket and followed her. They left the house in silence and Anne walked down the avenue, a fierce frown between her fine eyebrows. Charles jogged along at her side.

'Anne, do wait.'

'I shall not. I think that monster must be buried on the beach, but I have to know for sure.'

'Anne! You're missing the crucial point.'

She shook her head. 'I don't know what you are talking about.'

'Johnnie said this person he saw fighting with Miss Crane *is still at Holkham!*'

Her footsteps faltered. 'Still here?'

'Yes,' Charles said, taking hold of her elbow and steering her towards the path that led up to the monument. 'If Miss Crane is on the beach, and whoever killed her is still here, you heading down to the dunes with a shovel is going to be a bit of a give-away, don't you think?'

She twisted away from him, wringing her hands in frustration. 'But I have to know if Lavender Crane's body is on the beach, Charles! You can't imagine what it's like. Ever since she left, I've been expecting to see her round the next corner, or see her in a crowd and especially here.'

'But Anne, your dance is in three days. The whole household has been planning for months. Even I've been roped in! We're going to use the old searchlights to light up the Hall. Paterson has made me an unofficial lighting director.'

She wasn't going to laugh at him today.

'But Charles!'

'Think of your family.'

She did. She was always thinking of her family. It seemed very strange that it was Charles who was reminding her to think of them now.

'What if we just look now? Do you have a spade or

something in your car?' She looked in the direction of the beach in horrified fascination.

'Anne, think, please do. If the body of Lavender Crane is under that dune, it is the scene of a crime and if there is any hope of justice we have to let the police excavate it in the proper way. Anne, we could destroy crucial evidence just blundering about.'

'I don't care about getting justice for *her*! She was a monster, a sadist. Did you know she taught at a school for disabled children in London before she came to Holkham? My God, if you think what she did to me, what on earth did she do to them! I want to dig up her bones and take them down there and show those children she's dead!'

'Anne! I'm not talking about justice for Lavender Crane!'

Anne stopped dead. 'You're talking about . . .'

'I'm talking about your grandfather and Johnnie Fuller. If we are right about what Johnnie's note means then whoever may have killed Lavender Crane is still at Holkham. I think your grandfather confronted him.'

Anne swallowed. 'Grandpa read the note and went to see Johnnie, and Johnnie told him who he saw here on the beach with Miss Crane. Oh, and if it is someone he trusted, Grandpa would confront him himself, you're right.'

'Then that person killed Grandpa, and went out and found Johnnie, too drunk to defend himself, and killed him too.'

'You don't think their deaths were accidents any more then, Charles?'

He looked terribly sorry, but he shook his head. 'I thought the thief was gone! But if he is still here . . . then the coincidence is too much. If we are right about Miss Crane then

I'm afraid this man must have killed your grandfather and Johnnie too. That means we can't risk doing anything that means that man might get away with those crimes. Whoever he was, he left no evidence in the Hall when he killed your grandfather, and none where Johnnie died either.'

'Then we call the police!'

'Call them *after* your dance. Just wait this extra few days. Whatever evidence might be found with Miss Crane, if she is here, will wait till then.'

She looked down the slope at the long sweep of the Hall. It was just as imposing in the early summer, dressed in fresh greens with the sun-soaked woods softening the swell and drop of the land around it, but she could hardly see straight.

'Why did he stay? Whoever this person is, why not just take the necklace and go?' she murmured.

'Anne, Johnnie said that this man is still at Holkham. I think that means he never got his hands on the necklace, even after it was stolen.'

'I think he didn't have the necklace.'

'What?'

'Think about it – it's the only thing that makes any sense! This man conspires with Lavender Crane to steal the necklace and replace it with a copy. Then one night they meet on the beach, and argue and he kills her. Any sane man would want to get as far away as possible, but suppose Miss Crane didn't have the necklace with her!'

'I saw her!' Anne said. 'Or at least, I think I did. Walking down the avenue late one afternoon, and she just had her handbag, not an overnight case. I was with Ruby, outside so it must have been while I was still ill. It might have been the evening she left.'

'Can you remember anything else?'

'It's all such a jumble, Charles!'

He thrust his hands into his pockets and scowled at the soft turf at their feet. 'Not your fault. If killing her was unplanned, a spur of the moment thing, think of his situation. He knows the real necklace is hidden somewhere in the house or grounds, but he doesn't know where. He's murdered for it now. He has to find it before he leaves!'

'You think he's been looking for six years?'

'Yes, and remember, we don't know when those manuscript pages were taken. That might have happened since.'

She sat down on the grass and put her chin in her hands and breathed slowly. He lowered himself beside her.

'And, Anne, I honestly believe you have a better chance of finding the necklace than he does. You knew Lavender Crane, the real Lavender Crane, better than anyone in the house. I know you hate to think of her, but can you imagine where she would hide it? Can you remember anything else about what was happening just before she left?'

'Charles, I know it's awful, but I want her to be dead so much.' She sighed deeply. From here she could see Smith, polishing the Bentley in the stable yard, the post boy bicycling up the avenue, with his bag bulging. Two gardeners were making their way from the kitchen garden towards the house, their wheelbarrows full of produce for the cook. All this work, trying to launch her onto the world. No, she could not go looking for graves today. 'Do you remember that story in *Hotspur* I told you about, the one about the maid who found the ghost's bones and that meant he stopped haunting the house?'

'I do,' Charles said.

'I wonder if we do find Miss Crane's bones on the beach, if it will be like that. If I see them, if I know she's gone and we bury her, then perhaps she'll stop haunting me. A kind of personal exorcism.'

'I hope so, Anne. Just keep trying to remember, will you? And whatever you do remember, when the dance is over we can lay the whole thing out in front of your father and let him decide what to do.'

30.

1943

For Anne, time became rather swimmy after she was rescued from the Ice House. When she woke up her head and arm hurt badly, and it was hard to think about anything much. Ruby was always there, usually trying to get her to eat or drink something. She tried, but sitting up tended to make her feel rather sick and exhausted, so she'd manage what she could, then go to sleep again. Eventually sleep began to feel delicious, rather than dangerous, and she was aware of being safe. That seemed to make her feel very tired too, but it became a nice kind of tired.

Ruby started reading out loud to her. Funny books about lords and ladies falling in love and getting into scrapes, and Anne's dreams started to empty of rats and ghosts and fill with beautiful colours, dresses, balls and music. Once she woke up and saw her grandfather. Miss Crane had disappeared, Anne felt as long as she stayed in bed and didn't say too much she might not come back.

'What have you got there, Miss Anne?' Ruby asked her one day as she looked up between paragraphs. It was probably morning judging by the light. Anne wasn't sure herself.

She looked down and found she was holding a rag doll. It had blonde wispy hair and blue eyes and was wearing a long white dress made out of thin cotton and had a bow-shaped smile stitched in coral pink. Anne tried to think, and she vaguely remembered it being put into her hands during the night, and a gentle touch on her forehead.

'Perhaps Lady Mary gave it to me,' she said. 'To say sorry for frightening me in the cellar.'

It was the longest sentence she'd said out loud since the Ice House. Ruby looked sceptical, but pleased. 'Well, that's nice of her I suppose. You look a lot better today. I'll ask Peter to bring us some toast.'

Eating toast made her think of Miss Crane. She tried to enjoy it, but after a few bites her stomach turned over and Ruby had to hold a basin while she brought it up again.

Once Miss Crane came to the door and opened it. She smiled at Ruby, who looked at her but did not smile back.

'How are you feeling, Anne?' she said.

It was like being locked in the Ice House again. Anne felt the soft body of a rat run over her ankle, her head swam and her hands ached from beating on the door. What she did or said, she wasn't sure, but slowly she became aware Ruby was hugging her and Miss Crane was gone.

Abner Mullins came to visit one afternoon while Ruby was trying to get her to eat something more substantial than broth. He was so interesting and nice, talking about Coke of Norfolk that Captain Horton had mentioned, and how Gainsborough painted him and took years doing it, that she forgot to feel squirmy and strange about eating food and making noise, only realising she had been eating when Ruby took the plate away. After that he or Mrs Warnes or Grandpa seemed to appear quite often at mealtimes and her appetite improved. Twice Johnnie came to visit. Both times he was wearing a tie and his face looked oddly clean. He brought comics with him and sat on the bed and they talked about the prisoners and spies and the party the Royal Engineers were planning and Anne was pleased to see him.

The doctor came and pronounced her much recovered.

When Ruby suggested they go out for a walk, Anne realised she didn't like the idea of leaving her room. She thought of Lady Mary, shut up for weeks and weeks, and rather wished she could do the same. But even Lady Mary had gone out in the end.

Ruby helped her dress and they walked downstairs together and out onto the terrace. Winter had arrived. Somehow when Anne had been sleeping, it had come roaring in and the whole of the park was frosty. The mist clung to the ground, making the whole landscape shimmer like sugar in a bowl. Up the slope a group of deer crossed from one patch of trees to another, their dappled skin seeming to carry the sunlight with them from place to place.

The Ice House was there too, its witchy outline slightly softened by white. Anne resolutely turned away from it and she and Ruby walked towards the conservatory and the lavender walk, though there was no lavender there now. In the little shelter, a bit like a temple, but open to the air, Anne began to clear away the leaves, that had fallen over the mosaic and turned to mulch, with the edge of her shoe.

'Don't you want to go and look at the gargoyles in the pleasure garden?' Ruby said, pulling her shawl around her.

Anne thought of rats and shook her head. Ever since that afternoon with Miss Crane even the gargoyles themselves seemed hostile, ready to bite off her fingers.

'Wait there then, Miss Anne,' Ruby said, 'I shall fetch a trowel from one of the garden boys and you can clean off those leaves properly.' Then she dashed off back towards the house.

Anne waited for her in the cold. The Royal Engineers must be on the beach, she thought, it was so terribly quiet, not even any bird song. She imagined the blackbirds and thrushes sheltering in the bare hedgerows with their feathers all puffed out, saving their energy for spring. She turned her back to the house and looked up into the evergreens of the arboretum to see if she could spot them.

'Anne?' Miss Crane, without her coat on and with her arms wrapped tightly around her waist, marched quickly up the path. 'You are a cunning little monster, aren't you? How long do you think you are going to be able to keep up this pretence of being ill? Everyone knows you are just being lazy. Lord Leicester thinks you are simple-minded, and he is only waiting for your parents to come back to England to have you put in a home! We know how to treat children like you there. But you are not just simple, you are wicked. I know that.'

She had come right up to Anne now, and she grabbed hold of her shoulder, digging her long fingers into her flesh, her eyes dark. Anne wasn't used to it. She cried out, a little yelping gasp.

'Miss Crane!' Ruby was racing along the path towards them, the trowel in her hand, lifting up her long skirt so she could run faster. Her hair was coming loose and her shawl lifted behind her like a cape or the trail of a comet. 'You are hurting the child! Get away from her!'

Miss Crane looked startled and took a step back, but Ruby didn't slow down or stop running until she was standing by Anne, her hand on Anne's shoulder. Anne leant into her.

'I was *not* hurting her! The child is playing games and how dare you speak to me in that way!'

'You hurt Miss Anne and I'll speak to you any way I fucking please,' Ruby said.

Anne was transfixed. She had no idea what that word meant, but she had heard one or two of the soldiers say it when they dropped something, but the look on Miss Crane's face told her it was a word of huge power. She went dead white, whiter than the statues in the gallery or the conservatory, then red, an ugly red, blotched with yellow. She lifted her hand, her palm flat, ready to hit Ruby across the face, and Ruby lifted her hand too, the hand holding the trowel. Miss Crane hesitated.

'I'll see you turned out on the street for this,' Miss Crane said in her worst and most angry hiss, but she lowered her hand. 'I'll have you fired without a name or reference.'

Ruby took a half step towards her. 'I don't know how you've got Mr Shreeve and Mrs Warnes dancing to your tune,' she said. 'But if you think they'll choose you over Miss Anne you're mad.'

'You're a thief!' Miss Crane said, her eyes sparking. 'You'll be taken away in handcuffs by the time I've done with you.'

'Oh, save your wind!' Ruby said. 'Now get away with you, and stay away.'

Miss Crane's upper lip lifted and she looked at Anne. 'This girl won't be here to protect you for long, Anne. You'll be alone sometime and I shall find you. Then you will answer for your behaviour, and hers, to *me*.'

Then she turned and stalked back along the path to the house.

Ruby, watching her go, handed the trowel to Anne. 'Don't you worry about her, Miss Anne. Now get on with your cleaning.'

She sat down firmly on the little stone bench and folded her arms across her chest. Anne crouched down to push away the mulch; the stones, bright and perfect when she pushed away the leaves, looked very lovely.

31.

JOHNNIE HAD BEEN keeping watch on the house and beach all the time Anne was ill, he'd told her as much when he visited. Anne had to do the same, not to protect England this time, but Ruby, who was just as important.

She knew that spark in Miss Crane's eye. It was the look she got when she had found a new way to be cruel, and Miss Crane's favourite time to be cruel was at night. Anne only pretended to be asleep that evening and as soon as she heard Ruby's light snore from her camp bed, Anne got up, slipped out of the room and sat in the cold at the top of the stairs. She must have dozed off, because the sound of Miss Crane's door opening on the floor below woke her with a start.

'The beach then if needs be,' she heard Miss Crane's voice say, 'but the maid will be gone by tomorrow. I can handle the child.'

The door closed again and the silence washed back around her, but Anne was very, very awake. What could Miss Crane have done to be so sure she'd get rid of Ruby? Anne sat in the dark at the top of the staircase and thought hard. If

Miss Crane was going to complain to Grandpa or Mrs Warnes about Ruby swearing at her, she'd have done it by now – just marched straight into the house and made her complaint. Then Mrs Warnes would have come out to speak to Ruby and they'd know by now. Instead, after cleaning off the mosaic and going up and down the walk a few times, they'd gone back to the nursery for tea. Then they had played Monopoly together. Ruby won, but was so happy and funny about it Anne was glad she had. Then reading and bed.

Anne remembered what Miss Crane had said about Ruby being a thief. That was when her eyes sparkled. It was a lie of course, but . . . Anne had never realised how evil some ordinary-looking people could be until she met Miss Crane. So what would an evil villain do in one of the *Hotspur* stories? Something to make Ruby look guilty. And Miss Crane had had most of the afternoon to think of that herself and do something about it.

Surely it would be best to check. Anne got up and felt along the wall opposite her own bedroom until she found the little handle to the maid's room. It was more of a cubby hole really, just big enough for a bed and a box with Ruby's name painted on the lid. Anne slipped inside and flicked on the electric light switch. The single bulb in its green cover came on, and cast a warm orange glow into every corner.

Anne opened Ruby's box. It had a tray in it that lifted out. On the top layer were Ruby's spare stockings and underwear, folded very neatly, her hair brush and the pins she used to keep her hair tidy under her cap when it was having a wispy day. Under the tray were bundles of letters, and a photograph of George Fuller looking handsome in his uniform. The photograph came in its own cardboard folder, which was rippled and patterned like freshly churned ice cream. Another folder held a picture of a man and woman standing in front of a painted garden. The man looked rather severe, but the woman had nice eyes. Ruby's parents.

It was under the letters that Anne found Miss Crane's silver necklace and her ring with garnets in it. When Anne looked at it, she could feel the pain of those little stones pressing against her.

Anne took the necklace and the ring and put everything else back in the box just as she had found it, turned off the light and closed the door behind her. She couldn't just keep the necklace and ring. Miss Crane would tell Grandpa that Anne was a thief then. Anne carried them downstairs to the nursery. The necklace she dropped behind the cushion where Miss Crane liked to sit while Anne was writing out Bible verses about the punishment of evildoers. The last one she'd been made to do was about fire and brimstone. Anne put the ring next to the chalk, then she went back to bed. Ruby turned over when she came in, but didn't wake up.

Anne had been having breakfast in bed since she got ill, just like she would when she was a grown-up. It was nice. Things came on a tray, neat little sets of plates, cup and butter dish all matching. Peter, the boy who was waiting on them, like a footman, half a footman Ruby said, told them that His Lordship would be glad to have a visit from Miss Anne this morning, if she was well enough. Anne wasn't completely sure she wanted to leave her room again, but Ruby was firm.

'Now, it's not lessons!'

Anne wanted very much to see her grandfather, so perhaps it would be worth risking leaving her room to visit him. Anne lifted up her arms so Ruby could slip her jumper on.

'Good girl,' she said, then she sat back on her heels. 'I can't wait to hear you chattering away again, Miss Anne. Maybe when you come back after seeing your grandfather you can show me the best photographs you've taken together so far and tell me about them.'

Someone knocked at the door, and Mrs Warnes put her head in.

'Ruby, can I speak to you outside?'

Ruby made a 'I wonder what this is about' face at Anne, then got up and followed Mrs Warnes into the hall. Anne put on her skirt and socks and opened the door in time to hear Ruby's exclamation of indignation.

'You know I would never do such a thing, Mrs Warnes!'

'I do know, Ruby, of course I do but it's a serious accusation, and I must look in your box, I'm very sorry, but I'd be neglecting my duty if I didn't.'

Ruby's voice was full of tears. 'I was sleeping in Miss Anne's room last night, what if that nasty cow put her jewellery in my box herself?'

'Ruby, do watch your language!' Mrs Warnes looked suddenly very angry. 'I will not have you speak that way. No matter what the provocation, I expect you to always keep your temper. Now let's get this nasty business out of the way.'

Anne slipped round the door and took hold of Ruby's

hand. Ruby held it hard, a bit too hard really, but Anne didn't mind.

Mrs Warnes's search didn't take very long. 'Well, there's nothing in your box, I'm glad to say,' she said, closing it and then looking at the lid. 'It did cross my mind Miss Crane might have got jealous of you looking after Miss Anne and played a nasty trick. But perhaps it was an honest mistake. Where Miss Crane's necklace is, I have no idea.'

'I think perhaps in the schoolroom,' Anne said. Mrs Warnes jumped.

'Anne, I didn't see you there. Why do you say that?'

'She plays with it when she is sitting in the window seat,' Anne said.

Mrs Warnes nodded, though a flicker of suspicion crossed her face. 'Good idea, Anne. I shall check, but you really shouldn't listen to adult conversations as a rule. I am sorry to have troubled you, Ruby.'

'Not at all, Mrs Warnes,' Ruby said and gave a little bobbing curtsey and the corner of Mrs Warnes's mouth twitched into a smile. 'I'll be taking Miss Anne to see His Lordship as soon as she's got her shoes on. Shall I come to the kitchen after that? I heard Mr Shreeve mention Peter might need some help with the silver polishing.'

'Excellent, Ruby,' Mrs Warnes said. 'Thank you for the suggestion, Anne. I shall check the schoolroom.'

Mrs Warnes found the necklace and ring in the schoolroom very easily. Far too easily. She thought of Anne's suggestion and wondered. Could Anne have worked out what Miss Crane was about and thwarted her? It would be a clever thing for a child her age to do. Mrs Warnes had no doubt of Ruby's honesty. How could she have thought of Lavender Crane as a friend? She was far too old to fall for the blandishments of a woman like that, but she had been fooled, then after Anne's escapade in the cellar, Lavender had shown what she was really like and had kept them all on a string ever since. Well, enough was enough.

Mrs Warnes walked into the steward's room and put the necklace and ring down on the scrubbed table in front of Miss Crane. Mr Shreeve, Abner Mullins and Mrs Rowse were there too, gathered by the invisible nervous system of the house to the right place at the right time.

'Tea, Mrs Warnes?' the cook asked.

'Thank you, Mrs Rowse,' she replied. Mr Shreeve looked stricken, seeing the glitter of the jewellery on the table, and Lavender Crane was exultant.

'I expect you to call the police, of course,' she said, fastening the chain holding the small silver cross around her neck, and slipping the ring onto her finger. 'Obviously one would prefer that these things be kept quiet, but I'm afraid I have to insist. Such behaviour must be punished with more than a simple dismissal.'

Mrs Warnes took her tea from Mrs Rowse and sipped, but did not sit down.

'There is no need to call the police, and Ruby will most certainly not be fired. She is a vital member of our family at Holkham.'

'What?' Miss Crane blinked rapidly and her face lost that feline smirk. 'She is a thief. You found the proof!'

'Ruby's box contained her own personal possessions,

nothing else,' Mrs Warnes continued smoothly. 'I found the necklace and ring in the schoolroom. You must have mislaid them there during your lessons.'

Miss Crane was, briefly, speechless. She looked, in fact, utterly baffled. Mrs Warnes was convinced in that moment that her suspicions had been correct. Miss Crane had tried to frame Ruby, and Miss Anne had been watchful and quick enough to turn the tables on her. Mrs Warnes did not intend to let a trump card like that go to waste.

'I did no such thing!' Miss Crane said. 'You must have told her you were looking for them and given her time to move them!'

'Who had a moment to do such a thing?' Mrs Warnes said. 'You only made your unfortunate accusation a few minutes ago. And I hope you are not accusing *me* of colluding in a theft, Miss Crane. Honestly, Lavender, I don't know what you are thinking of!'

The governess looked at the senior staff in angry appeal. 'I am sure that Lord Leicester doesn't know half of what goes on in this house. I would hate to upset him, of course, but if it is my duty to inform him of what has been going on . . .'

Then of course, they had another trump up their own sleeves. Mrs Warnes glanced at Mr Shreeve, her eyebrow raised to see if he would like to play it. It seemed he would.

'If you wish to make a fool of yourself making further wild allegations to His Lordship,' Mr Shreeve said, his voice a perfectly pitched mix of disdain and disbelief, 'I'm sure there is nothing we can do to prevent you, Miss Crane. But I would advise against it. There is nothing happening in this house that would disturb or surprise His Lordship one jot.'

'Really?' Miss Crane said, a nasty smirk on her face as she looked between them. 'Well you have all changed your tune!'

'Not at all,' Shreeve said firmly. Miss Crane's neatly painted lips puckered with distaste, then she got to her feet and swept out of the room.

Mrs Warnes handed back her tea cup to the cook.

'Should Miss Lavender get the same lunch as the rest of us today, Mrs Warnes?' the cook said carefully. 'No extra treats from His Lordship's table?'

'No,' Mrs Warnes said. 'All treats you can manage should go to Miss Anne, while she is recuperating, don't you think?'

That was the last day. Anne and her grandfather took photographs and developed them and when it was time for lunch, there was Ruby to serve it. After lunch they went, by invitation, to see the Royal Engineers in the stable yard. The plans for the Christmas party seemed to have got very elaborate. The children from the village would be able to throw darts at German bombers and fighter planes as well as at Hitler and his henchmen. The smaller children would be invited to hook painted ducks out of an old tin bathtub, almost as good as the fair, and there was to be a raffle too, but they weren't sure what the prizes should be.

They stayed so long, looking at everything and helping the soldiers work out difficult things like where to display the prizes, it was nearly dark when they came out of the stable yard and walked round towards the front of the house.

'Wonder where she is going?' Ruby said. Anne turned. Miss Crane. The sight of her made Anne jump. Ruby noticed and took a step back so they were hidden by one of the big stone lions who guarded the drive in front of the house. Miss Crane passed by them, a few feet away. Anne could smell her scent in the frozen air. She was wearing her long coat, a tiny handbag over her arm.

'Probably off to visit her many friends in the village,' Ruby murmured. 'She does pop up all over the place, doesn't she? I think I'd rather have Lady Mary following me about.'

Did she have friends in the village? Did that mean that even the village wasn't safe? Anne put her hand into Ruby's. Somehow, seeing Miss Crane walking towards the village, she suddenly realised Miss Crane would work out that it was her, Anne, who had moved the things from Ruby's box and put them in the schoolroom, and as she was getting better now, lessons would start again and Ruby wouldn't be there any more. Anne would be alone, and Miss Crane would be waiting.

'Miss Anne, you're shaking!'

Would Ruby still sleep in the nursery wing, or would Anne be there alone again, every night, with Miss Crane?

'Miss Anne!'

Anne blinked at her.

'Goodness me, I thought you were having a bit of a turn then and you are still shivering! Perhaps we've done too much today, all this excitement. Let's get you back to your room and get some tea in you. Honestly everyone will have my hide if you get sick again.'

Anne had a nightmare that night and woke to find Ruby

holding her hand. In the morning she couldn't remember what it was, but it had scared Ruby enough to ask Peter to pass word to Mrs Warnes, then Mrs Warnes came up herself to fetch down the tray and tell Ruby she'd been on the telephone to the doctor.

'He says occasional nightmares are probably just part of the healing from that bump on the head. Do you remember them, Miss Anne?'

She shook her head.

'She just sounded very scared,' Ruby said, 'and as if she was in pain. Ghosts perhaps? Though I think that new doll of hers looks like Lady Mary and she loves it, don't you, Miss Anne?'

'Does she?' Mrs Warnes smiled. 'I shall let the lad who made it know.'

'One of the POWs, was it?' Ruby asked.

'Indeed,' Mrs Warnes replied and picked up the tray.

Ruby followed her to the door. 'She's still hardly saying a thing, Mrs Warnes. What she said to you about Miss Crane yesterday and where her necklace might be is the most words I've heard her say for days.'

Mrs Warnes replied in the same low tone. 'Shows she can speak, and think perfectly well and that's the main thing. But none of us need to worry about Miss Crane's tricks any more. She is gone.'

'What?' Ruby said, beaming.

'Yes, Peter took her breakfast tray to the schoolroom, came back with a note. Family emergency, she said. Asked for her luggage to be forwarded.'

'Good riddance,' Ruby said.

'Ruby!' Mrs Warnes didn't sound cross this time. 'His Lordship will explain to Anne later. He wants to tell him herself about when the Viscount and Viscountess are coming home.'

'What a thing! Just to go like that. I saw her heading towards Holkham village last night. Maybc her family emergency came to pick her up!'

Mrs Warnes half laughed. 'I must get on, lot to do before the rest of the family arrives. They'll be here in the Chapel Wing over Christmas.'

Ruby came back, and they got on with the business of getting washed and dressed. She had a lightness about her. Anne wasn't sure though. Miss Crane had lied about Ruby stealing, what if she lied about leaving? She couldn't really take it in when her grandfather told her Carey, their beloved new governess, Billy Williams, and Mum and Dad would be at Holkham in ten days' time. She had been told to walk back to the Chapel Wing by herself, and was afraid Miss Crane would be waiting for her.

32.

Mrs Warnes rose well before dawn, and went to bed after midnight for the next ten days. Not that she begrudged an hour of it. Whatever extra work three more people to cook for and clean after made, it would be a pleasure to have Lord and Lady Coke home, and an excuse to make this year as close to a proper Holkham Christmas as they could. They all came up together from London by car, and the whole staff lined up on the drive in the freezing cold to meet them with Miss Anne at the top of the steps in her Jaeger coat, holding hands with her grandfather.

Carey, Anne's little sister, climbed out of the car first, and before Billy could stop her, she rushed straight at her sister with a shriek of delight and hugged her. Anne stiffened when her sister touched her, then Carey was kissing her grandfather and telling him about something very important and funny to do with a goat they had seen coming through Burnham Thorpe, then she tumbled into the house and Anne could hear her running up and down the steps in the hall as if to check they were all still there.

Anne blinked. There was darling Billy Williams, who was

almost as nice as Ruby, organising the unpacking of the car, and there were two adults, who Anne knew must be her parents, greeting each of the members of staff in turn as they approached the doors. The man, her father, came first. When he reached the top step he spoke.

'You're looking well, Dad. Carey, stop clattering about.'

'Good journey?' Grandpa said, and the two men shook hands. 'We delayed tea. Thought we'd have it in the library. Only room we can keep warm at the moment.'

'Not a bad run, tea would be excellent. Now,' Anne felt this man's attention turn to her, 'is this my older daughter?'

Anne put out her hand and her father shook it. 'Welcome home, Dad,' she said quietly.

'Thank you, Anne.' Then he called over his shoulder. 'Shreeve, can you make sure the pale green case is opened first? It has my shaving kit, and I'd like to make myself decent after tea.'

Anne looked up at him sideways. He looked very sharp, as if made of straight lines. He ruffled her hair and then started talking about roads to Grandpa.

'Hello, Anne. Do you remember me?' A very pretty woman was crouching down in front of her. She had a fur stole round her neck and a hat with a tiny veil.

Anne shook her head.

'I'm your mum!'

Anne put out her hand. The very pretty woman laughed. 'Oh no, handshakes aren't enough for me!' She put her arms around Anne and Anne went stiff, waiting for a pinch or a twist.

'Not used to hugging, Anne?' the pretty lady said, still

holding on to her hard. 'I'm afraid you'll have to get used to it because I have three years of hugs to catch up on.'

The stole was very, very soft against Anne's cheek and the lady's, her mother's, hair smelt of something tangy and dark that made Anne feel safe. She relaxed a little.

'That's better,' the lady said and hugged even tighter. Anne felt something well up inside her, it made her want to cry with happiness.

'Elizabeth, come in and have tea before everyone freezes to death!' Grandpa said.

'Coming, Tom!' she called back, still hugging Anne. Then she took hold of Anne's shoulders and held her at a slight distance. 'What a beautiful daughter, I have! We are lucky!' Then she winked. Miss Crane had never winked. 'Come on, darling. Tea and then you and Carey can help me arrange all my clothes and we'll see if your father and I might have found you a present or two in Egypt.'

Mrs Warnes watched the family climbing the stairs in the Marble Hall. 'Like a light's been switched on, isn't it?' she said to Shreeve.

'It is, Mrs Warnes, it is.'

The Christmas party was a great success. It began with the children of the village singing, and Anne's mum and dad and Grandpa applauding, then the games the Royal Engineers had set up, which were exactly the right mix of noise and laughter. Anne and Carey handed out the prizes in the end, and Johnnie did so well on the darts he got the best prize of a real penknife.

It took ages until Anne got a chance to speak to him.

'Miss Crane has gone,' she said. 'She went away because of a family emergency.' Talking had got easier since Mum and Dad had got back, and Mum in particular always seemed so interested in whatever one had to say, the words just came out.

'Oh, your governess!' Johnnie said. 'I see. Oh, I bought you a present.'

He went and fetched his satchel, and produced a bundle of *Hotspur* magazines.

'Don't you want to read them again, Johnnie?'

He shook his head. 'They are a bit babyish actually. And I might not be able to play with you so much any more. I'm going to play football.'

'Oh,' Anne said, and was wondering if she should feel hurt or offended, when he suddenly grinned again. 'But you and Carey can use our redoubts in Donkey Wood if you like, and I wanted to tell you – Mum liked that picture you gave me so much, she's put it in a frame and hung it on the wall!'

Then it was time to go to the Marble Hall to see the Christmas tree, decked in white candles all aflame, and Grandpa handed out presents, wooden toys made by the Italian Prisoners of War, to all the children. Miss Crane did not appear like a Dickens ghost, and though Anne's heart stopped from time to time when she sensed a movement in the shadows or thought she heard a voice behind her, Miss Crane was never there. On Christmas Day they had turkey and a proper cake. Anne and Carey embroidered handkerchiefs for their parents, and both got new books and notebooks and Anne got a fountain pen because she was about to go to boarding school.

By the time Anne came back from her first term, she had almost forgotten why certain parts of the house and grounds made her nervous, and why she was not entirely comfortable when she was alone at Holkham. Her family told her she was afraid of ghosts, and she began to believe them.

33.

1950

IF ANNE WENT through the day of her dance in a bit of a haze, everyone just assumed it was nerves. The house was busy from dawn, but it was a different kind of busy from her grandfather's funeral. That had been serious and sombre; today felt bright and cheerful.

'I cannot get the sound of violins tuning up out of my head,' Elizabeth announced when she came in to find Anne just after breakfast. 'I feel like one does in the theatre just as the curtain is about to go up, and I can't tell if I'm in the audience or on stage.' Anne climbed out of bed and began to dress. 'You, Anne, are most definitely on stage,' Elizabeth went on. 'Oh, and the stage is Holkham, and your father, Carey and I are your supporting players. It will be a wonderful evening.'

'Do you really think it will be a wonderful evening, Mum?' Anne said.

'Darling, it's going to be marvellous. We are all just beginning to struggle free of the war, and this dance is a manner of grand return for the whole county! Every house within fifty miles is full of guests. It will be blissful.' She looked out of Anne's window with a dreamy look on her face. 'Everyone is just dying for a bit of colour and light relief! And thanks to your communist, the house is going to be lit up like fairyland. Then there's the champagne of course, and the band. Everyone's going to be so pleased to see each other at a proper party again! All you need do is look pretty and don't drink too much.'

'I think I can manage that,' Anne replied.

Elizabeth sat on one of Anne's armchairs, her long slim legs straight out in front of her and crossed at the ankle. 'I think even Lady Mary is excited. She's been pinching the maids and whispering at the house carpenter till he thought he was going mad, you know.'

Anne sat down at her dressing table, and her mother got to her feet again at once, picked up the silver-backed hair brush and ran it through Anne's blonde curls. 'Do you hear her at all, darling?'

Anne smiled at her in the mirror.

'Lady Mary? I'm not sure I ever did, Mum.'

Elizabeth bent down so she could look at Anne's reflection properly. 'Who knows? Don't worry about tonight. You are looking very lovely already and you haven't even got your dress on yet.'

The day went by very slowly and very, very fast at the same time. After Lord and Lady Leicester and their house guests had dined the musicians, Tommy Kinsman and his orchestra, set up in the long gallery and outside, in the soft dark of a midsummer night, the lights were turned on.

'Do come and look, Anne!' Carey called. Anne joined her

by the window in the salon and the two sisters looked up the avenue towards the obelisk.

The searchlights played over the house and avenue in pink and blue, and a pale green that was just the colour of Anne's parachute silk ball gown.

'It's absolutely spellbinding!' Carey breathed.

On cue the band started playing and Carey took Anne's hands and twirled her around, the dress swung beautifully.

Her father appeared. He had settled his friends around the state rooms and made sure they were being taken care of. 'Anne, I'm going to meet the King and Queen at the south gate. You and your mother better start receiving people, I think.' Then he looked her up and down. 'Hmm. You'll do.'

Elizabeth entered from the direction of the Family Wing. Her dress was a pale purple and she seemed to float rather than walk. She put her arm round her daughter's narrow waist. 'Show time, darling.'

For the first hour or so, until it was close on midnight, Anne remained at the top of the stairs in the salon, greeting a bewildering number of people and being looked at. The King and Queen both told her she looked well, and Princess Margaret was quite friendly – but very grown-up and sophisticated now. She told Anne her dress was just the thing, before being carried off onto the dance floor by the most handsome men in attendance.

When Elizabeth told Anne she could go and dance, she walked into the drawing room and felt rather baffled and bemused by the noise and the music and very shy of launching herself into the middle of it.

She turned round and walked out of the dining room and round the Marble Hall, heading towards the old kitchen. It was still not in general use, more repairs would be needed, but they had opened it up for tonight and the huge table was polished and crowded with bottles of champagne. Mrs Warnes was marshalling the whole enterprise, issuing instructions to the waiting staff and neatly ticking through the lists in her notebook. She looked up and saw Anne.

'Lady Anne! Is everything all right?'

'Yes, it's all absolutely lovely,' Anne said. 'I was wondering if I might take some champagne out to the men operating the searchlights. To say thank you.'

'An excellent idea.' Mrs Warnes said something to one of the waiters, and like a fairy godmother she seemed to summon a tray with a bottle and glasses on it out of thin air. Anne thanked her, and carried it carefully out onto the terrace, the silk of her dress whispering round her ankles.

Charles was standing with two of the gardeners by the huge searchlight that washed the front of the house in pink. He took his glass, and the two gardeners took the tray and the champagne off to the others, promising to return the tray to the old kitchen when they were done.

He sipped the champagne and his eyes widened with pleasure.

'I could get used to this. I fear your family will corrupt me in the end.' They looked up at the portico; the sound of the band, playing songs from musicals that blended seamlessly into big band jive tunes, poured out of the open windows and across the terrace. It mixed with the sound of laughter, and Anne could see the state rooms glittering and thronged with people.

'Your public awaits, Anne,' Charles said. 'Come on, you've done the being presented at court and been to that ball at, where was it?'

'Londonderry House,' Anne said distractedly. 'Being presented is just a lot of queuing with other debutantes, really.'

'I shall have to take your word for it. Armstrong at the Nelson cut out the picture of you and all the other debs on the staircase and stuck it behind the bar. Go and dance!'

'But Charles!'

'Anne,' he sounded quite serious, 'I am sure we are right, about Lavender Crane being buried in the dunes, about the Coke necklace still being somewhere on the grounds and someone still searching for it, but you can't worry about that tonight. The King and Queen are here! You and your family are safe for now, so just enjoy it.' He finished his champagne and made a great smacking noise with his lips, and wiped his mouth with the back of his hand. That made her smile. 'Who knows, perhaps thinking about other things for a few hours will give you a chance to remember more. Now, off you go!'

'Oh, very well,' she said a little huffily, then made her way back into the house, going past the old kitchen into the Marble Hall and lifting up her ball gown as she climbed the stairs.

'Lady Anne!' She turned round to see Carstairs with a couple of other men in their thirties all in white tie with their chests stiff with medals just arriving behind her. 'What a stroke of luck to find you! I claim this dance!' He jogged up the stairs to join her and she took his hand with relief as he led her into the salon.

Carstairs was a very good dancer, which made the next few minutes a lot easier and more fun.

'The band are terribly good!' he said, loud enough for her to hear over the brassy blast of the trumpets standing to play a chorus. 'Are you having a good time?'

She liked his smile, so felt able to answer honestly. 'I think so! I'm not sure I absolutely love being the centre of attention, but I hope I look all right?'

He laughed. 'You most certainly do! *Tatler*'s debutante of the year too! Is your sister jealous?'

Anne laughed. 'I think she might be a little, apparently it can be very annoying being the younger sister and not getting to do anything first, but I think she is having far too much fun tonight to worry about it.'

He spun her round under his arm as the band let off a final blast, which made her feel for one moment utterly marvellous, then with a bow he invited her back into his arms as the band started a more gentle foxtrot – the sort of thing where you could dance and talk more easily.

'Lady Anne, that young man, Johnnie Fuller, has been on my conscience since we spoke. I hope I won't spoil your evening by mentioning him.'

'No,' she said. 'You won't spoil my evening talking about Johnnie. I am sorry to say his wife is not mourning him very much. She has moved to Norwich to be near her brother-in-law and his wife, Ruby. She used to work here too and is rather a heroine of mine. But why would Johnnie be on your conscience?'

He turned her round, moving smoothly through the crush of other dancers as if they weren't there at all. Anne was suddenly aware that he was the kind of dancer who knew how to make his partner look graceful and easy without even trying. She didn't mind if people looked at her now.

'I was wondering why the lad was so convinced he had seen spies all over the estate, and then it came to me. Have you heard about the auxiliary units?'

She shook her head.

'They were set up early in the war, a secret network of them operating under the cover of the Home Guard, but much better trained, and trained in all sorts of guerrilla tactics. They were there to fight on if Hitler invaded and our conventional forces were overwhelmed. There was one at Holkham, based out of your temple.'

Her eyes widened. 'Really? My goodness! I always thought if Hitler turned up at Holkham it would rather have been up to me and Grandpa to deal with him.'

He steered her past another couple, guiding her with a gentle pressure on her waist or hand that meant she could follow without thinking.

'You would have had a very effective ally in Lieutenant Ketteringham. Anyway, one of the things the auxiliary units did was maintain secret weapon caches around the place and make sure they were intact and secure at regular intervals. I imagine if Johnnie had seen something like that he could well have thought he'd fallen on a nest of spies.'

'Oh, yes, I think that could well have been the case. Are you sure you are allowed to be saying such things to me?'

'Quite sure. It took a while to recover all of the weapons

around the country, and the auxiliary units couldn't be spoken of till that was done, but we are not too worried if people hear about them now. In fact, the work that Ketteringham and his men did should be acknowledged and celebrated, I think. Your grandfather always knew they were on the grounds. We consulted with him after you went to Scotland and your parents were in Egypt. That's when I first got to know the house.'

'You knew my grandfather well, didn't you?'

'I like to think so.'

'And he knew he could rely on your discretion?'

This time he only nodded.

'Did he ever mention the Coke necklace to you?'

For the first and only time he faltered slightly in his steps.

'He did. In 'forty-seven. He was sorry to learn that his son had sold it without telling him towards the end of the war.'

Anne gasped. 'My father did not do any such thing!'

'Are you quite sure?' Carstairs frowned. 'We were talking about ways of keeping the different collections of Holkham together. He had been told his son sold the Coke necklace soon after his return from Egypt, and he had only just found out. The man who told him was the one who handled the sale for the current Lord Leicester.'

Anne swallowed. 'He didn't say who that was, did he?'

'No,' Carstairs replied. It was almost a relief he could not tell her. 'He did not. Only that he had only discovered the necklace was gone the previous day. It was when Princess Elizabeth's wedding had just been announced.' He looked down at her with narrowed eyes. 'Shall we stop dancing, Anne? Perhaps you need a glass of something.'

She sighed and lowered her eyes for a moment, then lifted her chin. It was another thing that could wait until morning.

'No, no thank you, I would much rather keep dancing for now!'

'An excellent plan!' he agreed with enthusiasm and entertained her with gossip and nonsense until her hand was claimed by her next partner. Time began to speed up, and Anne felt the darkness driven away by the music and the many pleasures that surrounded her.

'Hello, Anne! What are you doing out here by yourself?'

Anne turned away from the view and smiled. After hours of dancing, she had escaped onto the portico outside the salon. She felt flushed, but still terribly happy. Princess Margaret looked as poised as when she had arrived. She fitted a cigarette into a long ebony holder, lit it and leant on the balustrade.

'Just admiring the view, ma'am. I hope you have enjoyed yourself?'

The Princess's eyes widened. 'Oh, Anne, what a wonderful party! Holkham has become alive again. I have enjoyed it so much and very clever of you to have asked so many of my friends – Colin, Billy, Peter – I was danced off my feet. It's so strange to think the last time we stood together on this portico was twelve years ago. I think we must have been thinking up something naughty but what fun we had.'

Anne laughed in spite of herself.

'Oh, Anne, look!' the Princess said and pointed. A flight

of geese had lifted off the lake and flew across the grounds between the house and the obelisk, the first sunlight of the new day reflecting off their wings. 'How lovely! What about you, Anne? Did you enjoy yourself?'

Anne shook her head. 'I'm honestly not sure, ma'am. I was terribly worried before, and it's so early in the season I hardly know anyone. Just a few cousins and school friends of my father's and Carstairs who keeps an eye on us on behalf of the British Museum.'

The Princess flicked the ash from her cigarette, then smoothed her long silk gloves along her slim arms.

'Oh yes, he's a darling. Don't worry, you'll go from not knowing anyone to being bored of the same old faces in a month. I will take you to The Four Hundred. It's much more fun than all the formal affairs. However I heard the King telling your father this will go down as one of the first great dances of the season after the war. Perhaps we are emerging from under the shadow of the damned war at last.'

'Dad will be terribly pleased to hear that. Do you remember, ma'am, riding our tricycles through the hall before the war?'

She giggled and rested her hand briefly on Anne's. 'Oh yes! And running around in the attics. It was such fun. Have you been back to the beach? I loved swimming there when we were little.'

Anne thought of the dunes, the taxis and Miss Crane.

'Too many ghosts,' she said quietly.

'What?'

'Sorry, ma'am. No, not yet. There is still rather a lot of barbed wire around and the odd landmine. Carey and I will be swimming in the fountain again this summer.'

'Could be worse.' The Princess turned round, looking back into the house. 'Such a friendly place, Holkham. I always thought so. Glamis is wonderful in parts. I know I used to boast when we went around looking for the ghosts there, but there are rooms I would never go into alone.'

Anne felt a stir of an idea in the back of her mind.

'Shall we have some breakfast, Anne? It is such a civilised habit to end an evening's dancing with bacon and eggs.'

'Yes, of course, ma'am.'

Anne followed her back into the salon.

34.

THE KING AND Queen left at five in the morning, and Princess Margaret just after six. The band played one last tune to serenade the dawn, and the final dancers made their farewells and piled back into their motorcars to return to the various houses in which they were staying. Anne kissed her mother, who declared the evening an unqualified success, and thanked her father, then went up to her room to shed her finery and get into bed. On impulse, she opened the bottom drawer of her wardrobe, and moved aside a few of her keepsakes – the presents her mother had brought back to her from the war, a picture of a Messerschmitt punctured with dart holes from the Christmas party, the copies of *Hotspur* that Johnnie had given her – and found it. The doll that had suddenly appeared in her room when she was ill. It did look rather like Lady Mary, not as she appeared in the portrait they had of her in Holkham, but as she looked after she became a relatively merry widow in London, a long white dress, with her hair tied up. The stitching was neat, but workmanlike, and the doll seemed to have been made with scraps of fabric of different ages and styles. Anne stared at it, thinking of those weeks with Miss Crane, how she had played on Anne's fears. She thought of all the men who had been in Holkham at the time, the Home Guard and Royal Engineers, Shreeve and Mr Mullins, the Prisoners of War, some of whom now worked at Holkham, and whoever that person was who had been hiding in the cellars. The poor boy. She thought of the list of losses, the dozen or so pages of illuminated manuscript now unmoored from their volumes, of the feeling of being watched, by the people of Holkham, by the portraits and ghosts, and what she had said to Charles about how finding Lavender Crane might lift this curse of fear, of nervousness, which she had lived with in the long shadow of that woman. Faces, eyes – it sparked something again. Miss Crane slapping her legs as she tied her up, hissing her dark, twisted fairy tales about the gargoyles. Anne put the doll back in the drawer and got dressed.

Charles was helping to load the musicians' gear into a truck in the stable yard when she found him. He grinned, and looked her up and down.

'Out of the party frock? Shouldn't you be in bed? That's where I am going as soon as this is done. Mrs Warnes just brought us all the remains of your breakfast and bottles of beer. I can't decide if it's knocked me out, or if I am going to get back to the easel and paint the best thing of my career.'

'Charles, I've had an idea.'

The foreman in charge of the band called out to them. 'All done here, Charlie! You need a lift anywhere? Morning, Lady Anne. Lovely do.'

'I've got my bike, John,' Charles called back to him. 'Safe travels!'

Anne raised her hand in thanks and acknowledgement. The man slapped the side of his truck, and the driver pulled away.

Charles turned back to her.

'What is it? Do you want to go to your father and the police about Lavender Crane now? Are you sure a few hours' sleep might not make it all a bit easier? I can hardly think straight and didn't have half the excitement you did last night.'

'No, it's not that. It's just . . . I got an idea about where the necklace might be and I can't rest till I've checked.'

'Are you sure? There must be a million places, the house is a rabbit warren.'

'Yes, it is,' Anne agreed, 'but it has not got as many safe hiding places in it as you might think! People are always coming and going. Even if the family don't often use the service corridors, the staff do, and all the cupboards and cubby holes are used to store things by the maids or daily ladies. And Lavender Crane would want to be able to get to the necklace quickly and easily, wouldn't she?'

'I shall take your word for it, Anne. So where?'

'I thought the Ice House at first, but it's too far away from the house, and of course the brickwork was tidied up last summer and the thatch redone this spring. The temple was always full of Home Guard. Then I thought the conservatory, but Grandpa had tea there sometimes right up until he died, even though it's rather falling apart. So too many people coming and going, just like in the house! But the pleasure gardens! Only the family use that.'

He glanced towards the gates. He looked a bit baffled with lack of sleep. 'Well – I suppose . . . Do you want to go and look now?'

She nodded. They crossed the stable yard, exchanging good mornings with the gamekeepers and gardener's boys.

Charles paused as she pushed open the gates. The light always seemed softer here, filtered through the leaves of all the different trees that made up the arboretum and the soft banks of ferns that lined the walkways.

'What made you think about this place today?'

'It was something Princess Margaret said, it reminded me of Miss Crane making me so afraid of certain places, I wouldn't go near them on my own even after the war. When Mum and Dad came home, it was much easier to pretend it was Lady Mary who I was scared of, until I believed it myself. Poor Lady Mary! I feel I've been terribly unjust to her.'

'Carey told me she is a hair puller. I don't think you need to feel too guilty.'

'I suppose so. Anyway, Miss Crane made sure I was very afraid to be in here.'

'How did she make you afraid?'

'I used to love the gargoyles. Then she told me once that their niches had rats nesting in them. I was terrified of them after that. And they always seemed to be watching me.'

She took the familiar path towards the grotto, while Charles looked up and around him.

'It's so different to the rest of the grounds! It's like being suddenly transported to Kew Gardens.'

Anne led the way to the centre of the gardens, the small

oval pond with the gargoyles watching over it, next to the little shell house. Anne hesitated, almost expecting to see Miss Crane sitting there, her book on her lap, watching Anne with those flashing black eyes.

'What is it, Anne?'

She shook her head. 'I know it seems silly, but even now after all this time, it scares me.'

She bit her lip and turned her attention to the gargoyles. She had thought perhaps, with a giddy sense of possibility, that she would find the necklace in the mouth of the gargoyle who looked as if he was catching snowflakes, but as she reached him, she felt a sting of disappointment, an odd vertiginous twist as memory and reality met, clashed and rearranged themselves. No matter the number of times she had seen it since, she still had the image of this grotto fixed in her eye from a child's perspective. She had imagined reaching up to the gargoyle, but now she found herself looking him in the eye. She had thought his mouth a great cavern she could put her whole hand in, but now she saw it was just a shallow depression. She felt round the back of the other gargoyle, the one with his chin in his hands, but it was a small space, and her fingers touched nothing but leaf mulch.

'Anne?' Charles said.

'Oh, there is nothing there! Why on earth would I think I could suddenly find the necklace, when someone has been searching for it for years and obviously not found it! I feel a complete fool.'

She leant against the rough, ivy-cloaked wall of the grotto and scowled.

'What about there?' Charles said, pointing. There was a small fountain in the middle of the pond, a very modest little thing compared with the battle going on at the front of the house. On a plinth formed by the top section of a Corinthian column sat a huge scallop shell, open, and with a giant stone pearl balanced on the hinge. The fountain had been turned off now, but the pearl still glistened with damp.

'But Miss Crane wouldn't hide it there! She'd have to wade through the pond to get it.'

'One of the chaps on searchlight duty said all the fountains were dry during the war,' Charles replied.

Anne had a vision of it on the day she had curtsied to them, when they were still friendly. The pond had been full of nothing but frost and dead leaves. 'Oh! Yes, he's quite right!'

Charles kicked off his shoes and peeled off his socks, then rolled up his trouser legs.

'Worth a look, I'd say. You could certainly hide something under that shell, under the hinge bit, and it might not be noticed for years.'

He took his first tentative step into the water. It was thick with weeds, but only came halfway up his shins. He peered into the darkness where the curves of the shells met.

'It looks like it might be solid stone, but I think whoever made this was better than that, I think he would have sculpted the full shell.'

He leant on the top of the column, and pushed his fingers into the darkness, then hooked out a press of rotten leaves.

'Is there anything there, Charles?'

'Do give me a minute, this is awkward.' Then his movements became quicker and more urgent.

'Charles?!'

'Hang on! Yes!' He carefully withdrew his hand and Anne could see he was holding something. It looked rotten and slimy, but it had a certain weight to it.

'Open it!'

'I shall not! This is for a Coke, my lady, foul as it is.' He sloshed through the shallow water towards her, his face shining with excitement, and she bent forwards and put out her hands.

'But it might just be something horrid!'

'Take a look, Anne.'

Whatever it was stank of slime and decay and felt soft and strangely heavy in her palms. He was still standing below her in the pond; he cupped his hands under hers as they began to tease the strange muddy mass apart, shaking off the rotted leaves. A cloth of some sort, a dark-coloured flannel, sealed in on itself by time. It was so eaten up by damp though it yielded easily to the touch of Anne's forefinger. A flash of light.

'It's the necklace!' Anne said, her voice rising in excitement. 'Oh Charles! We have found it!'

'I say, very well done!'

Anne looked up. Captain Horton was coming towards them along the path, one hand in his pocket and smoking a cigarette.

'Good morning, Captain Horton,' Anne said delightedly. 'I'm sorry I can't stop to explain, I really must take this to my father at once.'

'No, Lady Anne. You will give it to me. Lucky my friend the gamekeeper saw you ducking in here. Just imagine how I would have felt if you'd whisked that necklace off to your father, right under my nose, when I've been looking for it for six and a half years.'

Anne felt her blood run cold. '*You've* been looking for it, Captain Horton?'

He nodded. 'Eight thousand pounds,' he said. 'That's how much I was told I could get for it when I first took your pictures down to London. I looked into it, and that was very nearly sufficient capital to set me up in Brazil. I wanted to grow something on my own land, you see. Not toil over someone else's. Lavender seemed very keen on the idea, but I'm not sure she would have made a decent farmer's wife. Not really.'

'It was you?' she said, looking at him, still unbelieving.

'I'm not entirely sure what you mean by "it", Lady Anne. But I suppose so.'

Charles took a stride towards him, sloshing through the shallows of the pond.

'Lady Anne means robbing the house and betraying and killing her grandfather!'

Then he stopped suddenly and raised his hands. Another figure had emerged from the trees on the edge of the path – the quiet gamekeeper. He carried a shotgun that was aimed at Charles's head and was looking nervously between Horton and Anne.

'I shall scream,' Anne said quietly.

'And it would be one of the only times in Holkham no one could hear you!' Horton said amiably. 'The stable yard has quite emptied out now, you know, and everyone else other than us is in bed, or putting the state rooms in order. You won't be heard. Now give me the necklace, Lady Anne. There's no need to make a fuss. My friend and I will simply tie you and Elwood up and pop you in the shell house. I only need a few hours. By the time anyone finds you I shall be flying to the continent, and be lost among the human wreckage of Europe. No need to make a fuss.'

Anne looked down at the necklace, then up at the gamekeeper.

'Who are you?' she said, her voice wondering.

'Just someone who owes me a favour,' Horton said. 'He can disappear in his own way. He's done it before.'

The clicks and traps of memory turned in her mind. 'You are Paul Mullins, Abner's son.'

The gamekeeper glanced at her. His eyes were flicking nervously between them all.

'You hid in the cellars during the war. It was you that made me my doll, wasn't it? Thank you.'

Horton looked impatient. 'Yes, yes. Lavender found out he was there after your escapade in the cellars and Shreeve confessed to your grandfather after the Ice House incident. He agreed to turn a blind eye, and after Lavender left, I got Paul false papers.'

'No wonder the staff think you are a good man,' Anne said.

'Seemed sensible to keep them onside,' he said with a shrug. 'Lavender enjoyed flaunting her power over them and they rebelled. Tactically unsound of her.'

'Lavender Crane didn't just leave. You killed her,' Charles said. He still had his hands above his head. 'Why?'

Horton took his hand out of his pocket. He was carrying his old service revolver. He glanced at his watch.

'Does it matter?'

'It matters to me,' Anne said fiercely.

He sighed. 'She got rather tiresome and twitchy when her attempt to frame the maid failed. She wanted to leave at once, before Lord and Lady Coke got home. I wanted to make sure we had enough to live on until we could leave the country and wanted her to lift a few more things. Those manuscript pages went for over a hundred pounds each, you know. Lord knows, I had ample time to take them myself in the end. Stopped me getting bored to death at least. Honestly, it was more than I could bear. All that money, good as bank notes, just sitting on the shelves. Anyway, Lavender felt the tables had turned and the staff were against her, I said whose fault is that? Hold your nerve! One thing led to another. I didn't mean to kill her, but there it was. I bundled her away and ran into Johnnie. Had to think fast, but he swallowed the story about secret spy catchers. I got back into the house to type up her resignation on Bartholomew's machine and pack her an overnight bag. That's when I first ran into Paul myself! Thought we were going to have a moment, then I told him I was looking for him because I thought I could get him papers. We've been firm friends ever since! There. Now you know. Throw the necklace over here and we'll get you squared away, shall we?'

'That was a hell of a risk,' Charles said, 'just leaving her body on the beach.'

Anne risked a look at Paul. He seemed upset and confused,

the barrel of the shotgun was wavering, and he was blinking very fast.

Horton shrugged. 'I tucked her away in one of those taxi cabs. And I knew no one would dare go near the beach till the war was over, not with the bombing practice and the mines scattered about. I knew which parts were safe though, which is why I got her to meet me there sometimes. Now, the necklace please, Lady Anne.'

'You will have to shoot me first,' Anne said.

'You'll have to shoot both of us,' Charles added.

Horton threw away his cigarette.

'I'd rather not, but if you insist. Either way I shall be gone before you are discovered.'

Paul made a noise, not words, but a twisted chirp.

Horton glanced at him. 'Funny, isn't it? I understand he was quite a clever lad before the war. Dunkirk addled his brain. Ran away, and has hardly said a word since the night he reached Holkham. Happened to some chaps in the Great War too.' He examined his revolver. 'Now are you quite sure? Remember, you could be tied up and live a full and happy life.'

'Did you kill Anne's grandfather? And Johnnie?' Charles asked.

'Must we go over this?' he said. 'It's really most unpleasant. Lord Leicester was disappointed to learn I'd lied to him about his son selling the Coke necklace,' he said seriously. 'Our disagreement became heated, and yes, I tried to prevent him telephoning the police. We struggled and he fell. He had told me about Johnnie, so yes, when I realised nothing could be done for Lord Leicester, I thought I'd better take care of Johnnie too. I did check, you know, before I left Leicester,' he added, his voice rather hurt. 'I had nothing against your grandfather, Lady Anne. But it was clear he wasn't going to survive.'

'He had the fake diamond necklace in his pocket,' Charles said.

Horton looked at Anne, as if it were she who had spoken. 'Oh, *did* he? Is that what set you and your pet communist off on your little detective adventure?'

'I am a *democratic socialist*,' Charles said between gritted teeth.

'If you say so. It's been very hard, you know, looking for that damn thing all these years. I've earned it.'

'Earned it? By going to find Johnnie and killing him? How could you, Horton?' Anne spat out, thinking of Johnnie and the photograph of him and his bicycle. 'You've been trusted here.'

Paul's sounds, his twitching chirrups, were increasing in intensity.

'Paul,' Anne said, 'you don't owe this man anything. He's been using you.'

'Do shut up. Last chance to hand over the diamonds, Lady Anne.'

'Go to hell!' she shouted.

'Shame.' Horton lifted the gun.

Charles leapt forward. The gun kicked in Horton's hand – a tight explosion of sound like a rim shot on a snare drum. Charles's body stopped in mid-air, caught by the invisible fist of the bullet, and he fell sideways. Horton pulled back the hammer again and swung the barrel towards

Anne. She dropped down into a crouch behind the fountain as the drum beat gunshot sounded again, and she heard the ping and zip of the bullet striking the pearl and ricocheting away. Horton cursed, then a deeper, booming explosion of a shotgun, then silence. Anne lifted her head.

Horton was splayed out on the path at the bottom of the pond. Paul was standing over him. Then she saw Charles, floating face down among the weeds. She shouted his name, then thrust the necklace into her pocket and clambered into the pond. He was so heavy, weighed down by water and weed, but she managed to twist his body round in the water, falling over herself with a great splash; then, pushing herself up again, she cleared the weed away from his mouth. The top of his shirt was red with a spreading stain of blood, but he coughed, and his body shuddered as he drew in air again, and let it escape with a groan.

'Charles?'

'Shot saving the bloody ruling classes,' he murmured. 'They will bar me from meetings.'

Paul Mullins was still standing over Horton, the shotgun raised to his shoulder. Anne watched in horrified fascination as Horton's hand reached for his revolver with shaking fingers. Paul stepped forward and put his foot on Horton's wrist. The fingers spasmed, then went still.

'Is he dead, Paul?' Anne said.

The gamekeeper nodded, but still stared down at Horton, his shotgun aimed at the dead man's head.

'Paul,' Anne said. 'Help me get Charles out of the pond, then go and get Shreeve please.'

The gamekeeper looked across at her, his eyes wild, unseeing and scared.

'He's dead, Paul. You saved us! Now please, come and help me, then go and get Shreeve.'

Paul seemed to wake as if from a dream. He set his gun on the ground and jogged round, lifted Charles out of the pond as easily as if he had been a rag doll and deposited him on the path in front of the gargoyles like an offering, then he ran towards the house.

Anne clambered out of the pond by herself. She was drenched, but the scarf around her neck was still dry. She pulled it off and used it to try to stop Charles's bleeding.

Shreeve arrived first. He took one look at the situation and sprinted back to the house to summon her father and a doctor. Seeing the stately butler move so quickly made Anne laugh, which made her realise, in a distant sort of way, she was in danger of becoming hysterical. Paul sat on the ground beside the gargoyle grotto and lowered his chin to his chest. Then came Mrs Warnes with her arms full of bandages. Lord and Lady Leicester and Carey appeared next, all wearing a jumble of pyjamas and dressing gowns and asking a thousand questions at once. Carey saw Horton and burst into tears. Elizabeth immediately bent down to check his pulse and shook her head at her husband. Then she ran round the pond to persuade Anne to surrender Charles into Mrs Warnes's sole care, and held her daughter, kneeling on the path next to her, her embrace as tight, as fierce and as miraculously healing as the day she had returned from Egypt.

'Who did this?' Leicester shouted, then he caught sight of Paul. 'Was it you?'

'He saved my life, Dad!' Anne said, her voice muffled by her mother's dressing gown. 'They both did. Horton fired at me, and Charles jumped in front of the bullet, then Paul shot him. For which I am *exceedingly* grateful.'

'That's enough for now,' Elizabeth said sharply. 'Carey, stop crying, no one has shot you. Tom, darling, call the doctor and I think that man Carstairs is staying at the Victoria. Do call him too. I suspect he might be rather useful. Oh, and Abner. Call Abner and tell him to come to the house straight away.'

'Come with me, Carey,' Leicester said, and took a firm grip of her hand. Charles was sitting up now, and trying to stand.

Elizabeth put out her hand and tapped Paul's knee. 'Paul dear, could you help Mrs Warnes take Charles into the house to wait for the doctor?'

Anne pulled away from her mother and looked at her in surprise while Paul obediently stood up, then lifted Charles onto his feet.

'I can walk,' Charles said, and started to fall over. Paul caught him, supporting him on his good side.

'Do let Paul help you, Charles,' Elizabeth said. 'You've performed enough heroics this morning.'

'Mum? You know Paul is Abner's son?'

'Yes, darling,' Elizabeth said, smoothing her daughter's hair from her forehead. 'Your grandpa told me about him just after the war ended. I was asking him where you got that doll from, and it all came out. I waited a year or two before I told your father, of course. We've been rather worried those missing pages you discovered might have been Paul or Abner getting funds to buy false papers. It seemed impossible to believe it of Abner.'

'Captain Horton got the false papers for him. And it was him that did the stealing. All of it. And he murdered my old governess. But I don't really mind about that, because she was an absolute monster, Mum, but I always thought it would be wrong to tell you that.'

'Ah, I see. Gosh, what a tangle we have got ourselves in. Such a lot goes on under one's nose and we have no idea!' She noticed the lost and rather startled look on Anne's face. 'It's a big house, my love, and we all have our secrets. Now let's get you into the house and cleaned up.'

35.

IT WAS A little after eleven when the family gathered in the long library. Carstairs joined them. He had spoken to the doctor, who had treated Charles and who had also pronounced Horton dead, as well as to Charles and Anne.

Anne explained as best she could. Her governess, Lavender Crane, had conspired with Captain Horton to steal the Coke necklace and replace it with a fake, then the thieves had fallen out and he had killed her. He had been searching for the real necklace ever since. Johnnie had seen Lavender Crane being killed, but only realised the significance of what he had witnessed very recently. Johnnie had told Lord Leicester, then on being confronted, Horton had covered up his crimes though it cost two more lives, the Earl's and that of the troubled young man in the village.

'And you found all this out by yourself, Anne?' her father said at last.

'I couldn't have done it without Charles,' she replied simply. Then she reached into her pocket. 'Sorry, it's terribly dirty, it's been hidden under the scallop shell in the pleasure gardens all this time, but here is the Coke necklace, Dad.'

She passed it over to him, a jumble of light and precious artistry in a bed of rotted linen and leaf mulch, neatly folded round by her own monogrammed handkerchief.

He stood up to take it from her and carried it back to the sofa to show his wife.

'Good Lord, Anne,' he said. 'Very well done.'

Anne looked down at her hands, the praise sounding through her like a distant church bell, rather beautiful, but a little sad.

'Well, Carstairs, what the hell do we do now?' Leicester said. 'You know the King and Queen were here last night. This is a Gothic tragedy and I'd very much like the Royal Family not to be caught up in it.'

'I'd rather your family weren't caught up in it either, Lord Leicester,' Carstairs said. 'I worked with some good local men during the war who I can trust. The sergeant at Wells, Bill Coogan, and Lieutenant Ketteringham. He went back to law after the war and is now the local coroner. Anyway, I think we may find a way through that will see justice done, but keep the full story out of the newspapers. You can of course tell the Royal Family whatever you see fit.'

'I have no idea how you can manage that,' Leicester said. 'And I will not have the local authorities lie on my behalf. Absolutely not.'

'It all does rather depend on your pet communist, Elwood,' Carstairs said. 'If he wants to go to the newspapers, we shan't be able to stop him. But if he is happy to say he is sporting a sling because he fell off his bike, then no one else need lie. Horton's death will be recorded as death by misadventure. I think everyone would agree that we would rather not expose Paul Mullins – it would be terribly unjust in the circumstances.'

'What about Lavender Crane?' Anne asked, and saying the woman's name, she found, did not disturb her at all.

'I think you'll find with Horton gone, it will suddenly be a lot more straightforward to arrange the clean-up of the beach. If her remains are there, they will be found in due course. At that point I would imagine a number of people will conclude that Horton killed himself when he realised her body was going to be found. I would imagine the family would simply refuse to speculate.'

Charles Elwood did not go to the papers.

The body was found three months later. Anne had spent most of the summer in London, staying with her grandmother and going from party to party, but she happened to be at Holkham that weekend.

The call that something had been found came from Mr Hudson at the Nelson, and Anne walked down to the beach to represent the family, picking up Charles from his favourite painting spot on the way.

'Do you think it's her?' he asked, while they stood on the path at the edge of the pinewood and looked down at the men who were working.

'I know it is. How is your shoulder?'

'Fine,' he said easily as he lit a cigarette. 'I can paint again, and Carstairs has turned out to be a bit of a benefactor. He's talked a few of his friends into buying some of my pictures. Even your father has commissioned me. A portrait of his eldest daughter. Good God, I hope I'm not being bribed!'

'None of us would dare to try and bribe a dedicated democratic socialist.'

'You can say it now! Do you want to find out more? Come to a meeting!'

'Certainly not. A portrait did you say?' Anne said, looking a little concerned. Charles chuckled.

'Don't worry, I can paint a nice, flattering portrait. You'll like it.'

The men on the sand had seen them. Mr Ketteringham, the coroner and Bill Coogan in his police uniform detached themselves from the group of other men and came towards them across the sands.

'It's a woman, Lady Anne,' the sergeant said. 'Can't say much more than that. Just a skeleton now.'

'I wondered, Sergeant,' Anne said, 'if it might be the body of a woman who was once my governess, Lavender Crane. She went missing in early December 1943. We thought she had left of her own accord, but given the family have never heard from her again . . .'

Coogan nodded. 'Oh, her! I remember *her*! Anything that might identify her, Lady Anne?'

Anne remembered the cold touch on her forehead. 'She almost always wore a small silver cross, on a chain. And a ring with garnets on it.'

The sergeant glanced back towards the men. 'Aye. Those are there.'

Anne looked in the same direction. She could just make out the shattered edges of metal, a wheel arch of the old taxi. She saw something being lifted out of the crumpled chassis and set carefully onto a linen sheet.

'Lady Anne,' Mr Ketteringham said, 'I hope you don't mind me asking. I've never been able to forget the way you reacted when your governess came in after Bill and I found you in the Ice House. Did she put you in there?'

'Yes,' Anne said. Strange, after all these years of fighting down the memories it felt easier to say it now. She had told her mother and Carey about exactly what Miss Crane had done soon after the discovery of the necklace, and Elizabeth had written a long letter to Ruby to thank her for defending her daughter when she was so in need of a friend. 'She did. It was her who dislocated my shoulder too.'

'I hate to say it,' the sergeant said, 'what with being an officer of the law. But I'm half inclined to tell the boys to pile on the sand again and leave her there. It's a better burial than she deserves.'

Anne smiled at him. 'No, Sergeant. Look on it as part of the clean-up of the beach.'

He snorted. 'Aye, well there is that.'

Anne thanked them, and the men, then turned back towards the drive. Charles followed her.

'How are you, Anne?' he said when they were a few yards away from the party on the beach. She stopped but looked away from the burial and across the wide golden sands of the bay, the pearl glimmer of the sea, the deep greens of the pines. 'Have the ghosts that haunted you here gone now?'

Anne lifted her head and breathed deeply. Salt, pine, the

metallic tang of seaweed and she could just catch the first notes of autumn in the air.

'I shall have to keep a watch out for Lady Mary, but yes, my personal ghosts have been exorcised, I think.'

'I'm glad,' Charles said, and he sounded like he meant it. He drove her back to the house, but turned down the offer of lunch to return to his painting.

Anne went in through the vestibule and Marble Hall and into the salon, then looked out of the window and up the hill towards the obelisk. Her mother was right. Holkham was a large house, and everyone in it had their secrets. She had not told Charles about the conversation she had had with Paul Mullins, sitting on the steps of the temple, the previous week. Poor Paul – still suffering terribly from his experiences at Dunkirk early in the war – spoke hardly a word at first, but eventually, under Anne's kind encouragement, he relaxed and they talked a little about the many weeks he had spent hiding in the cellars at Holkham. Paul had always felt sure he was not alone down there. He told her, shaking his head hard, that it was not him in the picture she had taken in the wine cellar. He had only known she was there at all when she blundered into his bed under the Strangers Wing. The doll he had made for her was of the lady, he said, the woman he saw in his dreams while he slept in the house and whose presence he felt, and whose voice he heard whispering to him from time to time when he was awake.

'Do you think it was Lady Mary?' Anne had asked him as the wood pigeons called around them in the soft summer air.

'I . . . I think so,' he had replied, then smiled shyly. 'She kept me company.'

Anne looked away from the window and checked her hair was neat in the mirror and for one moment she thought she saw a movement in the air behind her. She turned round, but there was nobody there. These moments did not frighten her any more. The strange presence in the house was her friend now. She had, it seemed, won Lady Mary's approval. On that day when Horton had been killed and Charles shot, when she finally got to bed, she had felt a hand on her forehead, a gentle tug on the curl of her hair and heard a voice so thin and so light one could hardly tell if it was real or not. She was sure she had heard it though, a mocking but affectionate whisper. *Remarkable girl.*

Anne glanced at her watch. She had time before lunch to tell her father that Lavender Crane's body had been discovered. He would, of course, tell the King everything, but there was no need for the newspapers to hear about it. The Coke necklace had been cleaned and was back in the safe where it should be, ready for her mother to wear at the next grand state occasion. Perhaps Anne herself would wear it on her wedding day. No need to think about that now though. She cast one more look out of the window enjoying the sight of the park in all its summer glory, then went to find her father.

Author's Note

A Haunting at Holkham is of course a novel, but firmly based on my memories of my life at Holkham during and after World War II. Readers of my autobiography, *Lady in Waiting,* will recognise many situations, places and characters as drawn from real life, and my family members are referred to by their real names. I hope that their many friends will recognise them from these pages. I've also drawn on many other memories of my grandfather and the times we spent together at Holkham in this book that space did not allow me to include in *Lady in Waiting.*

For those not familiar with *Lady in Waiting,* I would just like to point out where I have changed dates and events for the sake of telling what I hope is an enjoyable story.

My younger sister Carey and I were sent to stay with my cousins in Scotland at the outbreak of the war when the danger of a German invasion on the Norfolk coast was a daily concern. My parents were living in Egypt where my father served with the Scots Guards. My great-grandfather, the third Earl of Leicester, died in 1941. At that time my grandfather became the fourth Earl and my father became

Viscount Coke. As readers of *Lady in Waiting* will know, I was unlucky enough to be left in the care of a sadistic governess while in Scotland, though she was clever enough to hide her cruelty from the family. Miss Crane is based on my memories of her.

After the success of the North African Campaign my parents returned to England in 1943 and made their home in Holkham village. My sister Carey and I joined them there. Once Carey and I were back in Norfolk towards the end of the war, from the Donkey Wood we did watch soldiers training on the beach and show off for the Italian POWs. We were at that time in the care of Billy Williams, whom we both loved. I actually went to boarding school in the autumn of 1943, rather than early in 1944 as I have it in the novel.

Though my grandfather was in residence throughout the war, he did share Holkham with the Royal Engineers, who took over parts of the Hall, and the Home Guard, who were based in the temple south of the house. The Italian prisoners were held on the edge of the park between the church, St Withburga's, and the lake. The last of their huts is now used as a chicken coop. German prisoners only arrived in numbers after D-Day, however there were German Prisoners of War held in Britain before then.

My family left the house in the village and moved into the Family Wing of Holkham in 1948. My grandfather moved into the Chapel Wing, but before that, as children we lived in the Chapel Wing and had our nursery and schoolroom there as is described in the novel.

My grandfather died in the summer of 1949, falling down

the stairs into the cellar. No diamond necklace, false or otherwise, was found in his pocket. The Coke necklace is real, however, and I wore it on my wedding day. On my grandfather's death, my father became the fifth Earl of Leicester. My coming out party was shortly before my eighteenth birthday in June 1950 and the King and Queen and Princess Margaret attended. The night did not end quite as it does on these pages, but the details of the party itself are as I remember them.

Lady Mary still haunts Holkham, and various staff and family members have had strange or unpleasant encounters with her. I've tried to reflect some of those experiences in these pages. The details of her biography included in here are all as the history records them. The Holkham Bible Picture Book was acquired by the British Museum in 1952 and is now in the British Library and viewable online. The Leonardo Codex, now known as the Leicester Codex, was purchased by Armand Hammer in 1980 and sold to Bill Gates in 1994.

Charles Elwood and Johnnie Fuller are entirely fictional, as are many of the other heroes and villains in my novel. Though names have been changed, and some characters are composite or have fictional elements added, the larger family of Holkham is also reflected in the novel. It always has been, and continues to be, a community as well as a home, and I hope I have preserved that truth in the framework of this fiction.

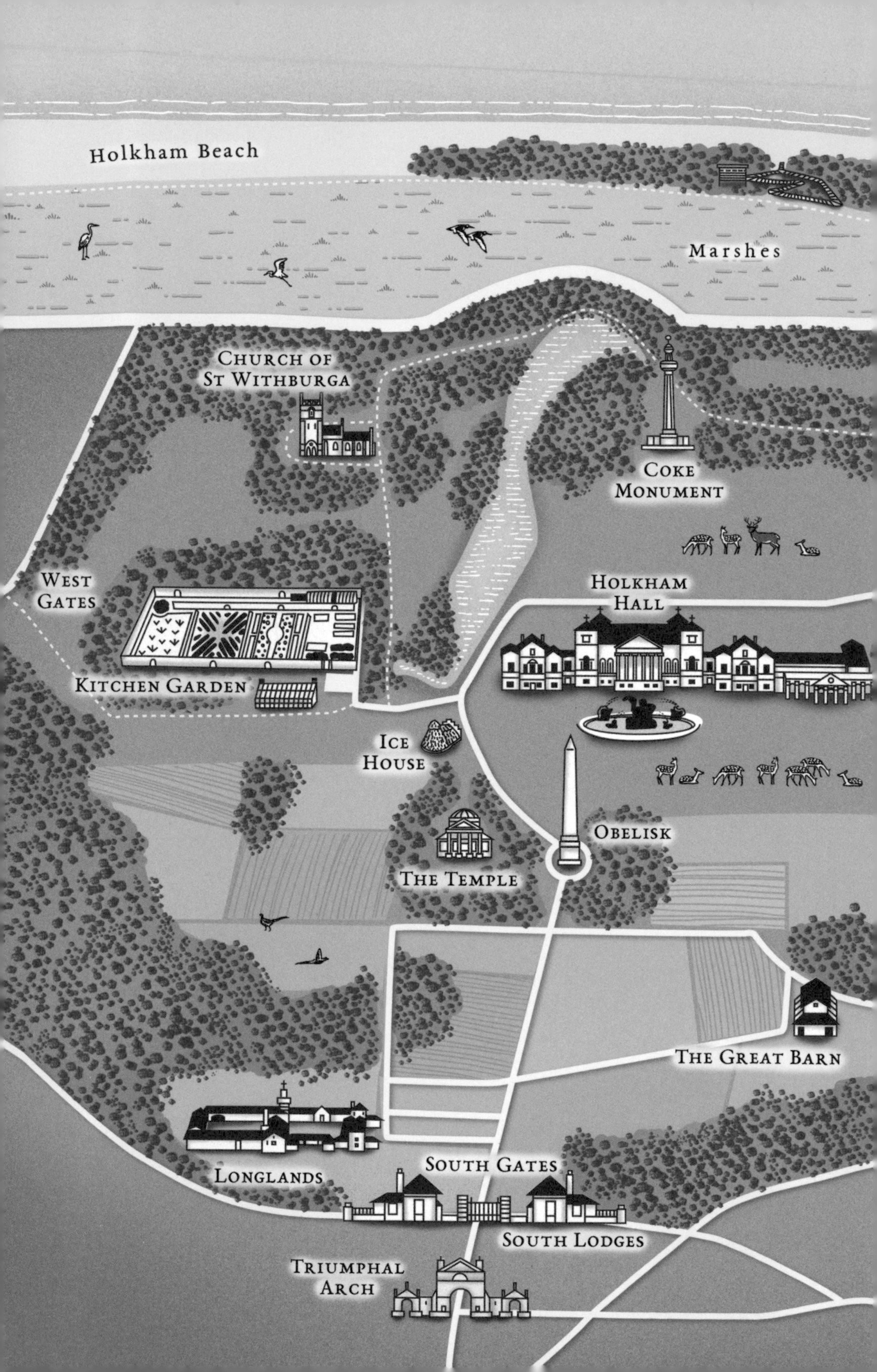
Holkham Beach
Marshes
Church of St Withburga
Coke Monument
West Gates
Holkham Hall
Kitchen Garden
Ice House
Obelisk
The Temple
The Great Barn
Longlands
South Gates
South Lodges
Triumphal Arch